PRAISE FOR KIERAN KRAMER
and *The Impossible Bachelor* series

"Impressive . . . engaging . . . vivid." —*Publishers Weekly*

"A delectable debut . . . I simply adored it!"
—Julia Quinn, *New York Times* bestselling author of
What Happens in London

"At once frothy and heartfelt, *When Harry Met Molly* satisfies! This book is better than dessert!"
—Celeste Bradley, *New York Times* bestselling author of
Rogue in My Arms

"Kieran Kramer pens a delightful Regency confection . . .
a wonderfully bright debut."
—Julia London, *New York Times* bestselling author of
A Courtesan's Scandal

"A delicious romp that will keep you laughing. A fun heroine and a sexy hero make this a delightful read."
—Sabrina Jeffries, *New York Times* bestselling author of
The Truth About Lord Stoneville

"I couldn't put it down . . . a charming delight!"
—Lynsay Sands, *New York Times* bestselling author of
The Hellion and the Highlander

"A wickedly witty treat . . . an exquisite debut!"
—Kathryn Caskie, *USA Today* bestselling author of
The Most Wicked of Sins

MORE . . .

"A delightful, page-turning read! New author Kieran Kramer will capture both your imagination and your heart."　　—Cathy Maxwell, *New York Times* bestselling author of *The Marriage Ring*

"In her exceptionally entertaining literary debut, Kramer deftly sifts deliciously humorous writing, a cast of exceptionally entertaining characters, an outrageously inventive yet convincing plot, and a splendidly sexy love story into a delectable literary confection that will have Regency historical readers begging for seconds."

　　—*Booklist* (starred review)

"Clever banter, stellar pacing, and appealing, exceptionally well-drawn characters make this fresh, sexy, and gloriously funny debut a knockout and a perfect start to Kramer's Regency-set quartet."

　　—*Library Journal* (starred review)

"You'll smile and even laugh out loud reading Kramer's delectable debut—even the title's nod to the famous film elicits a grin. With her perfect sense of pacing, comic timing, poignancy, and marvelous characterization, this utterly enchanting new voice will have you eager for more."　　—*Romantic Times BOOKreviews*

If You Give a Girl a Viscount

KIERAN KRAMER

St. Martin's Paperbacks

This is a work of fiction. All of the characters, organizations, and events portrayed in this novel are either products of the author's imagination or are used fictitiously.

IF YOU GIVE A GIRL A VISCOUNT

Copyright © 2011 by Kieran Kramer.

All rights reserved.

For information address St. Martin's Press, 175 Fifth Avenue, New York, NY 10010.

ISBN: 978-0-312-37404-4

Printed in the United States of America

St. Martin's Paperbacks edition / November 2011

St. Martin's Paperbacks are published by St. Martin's Press, 175 Fifth Avenue, New York, NY 10010.

10 9 8 7 6 5 4 3 2 1

To Rob and Maryellen

May you have many happy years together!

ACKNOWLEDGMENTS

This journey through my first book contract was a thrilling, unforgettable adventure—all because I'm fortunate to work with my dream team: Jennifer Enderlin of St. Martin's Press and Jenny Bent of The Bent Agency. Thank you, ladies, for your unfailing support and guidance.

I'd also like to thank all my readers on Facebook, as well as my Twitter friends and visitors to my blog. You've brought so much joy to my life as a writer!

Finally I'd like to thank my friends and family. You're always there for me. I'm a lucky lady.

CHAPTER ONE

On a sunny afternoon high in the left turret of a small, crumbling castle in the northwest of Scotland, Highland lass Daisy Montgomery scrubbed the hearthstones in her bedchamber and dreamed of finding her prince. *He'll make me laugh,* she thought, wringing out her rag in a bucket of cold water. Then, as she applied all her muscle to the coal-black stone, *I'll make* him *laugh.*

"You need to clean between the keys of the pianoforte," her stepmother told her from the door in that cool, deliberate way she had.

And he'll transport me, Daisy hastily added to her mental list. She'd read that in a gothic novel once. *He'll transport me anywhere the shrew behind me* isn't. *And I'll transport him to a place he* wants *to be. But I'll go to my place first. He'd be the sort to understand.*

Wishing with all her might that she didn't have to, she turned to look at Mona. "I just cleaned the pianoforte a few days ago."

"You're lying," Mona snapped. "Cassandra hit a flat note today, thanks to you. Use a string wrapped in flannel, and be sure to change the flannel after every third key. I'll know if you don't."

Daisy forced herself not to cringe. "Very well," she said in even tones, "as soon as I'm done here, I'll do it again."

"Oh, you're done, all right," Mona replied in a low register, which meant that if Daisy didn't stand up immediately, she'd be pinched by the woman's long talons.

Daisy dropped her rag and stood. "I suppose I'm finished then."

Mona stalked down the gray stone corridor in her beaded black sheath with a preposterously low neckline. It was completely inappropriate for daytime, but that was typical of Mona. It went without question that Daisy would follow her.

"It's exhausting dealing with you," Mona said. "You're so—" She waved her claws about.

"Braw?" Daisy whispered in a sad voice.

Mona hailed from Cheapside in London, and her Scottish vocabulary wasn't exactly extensive. *Braw* was a compliment meaning fine, good, even brilliant.

"Close." Mona laughed in a mean way. "God, you were *braw* to high heaven yesterday after you finished cleaning the scum off the top of the moat."

"Very well." Daisy sighed. "Perhaps you mean . . . *bricht*."

Bricht meant bright, which seemed obvious to

Daisy but was somehow not to Mona, who'd never adapted to the Highland way of life.

Daisy knew it was childish of her to take these subtle jabs at her stepmother, but it was her only solace, other than sitting with Joe and Hester in the kitchen, where each night they'd dunk shortbread in warm milk and talk in low tones about their day.

Mona nodded. "It's despicable how *bricht* you are, you sulky miss. You ought to be like my girls. Charming. Ever ready with a nice word."

The woman's deluded, Daisy thought. Perdita and Cassandra were *awful.*

But Daisy was a survivor, and she knew the servants' futures also lay in her hands, so she said, "I'm sorry."

"You should be," said Mona. "I've half a mind to give you bread and water tomorrow as punishment."

There was only one way to deflect such a punishment: pretend to be jealous of Mona.

"*You'd* never be *braw,*" Daisy told her stepmother wistfully as they passed under a portrait of Papa as a boy. "Or *bricht.*"

"Right you are." Mona's breasts led her like two roly-poly foot soldiers carrying bayonets into her bedchamber. "I'd be ashamed to be. Now brush my hair five hundred strokes, or I'll see to it that you get no supper and that you're locked in your room until morning."

Although she was thoroughly disgusted, Daisy refused to wince, not only at the threat and the prospect of a distasteful chore but at the changes Mona had wrought to the master suite Daisy's parents used to share. The hangings were a garish scarlet with black lace trim instead of the pretty sage-green-and-ivory toile they'd been before. And all the lovely, light figurines and paintings Papa and Mama had collected over the years had been replaced with crouching gargoyles and dark paintings.

As she brushed Mona's lank locks, Daisy tried to pretend she was somewhere else. But it was difficult when her stepmother kept slapping her hand and telling her she was either brushing too hard or not hard enough.

The worst came when Mona demanded her usual compliment. "What do you think of my hair?" she asked Daisy.

"It's lush and luxuriant," she replied.

It was the required response, even though Mona had bits of scalp showing through. The first several times Daisy had said anything else, she'd been sent to bed with no supper.

Mona smiled, close-lipped, into the looking glass, seemingly satisfied.

Inside, Daisy said *ugh*. And then a mote of dust flew up her nose and made her sneeze.

The looking glass reflected Mona's narrowed gaze. "Sneeze one more time, and you'll sleep in the byre tonight."

Daisy widened her eyes on purpose. She knew it made Mona happy to see her afraid. "Not the byre," she said in her best fearful tone.

"Indeed, the byre," Mona replied. "It's cold out

tonight, too. You'll have to snuggle up to those pigs."

Mona closed her eyes, no doubt contemplating the glory of that scene in her head, and promptly fell asleep. It was happening more often . . . Mona had always sneaked whisky. She'd made Daisy get it for her when Papa was alive, but since he'd died, Mona drank it openly, sometimes starting before noon.

Daisy laid the brush aside. She'd made it only to two hundred fifty-two strokes this time. She lifted her stepmother under her arms and dragged her to the bed, where Daisy proceeded, through much effort, to roll Mona on top of the gaudy satin coverlet.

The grasping woman who'd taken advantage of Daisy's grieving father began to snore. Much relieved, Daisy crept from the room and shut the door.

You'll be doing this forever, a mocking voice in her head said. It sounded exactly like her stepsister Cassandra. Cassandra was able to get to her in a way Mona couldn't—because Mona was rather stupid.

Cassandra wasn't. She was clever.

But Daisy refused to listen to Cassandra's voice in her head.

She couldn't. If she did, she'd cry.

And the last thing she wanted Mona or her daughters to see was her crying. The one time they had, when she'd fallen off a horse and broken her arm, not two weeks after their arrival, their jeers had haunted her for months.

Of course, Papa had been nowhere near at the time. Daisy was sure that Cassandra, who'd been standing near the small jump, had somehow spooked her mare into tripping over it.

But Daisy had learned—oh, how she'd learned!— to keep her tears to herself.

She'd learned so well, she hadn't cried at Papa's funeral. The night he'd died, her private grief had been wretched, a pain so deep that she never thought she'd be free of it. She still wasn't.

And she knew she never would be.

In the kitchen, she washed her hands in a bucket of clean water, dried them on a clean piece of linen, kissed Hester's cheek—appreciating how lovingly it was offered to her—and formed a bannock of oatmeal dough for Hester to bake on a griddle.

"Bake it extra hard, Hester," Daisy said. "I'm hoping Mona will break a tooth on it."

"Has she been worse than usual today?" The housekeeper was as soft as a freshly baked bun herself.

"Not really. But for some reason, I felt more provoked than usual." Maybe because Mona had interrupted Daisy's daydream about her prince. "She's sleeping right now and will no doubt wake up just in time for dinner."

Hester tsk-tsked. Daisy went out the kitchen door and down the steps to check on her potted lemon tree, the one she'd grown from a seed Papa had brought her back from London. One lovely lemon was growing on it—it was the first one ever, and she wished Papa could see it as she'd grown it especially for him.

But it was too late. He was gone. And Mona's hatred of her, which Daisy had always been keenly aware of—even when Mona used to smile at her and hug her in front of Papa—had come out into the open since his death and was stronger than ever.

The truth was, Papa would still be here today if it weren't for Daisy and her carelessness.

The old guilt came back, spreading through her like a pool of black bog sludge. And then, as it always did, it became guilt coupled with sorrow as thin and sharp as the blade on Papa's old *skean dhu*.

Then . . . guilt, sorrow, and anger—a lumbering, suffocating anger that was always the same: accusing. Cruel. Unreasonable. Unaccepting.

She tried to breathe.

If only!

She let out a little sigh.

If only.

She was angry at herself—there was always that—but there was the beginning of something else surging in her, tendriling up from the depths of her despair and demanding notice.

She'd give it time. She must be patient. Because it might be her only lemon, too. She couldn't afford to waste it.

Which was why moments later when Cassandra and Perdita called her into the drawing room, she straightened her spine and went to them without complaint.

"Yes, sisters?" she said in her most pleasant tones. Not because she felt like being polite but because she knew it annoyed them no end, how sweet and kind she always was to them.

Cassandra was a stunning young lady with glossy black curls and fine gray eyes. She and Daisy were almost the same age. Perdita, a year older, appeared to be a man dressed in women's clothing, and she sounded like one, too.

"You blondes *are* dimwitted, aren't you?" Cassandra said to Daisy. "I require tea and cakes immediately."

Hester walked in then. "You're impatient, lass," she told Cassandra with a placid smile, and placed a tray of cakes upon a low table. "You've already asked *me* for tea. I'll have you know the kettle has not yet boiled, but here's something to pique your palate."

"Your old bones will be fired, Hester," Cassandra replied in sharp tones, "if you insist on being so slow. You and your simpleton brother with you."

Daisy's whole body stiffened with rage. How dare Cassandra threaten Hester and Joe—and then insult him so! No one had been here as long as he. For the past fifty years, the people of Glen Dewey could look up and see him, regular as clockwork, tending his sheep with loving care on the side of Ben Fennon.

He was the heart and soul of Castle Vandemere.

Hester, his younger sister, and still a fierce Highland lass beneath those wrinkles forming about her eyes, merely folded her hands in front of her. "Miss

Cassandra," she said in a gentle but firm tone, "I'm doing my verra best to serve you."

And then she curtsied out of the room, but not before she gave a small wink to Daisy.

Winks always meant the same thing: *may the Furies rot in Hell.*

Hester had read about the wicked threesome in Papa's big book of Greek mythology. Scots believed in education for all, and Hester was no exception. They also believed in calling a spade a spade, and if anyone could be compared to the three Furies, it was Mona and her two daughters.

Only because Hester was able to do so, Daisy also held her temper as Perdita ate an entire cake whole and then another. But these days, as the first anniversary of Papa's death came near, Daisy couldn't help thinking, *When will it be my turn?*

Her turn to be in charge? Her turn to make Cassandra and Perdita uncomfortable? Her turn to oust the vermin living in her ancestral home, the ungrateful English family who'd so bamboozled her father and made her life, Joe's, and Hester's a living hell?

Joe knocked at the drawing room door.

"Come in," she said, admiring the way the aged shepherd's eyes sparkled so blue in his swarthy face. Not a day went by that he didn't say—

"It's a *braw, bricht* day, Miss Daisy," in his thick burr.

He did so now, and as always, his gaze was innocent and his demeanor shy. He clasped his cap to his breast and looked at her hopefully.

She gave him the response he loved. "It is, indeed, Joe," she said with spirit.

He grinned. It was a *braw, bricht* day to Joe even when a cold rain was slashing his face, or snowflakes found their way between his neck and the collar of his faded woollen coat. It had even been a *braw, bricht* day the day after Papa had died, and Joe had said the words with tears streaming down his cheeks.

Like their mother, Cassandra and Perdita showed no interest in their adopted country. Neither had ever bothered to learn any special Scottish words or ask to hear stories about the old clans. And they didn't give a fig for anyone at the castle or in the village of Glen Dewey.

Cassandra held up a hand. "Joe, don't you dare come in if you smell of the byre."

"Or sheep dung," Perdita added, with crumbs falling out of her mouth.

"Those sheep," Daisy said pointedly to her two stepsisters, "put food on our plates and a roof over our heads." She looked at Joe. "Come in, dear, and you're very welcome."

"Ta, Miss Daisy," said Joe, and limped over the threshold, his weak leg dragging behind him. From beneath his cap, he pulled a folded note and held it out to her. "The mail coach came to Glen Dewey today. And this was on it."

Cassandra jumped up faster than Daisy had ever seen her move and snatched the missive from Joe before Daisy had a chance to take a step toward him.

"No!" he remonstrated with Cassandra. "Tha's not for you."

Cassandra held the paper triumphantly over her head and giggled. "Finders keepers!"

Joe looked worriedly at Daisy.

"It's all right," she told him with a small smile to send him on his way with a light heart.

He still looked doubtful but retreated, no doubt to visit Hester in the kitchen before he went back out to Ben Fennon. The baking bannock was creating delicious smells that had wafted on the ever-present draft to the front of the castle.

Meanwhile, Daisy's smile disappeared and her heart raced. The letter could only be from one person: her godmother. Daisy had never met her before and had only just discovered she had a godmother two months ago, when she'd been reading from one of Papa's books and a letter had slipped out.

It had been dated from before Papa was married to Mama and had come from a Lady Pinckney. She'd said that if Barnabas ever married and had a daughter, she yearned to know of the news and was highly desirous of being the godmother. Those had been her exact words: *yearned* and *highly desirous*.

Daisy could tell from that letter that Lady Pinckney must have been one of Papa's old paramours.

Now Cassandra threatened to burn the letter in the fire. She looked back at Daisy with glee in her eyes. "What will you do if it goes up in flames?" she asked in a wheedling tone.

That green, pushy thing growing inside Daisy

shot up another inch. "I'll break *your* arm," she said, "the same way you broke mine."

Cassandra sucked in a breath and stared at her. Perdita let half a cake fall out of her mouth onto her lap.

Daisy strode toward Cassandra with her hand outstretched. "Give it to me now, or rest uneasy tonight."

Cassandra blinked repeatedly. "Why, you—you—"

Daisy snatched the letter out of her hand. "Cat got your tongue for once?"

Cassandra's mouth gaped even wider, and she blinked more and more rapidly, and then her chest started heaving.

Daisy had a sneaking suspicion Cassandra was trying not to cry.

"What's happened to you?" Perdita roared at Daisy.

Perdita couldn't help roaring. It was simply her way. Everything she said came out as a roar.

Daisy turned to look at her, feeling powerful with that letter in her hand. She didn't even know what it said, but it was from her godmother, by God, and that was something.

It was something, indeed.

"Nothing's happened to me, Perdy," said Daisy. "But something may happen to *you*."

"What do you mean by that?" shrieked Cassandra.

Perdita merely gave a soft roar, which was as close to a whimper as she would probably ever get.

Daisy turned her back on them and walked out

the drawing room door and up to her bedchamber. For the first time, she looked at the writing on the note.

Her heart sank. It was from a man. The handwriting was strong. Even fierce.

Some of the concern came back. What would Cassandra and Perdita do to her after that scene in the drawing room? She'd gone a bit far, hadn't she?

But it had felt good. It had felt *right*.

Still. She'd never done it before. It had been the letter that had given her courage.

Pushing down her worry, Daisy closed the door behind her, broke the wax seal on the paper, and unfolded it, all the while wondering what the man in the letter would want of her.

After she finished reading, she folded the long-awaited note back up and stared into space. "I've been given a viscount," she murmured, testing out the words.

But she hadn't *asked* for a viscount. She'd asked for a godmother.

He'd be here any day now. His name was Charles Thorpe, Viscount Lumley, and he was Lady Pinckney's grandson.

What in God's name was Daisy to do with him?

CHAPTER TWO

A month earlier

Charles Thorpe, Viscount Lumley, held up a missive written in a feminine hand to show his three best friends, all of them Impossible Bachelors, who'd been designated by Prinny as experts at both charming women and avoiding the marriage altar. They were seated in a private room at their club in London.

"As you know, I'm taking care of Grandmother's business while she's gone," Charlie said in his best leading fashion, which really wasn't very leading at all.

Not known for nuance, he was now the most physically imposing of the Bachelors—and rumor had it the most menacing when his ire was up. All the amateur boxing matches he'd trained for and won under the tutelage of Gentleman Jackson the past several years attested to that.

Harry Traemore, second son of the Duke of

Mallan and the first of the Bachelors to get leg-shackled, barely glanced at the letter. He even let out a tremendous yawn and settled deeper into his club chair. "Lady Pinckney's a spitfire, but it can't be too taxing looking after an elderly woman's affairs, can it? At least in comparison to your usual endeavors."

"Wining and dining widows and actresses, and making money hand over fist, you mean," interjected Stephen Arrow, a captain in the Royal Navy who was now on a new adventure as a landlubber—a married one, at that.

In the old days, Charlie would have chuckled at Stephen's comment. But he was far too cynical and jaded these days to do that. "You must admit it takes some skill to do either." He paused. "Especially at the same time."

"Is that possible?" Nicholas Staunton, the Duke of Drummond, who'd also succumbed to marital bliss, lofted an enigmatic brow. Being mysterious was a passion of his.

"No doubt with Lord Lumley, it's doable," Harry said.

"I won't deny it." Charlie shrugged. "But now my greatest task is to send round *no*s to all Grandmother's invitations."

"Feed her canary," Stephen added.

"Walk her poodle," Nicholas said.

Charlie acknowledged their repartee with a tip of his head. "But this is Lady Pinckney, not your typical elderly female. Did you know she has seven goddaughters?"

"Seven?" Harry stirred himself. "That does seem a bit excessive."

"She collects them the way you collect boats, Arrow," Charlie said, "or you accrue your horses, Drummond." He snorted. "Or you collect children, Harry."

Harry winced. "Three at the moment. I suppose that *is* considered a collection, eh?"

Nicholas shook his head. "I'm fast on your heels, old man, with my twins."

"And don't forget, I'm just getting started with my little sailor," Stephen said. "I'll catch up soon enough."

"You forgot to boast that they all have me as their adventurous uncle," Charlie reminded them, "the one with no rules. Speaking of which, I've got a fresh situation on my hands, a rather awkward one. Before I take action, I could use your counsel."

"Here's mine," said Harry. "Take a moment to recover from the last situation before you move on to this one."

"Nursemaid's advice," Charlie promptly told him. "Is that what comes with settling down?"

"Point taken, old friend." Harry's tone was dry. "Please. Go on chasing the wrong women as long as you like while I remain settled down, as you say, with a lovely, loyal wife who doesn't pocket the expensive baubles I give her and then walk away."

"Touché." Charlie considered his most recent romantic folly. "At least you're the only ones who know. Outside my family, that is."

"Are they speaking to you yet?" asked Stephen.

Charlie shook his head. "Only Grandmother."

"Perhaps her heart was broken once," suggested Nicholas.

"Or more than once," added Stephen, no doubt alluding to the fact that in the past two years, Charlie had had lengthy affairs with three women.

"Rest assured," Charlie said, "I may have been involved with more than my fair share of grasping females, but my heart's never been broken." Dented, maybe, but that had only made it more impervious to hurt. "At the moment, I've got a bigger problem on my plate."

"What's that?" Harry asked.

Charlie was loath to tell them. "I've been completely cut off from the family coffers." He felt quite bitter about it, too. "My parents believe that as the heir, I need to stop throwing money about carelessly."

"Interesting." Harry nodded, quite as if he understood.

Which rather riled Charlie. "I excel at investing on the family's behalf."

Harry and the other Bachelors exchanged neutral glances.

What's that about? Charlie wondered.

"Lord and Lady Frampton"—he referred to his parents testily—"say that no matter how rich I make the family, thoughtless spending will eventually lead to my ruin." He waited for someone to say such a claim was ridiculous. "Can you believe that?"

The ensuing silence enveloped him like a heavy cloak.

Charlie leaped from his chair, almost toppling it backward. "What the devil is going on here?" He stared at his friends. "What aren't you saying?"

"Is there more?" Harry asked quietly.

Charlie looked into the fire, remembering that excruciatingly uncomfortable moment with his parents. "They also said"—his voice was a bit raspy at this point—"that buying a ruby and diamond pendant . . . for a wench who turned right around and absconded with it to America . . . was the last straw."

The flames flickered higher, mocking him with their brightness.

Good God. Where had his head been?

Firmly in the ground, that's where.

"My parents are right, aren't they?" he said calmly. "They're absolutely right."

No one disagreed.

It *had* been the last straw.

He'd been a fool.

Looking round at his friends, he saw that no one excused his behavior, yet their gazes were sympathetic.

Slowly, Nicholas stood and joined Charlie at the hearth. "Well, then," was all he said.

Charlie glared at him. It was better than showing his embarrassment. But of course his friends understood. They'd made fools of themselves, too, on occasion, and every one of them had had a devil of a time admitting it.

Harry gestured to Stephen, who generously refilled their glasses from a second bottle of fine brandy.

"Let's raise a toast to your new adventure, shall we?" Stephen passed round the drinks, and everyone raised them.

"To living within new, limited means at Lady Pinckney's," Nicholas announced.

"For the nonce," Stephen clarified.

"And here's to sharpening your skills when it comes to choosing female companionship," added Harry.

"A challenge for any man," Nicholas said.

Truer words had never been spoken.

Stephen leaned against the mantel, a grin on his tanned face. "It's often the bon vivants of this world who have the highest standards and are most often disappointed," he philosophized. "It's why we become bon vivants in the first place."

"There's something to that," Harry agreed.

Nicholas raised his brandy higher. "To Impossible Bachelors."

"Here, here," came a chorus of assents.

The foursome clinked glasses and drained them.

"Every woman I meet from now on," Charlie said, "will have to jump through proverbial hoops of fire to even be considered an acquaintance. Not only that, my heart is firmly locked up, and I've thrown away the key."

"Don't go that far," said Harry. "We'll hold the key for you for a bit. Someday you'll want it back."

"I doubt it." Charlie's tone was dry. "I think I'm

the Impossible Bachelor destined to remain so. But let's get back to Grandmother. How plebeian you must think me, to be satisfied with walking poodles and feeding canaries. I've got loyal friends willing to take over those tasks for me—your wives."

"Our wives?" Harry drew in his chin.

Nicholas and Stephen exchanged wary but amused glances.

"Indeed," said Charlie. "I've already contacted them, and they've assured me they'd be delighted to turn down Grandmother's invitations and tend to her pets on my behalf. They even suggested they might get their husbands to perform those chores for them."

"No!" all three of his friends cried at once, and then chose their own favorite curses to heap upon his head.

Charlie laughed. "You'll be more amenable to the idea once you hear about the important mission I've got to do on Grandmother's behalf. I refer you once more to a letter from one of her goddaughters."

He held the missive in the air again.

Nicholas sat up higher in his chair. "Where is this goddaughter?"

"The north of Scotland," replied Charlie. "Somewhere near a village called Glen Dewey."

"Ah," said Harry. "Yes."

"You've heard of it?" Charlie was curious to know more.

"Of course not." Harry barely flinched at Charlie's punch to the upper arm. "When was the last time I left London?"

"Sounds as if it's at the back of beyond," Stephen commented.

"It is," Charlie agreed. "But I'm going there."

"What for?" Nicholas swirled his brandy in his glass and waited.

"She needs help." Charlie looked around at all three of them. "She doesn't say what's wrong, exactly. Only that she's in dire straits."

"Poor girl," Stephen murmured.

"You know what that means." Charlie sighed. "The odds are good she needs money."

"If she does, you'll give it to her," said Nicholas.

Charlie's brow shot up.

"Oh, right." Nicholas winced. "You're impoverished at the moment."

"We can fund your trip," said Harry.

"Right," said Stephen.

"How much do you need?" Nicholas was already reaching into his coat.

Charlie drew in a deep breath. "Thanks, but no thanks. I've got to do this on my own. I may have only severely limited funds to throw at the problem, but I'll find a way to sort it out."

"I like that attitude." Stephen, a self-made man himself, nodded his approval. "In fact, take it a step further. See if you can survive on this journey north—and thrive while there—without even a tuppence to your name. That will show your parents—and remind *you*—that you're worthy of access to the family fortune."

Charlie didn't know what to say. Life with no money at all seemed unfathomable, really.

"Maybe you'll learn what you're made of," Harry suggested.

"Stern stuff." Nicholas thumped a fist on his chest.

"We're best friends with a viscount of tremendous character," Stephen pronounced.

"A man who can solve problems using his own ingenuity," added Nicholas.

"What's his name?" Charlie said with a little chuckle.

Everyone had a comfortable laugh with him. But not for long.

"Perhaps my parents are right." Charlie felt very serious as he gazed round at his friends. "All that money has made things too easy for me." He thought of his life, one of supreme comfort with very little accountability—to anyone, to anything.

What was he passionate about these days? When had he become a man with very little resolve?

"I've lost something," he admitted. "And I need to get it back."

"Right." Harry gave him a stern look. "Starting now—till after you've solved the girl's problem—you can't spend a penny of your own money or borrow from anyone else."

"You might as well leave for Scotland tonight," said Nicholas.

"We're serious," Arrow added.

For a moment, no one stirred.

Then Charlie said, "Zeus take it, so am I."

A feeling of excitement gripped him. Without hesitation, he reached into his coat pocket and removed a leather pouch full of coins. "It's barely enough to get me to Scotland and back, and only if I stay at modest inns."

"That's still too much," said Harry. "Hand it over. And don't go back to your grandmother's. You probably have banknotes stashed in your pockets there."

"I do." Charlie slapped the purse into Harry's palm.

"Next time you see us, you'll be a different man," said Stephen.

"Who knows what adventures you'll have meanwhile?" asked Nicholas.

"I wish I could go." Harry sounded a bit wistful.

"Huh," said Charlie. "I'll be sleeping in haystacks while the three of you go back to your wives and the cozy beds they're keeping warm for you."

Harry and Stephen were quick to shake his hand, but when Charlie came to Nicholas, his friend said: "Let's make this even more interesting. What will you forfeit—besides your honor—if you don't follow through to the very end?"

"You're setting high stakes, are you?" Charlie thought for a moment. "How about the prime goer I bought last week? You can draw straws for him."

Nicholas waved a hand. "Much as I admire his bloodlines, it's not enough."

"It's got to be something you truly can't replace when your bank accounts open again," Harry said, "as I'm sure they will."

"His freedom," Stephen said flatly.

"What?" Charlie felt like pulling at his cravat, but he restrained himself.

Nicholas let out a whoop of glee. "Exactly. You'll enter the Marriage Mart, once and for all."

Charlie shook his head. "Please, no."

"Yes!" said Harry.

Charlie felt slightly ill. "If your wives get wind of this, they'll start lining up all sorts of dull, proper ladies well in advance. I'll feel them encroaching— even when I'm far away in Scotland." He shuddered. "I can feel them already."

"Poor sod." Harry's eyes gleamed with amusement.

Charlie narrowed his eyes. "Don't be so quick to pity me. I plan to win. And when I do, what will I receive from you?"

Stephen chuckled. "You mean, in addition to our undying admiration?"

"Yes." Charlie noted that none of the three immediately came up with an answer.

"We'll ponder it while you're gone," Nicholas finally said.

"It will be . . . a surprise," Harry added.

"All right, then." Charlie grinned. "But make it good," he warned. "Because I intend to claim it."

And with that, he saluted them and left the cozy chamber within their club. It was the same room in which they'd encountered Prinny and his mistress, who'd appeared from behind a panel in the wall a long while ago. So much had happened to the other Bachelors since then—namely, new adventures in uncharted territory. Marriage to women they loved. A certain wisdom and maturity. And children.

Now Charlie was ready for something to happen

to *him,* even if it was only an escapade to the far north.

He shivered in his coat when he opened the club door to the dark London night and trotted down the steps. He'd done it thousands of times before. But this time, when his right boot hit the pavement, he made sure to note that it was his first step on a journey to Scotland—

And what he dared to hope would be the adventure of a lifetime.

CHAPTER THREE

He was here. Daisy's viscount. The one who'd told her in his commanding scrawl that he'd be at her beck and call when he arrived. After her initial disappointment that her godmother wasn't available to assist her, she realized she'd never had anyone offer to be at her beck and call before.

She couldn't help but feel a bit excited. Although it probably wasn't done to be excited about receiving a viscount as a temporary gift—

Was it?

She wore a dress of faded strawberry-red striped chintz she'd sewn from the least faded cushions and the back of the old settee that had finally fallen apart in the sitting room. And she'd made sure that Mona, Cassandra, and Perdita were still tucked in their beds. It had been easy enough—the evening previous, Hester had told them the vicar needed them to wash altar cloths at the local kirk the following morning. And as Daisy knew they would, they all claimed colds and had yet to appear downstairs.

Now there was a deep voice in the hall. Clipped. Cold. Very masculine. And then Hester's thin, rabbity answer.

Oh, dear. Couldn't Hester work up a bit more nerve?

Daisy clung to the sides of the chair, her palms sweating. The pleasant smile she'd fixed on her face was gone. She'd never been good at playing a part anyway.

Daisy Alice Montgomery! Papa's voice came to her. *Be brave.*

Channeling *brave* with all her might, she loosened her grip, adjusted her curls, and wished for a sudden boost of radiance to infuse her person.

It didn't work. She didn't feel radiant in the least.

Not that she had time to worry about the matter. The next moment, Hester flung open the door and walked in, her eyes wide and blinking, her hand curled to her mouth. "Viscount Lumley of London," she gasped.

And then she scuttled off.

Daisy bit her lip. Why was Hester so jumpy?

When a man strode through the door, Daisy had to wonder—with her heart in her throat—if perhaps the housekeeper had seen what she was seeing now.

There was a fable associated with Castle Vandemere: *The Legend of the Two Lovers at the Ceilidh on the Last Night of the Hunt.* It was an awfully long name for a legend, but if it held true, it deserved such a title. The story went that long ago, a Golden Prince and his Golden Girl had found true

love at the *ceilidh*—an evening of Scottish dancing—
always held at Castle Vandemere on the last night
of the great hunt.

Of course, when the hunt and games had been
moved to the newer and grander Keep two centuries
ago, the legend had faded away. But a lovely stained-
glass window with the images of the Golden Prince
and the Golden Girl still adorned the west wall of
the drawing room, and on particularly fine evenings,
the sunset's glow lit up their faces.

The viscount looked like the Golden Prince.

Almost.

In his state of disarray, Daisy rather thought he
looked more like the Golden Prince's bad twin.

He wore muddy black high-top boots, snug but
ripped buckskin breeches, and a form-fitting coat
missing all its buttons. Daisy also noted the complete absence of a cravat over the stained white
shirt.

But like the Golden Prince, he had the same deep
brown hair—wavy and thick—touched with flecks
of gold, and eyes the tawny brown color of the ha-
zelnuts heaped in the white crock in the kitchen.
He also had the Golden Prince's square jaw, aqui-
line nose, proud bearing, and assured stance.

Indeed, if one didn't count the ghastly black eye
and a bloody scab on his nose, the visitor was far
too handsome for his own good. Daisy had never
seen such a handsome man (who'd obviously been
in a brawl. Or two).

Her heart raced not at his good looks, she told
herself, but at the insolence in his manner and the

scowl on his countenance. He also reeked of cheroots and stale ale.

She shut her gaping mouth and looked full-on
at the gentleman. "Welcome to the Highlands," she
said. "I'm Miss Montgomery, daughter of the late
Barnabas and Catherine Montgomery."

"And I'm Lord Lumley," he said softly, in a take-
no-prisoners tone, returning her gaze with cold equa-
nimity. "It's been a harrowing journey north, as
I've gotten here by hook or by crook—"

"By hook or by crook?"

A small turnip fell out of his coat.

"What's that?" she couldn't help asking.

"A turnip," he replied in bland tones.

"I know, but why—"

"Don't ask," he muttered. "I beg of you. Please."
He held up a palm. "It's better forgotten. The whole
journey."

"Very well." She nodded quickly. "If that's what
you'd prefer."

"Indeed, it is." He kicked the turnip under a sofa.
"The point is, I *am* here. And I'm at your service."

At her service?

Daisy put her hand on the back of a chair to
steady herself. "Do you really mean that?" she asked
in a rush.

"Of course." His gaze was still hard.

"Good. *Very* good." She gulped, not sure how to
say what she must. Oh, bother, she simply would.
There'd been that turnip, after all. Things weren't
quite the usual. It was the perfect environment to . . .
let loose.

Besides, her passion for her cause was making her desperate. Strong feeling had always been her downfall.

She's impulsive. Those had been her mother's words to her father.

Madcap. Her father's words to her mother.

Thoughtless. Her stepmother's take on the matter.

Harebrained. Stepmother again.

Selfish. Cassandra's refrain.

Daisy held tighter to the chair. "I need you, Viscount."

She really, really did!

"Need me?" A spark of something fierce and frightening flashed in his stony gaze.

His disdain almost made her flinch. But she couldn't. She wouldn't. She must be bold.

The words burned to be said: "I need your help procuring my godmother's money. Gobs of it."

Of course.

She wanted money.

Wait until the boys hear about this, Charlie thought, and tried to ignore the fact that he felt an embarrassing sense of disappointment that for a moment there, he'd thought she'd needed *him*—followed swiftly by a ripple of unwanted interest in her that had nothing to do with her brazen speech.

Were all Highlanders so . . . raw?

Her hair, yellow as freshly cut straw, was scraped back into a tight bun. She had a weary, gaunt expression about her eyes, which she didn't bother to disguise. And her skin was pale, almost translucent, like rice paper, over cheekbones that were high and sharp.

She exuded neediness.

Yet there was no cringing, no wheedling in her voice. She'd made her outlandish request in a brisk, businesslike manner, as if she'd been negotiating the price of a ribbon at market.

Even so, there was something rich and full that drew his notice. Perhaps it was the sound of her voice. He couldn't help thinking of buzzing bumblebees and honey. Cozy, unmade beds with feather pillows. Rich blue velvets, the same sky blue color as her eyes, and glossy fur muffs with deep silken pockets—even though she was wearing a threadbare gown.

"We can't solicit my grandmother for anything," he informed her. "She's abroad and left me no authority to open her accounts."

The girl didn't even attempt to hide her disappointment. "Oh, well, that's a shame. I'd so hoped."

He had trouble breathing for a moment. He was flummoxed. Thoroughly flummoxed. He was tempted to shake his head in wonder that he was dreaming. No one—save the burly highwayman who'd held a pistol to his head on the road north—had ever, *ever* petitioned him for money in such a direct manner. Even street beggars touched their forelocks or looked at the ground when asking him for a farthing.

"You so hoped to meet my grandmother . . . or so hoped to draw from her accounts?" he asked smoothly to cover the fact that he was sorely rattled.

And oddly fascinated.

She made a wry face, which made her look a bit like a naughty pixie, then let out a short sigh. "Both. I'll admit when I saw the name Lady Pinckney in your letter, I had a small, happy vision." She spread her sturdily booted feet a delicate space apart and put her small palms up in front of her as if she were setting up a glorious story. "A vision of a doting godmother hugging me close. Followed swiftly by another vision of her opening a trunkful of gold, the coins spilling into my lap, and all our troubles ending because I'd restore Castle Vandemere to its former glory."

"Is that so?"

"Yes, which would mean silken pennants flying from the turrets, a repaired drawbridge, and new drapes. Yes, new drapes in every room. And perhaps a massive sideboard, in the great hall, and a new suit of armor. Ours is so shabby. The left arm fell off last week and suffered yet another dent, thanks to Jinx, our overly curious tabby cat, knocking it over again." She paused, lost in her daydream, then said, "Of course, the castle will never be as grand as the Keep, but there are possibilities here. Distinct possibilities."

This was theater, wasn't it? A woman prosing on about how to spend his family's money?

"Do go on," he said, highly entertained in spite of himself.

"Oh, yes," she replied with enthusiasm. "I never mentioned the bedchambers. All of them need renovating."

"What good ideas you have."

"I must admit I do," she said. "But I see now that such a perfect scenario is merely a silly fantasy."

"Indeed, it is." His voice was rough now. "I'm appalled at your avarice. You do nothing to hide it. I've never met a lady as audacious as you."

"Then you've not met my stepmother," Miss Montgomery replied, unfazed.

He nearly choked. "She's *worse*?"

"Tenfold. But unlike her, I'm not greedy in the least. Nor would I have accepted your grandmother's charity. It would have been a loan only, I'll have you know, and I'd only have done it because I'm responsible for other people's welfare." Her cheeks were bright red now. "So you can stop your rude judgments of my character. I could say plenty about your own, by the way, but I won't. Because you look *awful*. If I were a man and looked as bad as you, I'd be rude, too. But after tonight, when you get a good night's rest, I'll not tolerate such boorish behavior anymore."

How had she done that? How had she turned everything around and made *him* look bad?

She was the grasping one. She was the one—

He opened his mouth to speak—he wasn't sure what he was going to say—but she put up a hand. "Enough with our disagreement. Let's appreciate the irony that in place of my silly fantasy, what I got instead is a quarrelsome man with a black eye, reeking of the tavern and the stables." She gave a genuine chuckle and clapped her hand over her mouth to restrain herself. But she couldn't stop. She let her hand fall away and laughed outright. "How funny life can be! Don't you agree?"

"Yes, it can be." What a compelling creature! Perhaps because she was being so blasted honest. He wasn't used to that.

That and she was almost enchanting when she laughed.

Not quite, of course, considering she was laughing at *him*.

But almost.

"Are you all right?" Miss Montgomery asked him. "I mean, you look as though"—she made an ungraceful looping motion with one hand—"as if you've been—"

"To hell and back?" He completed the sentence for her.

"Well, yes. Surely someone who's been to hell and back requires tea." Her tone was pert.

A very small corner of his mind was still hale enough to find her lack of artifice amusing.

"Brandy would do better," he said.

"We've none of that. We have some whisky, however. But"—she paused—"are you sure you need . . . *more*? You don't look as if more would help. Perhaps less would be better. Or none." She inhaled. "None is what I meant, actually."

"There's a tipping point, you know," he told her. "Forbearance would be counterproductive at this stage. It might lead to a massive headache."

"You don't have one already?"

Devil take it, must she remind him?

He'd try for a new subject. "It was a long trek up

the hill from your village. Glen Dewey must be the remotest outpost in the Highlands. I had to walk the last three miles to get to it from the main road."

"Yes, we're isolated here." Miss Montgomery didn't sound at all apologetic. "I'm shocked you found us at all."

She smiled at him, ignoring the fact that he refused to smile back at her.

"You're in pain," Miss Montgomery remarked. "Please, my lord. Do sit down and make yourself comfortable. I promise I won't—"

"Mention money?" He lowered himself onto an ancient sofa.

She winced. "Yes. At least for—at least until you feel *better*."

He longed to tell her that his stomach ached from lack of food, too much drink, and not enough sleep. He'd also love to confess that he'd played cards all night with a roomful of crofters just to get here today. He'd lost his last gold button and then—

His lucky penny, the one responsible for all his good fortune . . . the one he'd hidden from his friends when they'd taken his last farthing. He hadn't had any compunctions about concealing it—it wasn't as if he were ever going to spend it.

It was merely a talisman, the lucky penny his Scottish grandfather had given him when he was but six years old. Granddad had said, "Here's your lucky penny. What you see is what you get. Dinnae forget that, laddie."

Charlie remembered clutching the penny in his chubby fist and crying when his mother had tried to remove it that night at dinner. And so he'd stowed it away in his pocket.

Every day.

For the rest of his life.

Through Eton, Oxford, Granddad's funeral, all the weddings of Charlie's friends, and every purchase of castle or property on behalf of his family, he'd had the lucky penny on his person. He was convinced that it had everything to do with the fact that whatever business prospect he touched turned to gold.

But by some odd chance, the penny had appeared on the faded green baize table last night. Had one of the barmaids removed it from his pocket? He still didn't know. The Highland whisky had been flowing freely and—

The next thing he'd known, the lucky penny had been won.

Won *away* from him by a toothless old man who'd roared at Charlie when he'd tried to win it back, "Stay away! It's mah lucky penny noo!" And had disappeared into the eerie white night of the Highland summer.

Charlie had watched him disappear around the stables and let him go. At the time, he could barely stand straight as it was.

Things had gone rapidly downhill. First, there'd been the fight over—nothing. He'd been in many of those the last month. People in dire straits tended to be in bad moods when they were hungry or looking for a place to sleep. And then after his black eye, a large-eared drover had required him to sing "Will

Ye Go, Lassie?" on the bartop before he'd allow Charlie on the back of his wagon. He'd been dumped at the nearest market town and fortunately picked up by one of several coaches filled with anglers heading north of Glen Dewey to the village of Brawton.

Miss Montgomery bit her lip. "I'm sorry. I'm being a terrible hostess." She ran a hand through her curls. "Let me get you a poultice for that eye."

"No, thank you." Charlie told himself that he was being curt, yet he couldn't help making excuses.

He was half drunk.

He was in an ill temper.

He was an Impossible Bachelor.

With no money.

It was hell being poor. He'd found no redeeming value in it. The irony was, whether he was in rags or in a London ballroom, he was pursued for his purse either way.

"You *need* a poultice," Miss Montgomery said. "To stop the swelling—"

"No poultices," he snapped.

He couldn't bother being pleasant. There was that low level of throbbing all over his head, coupled with the fact that he had no desire to be his grandmother's emissary anymore. The trip had lost its luster after the third or fourth time he'd seen his life flash before his eyes in the numerous perilous encounters with man or nature he'd had since leaving London.

The girl halted. "All right," she said. "Have it your way."

Her tone was just dry enough to suggest that he was spoiled, which he certainly was *not*.

All right, perhaps he was, but he was new at the discomfort business, wasn't he? That night at his club in London when he'd agreed to leave off money for a while, he'd been thrown to the wolves, as it were, and was simply glad that he'd made it this far north in one piece.

"You will have received my note," he said. How brazen the young lady must think him, to assume that a letter of introduction written by his own hand from a seedy inn days before would excuse his present appearance and behavior. He knew it did not.

Nevertheless, there was a moment's awkward silence which he took pitiless pleasure in not breaking. But for this woman, he'd be happily ensconced in a chair at his club in Town. And he wouldn't have lost his lucky penny. In other words—

Everything was all her fault.

But Miss Montgomery didn't seem to notice his resentment.

She took a breath and crossed her arms over her modest bosom. "Yes," she said breezily. "Do you care to explain your letter further? You said that per your grandmother's wishes, you'd be at my ceaseless beck and call."

"Ceaseless?"

"Don't you remember? And you went on to say that noble words and deeds are what define a man, not the depth of his pockets. An admirable sentiment."

Did he really say that? He'd been in his cups when he'd written it. It sounded like something Arrow would profess.

"It's true," he said, trying to gain his bearings. "It's true that a man shouldn't be defined by how rich or poor he is."

"I had no idea you meant it quite so literally." Her face took on a regretful expression. "How kind of you to journey all the way up here—to suffer such indignities"—she cast a swift glance under the sofa where the turnip now lay—"when you're obviously short of funds."

She made an effort to look sympathetic, but her disappointment was palpable.

"Of course, there's always the chance you keep your coins in a very deep pocket," she added, her face brightening.

Good God, the woman was unashamedly transparent. She was after *his* money now.

"I'm penniless at the moment." He merely shrugged. "As for the journey, it was nothing."

Nothing, his arse. It was damned well something, and he never wanted to go through it again. He couldn't wait to leave this place and get back home to his luxurious town house in London.

"You've shown true dedication to the responsibilities inherent in being a godmother," she managed to compliment him.

He not only questioned her sincerity, he seethed under such an incongruous label. "I'm merely the emissary, if you'll recall. It's my grandmother you should admire. The woman has an unnatural penchant for collecting goddaughters."

"Does she?"

"Yes."

"Have you ever helped one before?"

"No."

Her brow furrowed.

"Miss Montgomery," he said, "you needn't worry. Yes, it's true that whatever your problem is, we'll have to settle it without my family's money. Due to an unfortunate series of events, I've lost complete access to it, and I've no idea if or when I'll get it back. And your godmother is inaccessible for a goodly while. But rest assured, I shall offer you my sage counsel, and I'm committed to staying until your dilemma is resolved."

There. He'd let her know in no uncertain terms that he could offer her no money.

So why did he feel more vulnerable than he had when he'd offered his paramours expensive baubles?

He had no idea.

But he did.

And he didn't like it.

CHAPTER FOUR

He braced himself for a dire response, but Miss Montgomery didn't appear as if she'd faint. Or cry.

She merely nodded. "Very well. We'll begin with our various talents, the eleven pounds I've already saved, and luck. And then we'll go from there. Surely we'll be able to amass four hundred pounds putting our heads together."

"Four hundred pounds?"

She might as well be asking for the moon!

He stood. "I can't stay long enough to help you amass such a sum. It could take years."

"I don't have years."

"Exactly why do you need so much? Drapes, sideboards, and drawbridge repairs shouldn't cost a tenth of that amount."

She sighed. "A very good question. The first one hundred pounds are needed immediately. They'll go to paying the annual *feu* duty to the landlord at the Keep. Without it, we could be removed from the property—as soon as the first of July, mere weeks away. Another hundred will be put aside for next year's *feu* duty. The rest will be invested in the estate, mainly in the sheep herd, to get us back on our feet so that we no longer have to suffer the indignity of borrowing from anyone."

"Pardon my mentioning this"—he looked round at the faded room—"but it's evident the castle's not in the best of condition. And the estate appears unwieldy for a young, untried lady to oversee. Surely it would be best if you moved elsewhere."

"No other place will do." She raised her chin. "I have people to worry about. Hester and Joe, the servants. They've lived here since well before I was born. And this is my home. My *home*, sir. Not merely an abode."

Her eyes glistened with a hint of moisture, but she didn't acknowledge the sheen of tears in the least.

He understood that sense of pride and attachment. He'd acquired many properties on his family's behalf, but not a one of them meant anything to him—other than his ancestral home in Devon.

"But you *do* comprehend," he said, "how much four hundred pounds is? It would take most citizens of Britain decades—many of them their whole lives, if ever—to earn such a sum."

"Oh, yes, I know. It's a bundle." She distractedly tapped a finger on her mouth while looking him over. "I'm perfectly willing to hope that even in your penurious—and I might add, downtrodden—state you'll be useful in acquiring it, however. What *can* you do?"

"Ride, fence, box, and . . . and sing. I'm very good at singing." How pathetic that sounded.

"I'm afraid riding, fencing, boxing, and singing won't be much use." She tilted her head. "Anything else you forgot to mention?"

He hesitated. "I know how to make money. But I can't do it from scratch. I need starter funds."

Miss Montgomery actually clapped her hands. "That's perfect." She grinned. "That's exactly what I need, someone who knows how to make money."

Somehow she'd wound up a mere foot from him. She studied him closely, and as she did, he couldn't help being fascinated by her blue eyes, the way they slanted up ever so slightly, as if she were a fairy.

"Do you have money to invest?" he asked her.

"No." She wrapped her thin arms around her too-thin body. "And you've already said you don't."

"No. Unfortunately."

Her expression drooped.

There was a short, sad silence.

"Now that you've been enlightened as to the stark particulars of our arrangement," he said, "no doubt you're sorry you contacted my grandmother at all."

She gave him a wan smile. "No, that's not it in the least. I'm disappointed because I need someone who believes we can make something from nothing." She sighed. "But you don't believe it's possible, do you?"

"I never said—"

"You rely on money to solve your woes," she said flatly. "Not that I blame you. I'm trying to reach the point that I have enough money to do the same thing. But there's one good thing about not having any. When you're poor, you develop a very good imagination. You need it to survive. To have hope. Because sometimes . . . there's nothing else."

There was a split second of silence, and she puckered up her brow, as if she were thinking.

Thinking hard.

It was rather adorable of her. And yet she'd unsettled him, too.

"That's not it at all," he answered, but inside, he felt she was dangerously close to understanding him. Surely it had been a lucky guess. "Have you ever considered that you're asking too much of a godmother—or a godmother's grandson?"

She tilted her head. "Isn't it a godmother's duty to demonstrate the great virtues for her charges? Courage, fortitude, nobility, and usefulness?"

"It might be, but must I remind you, I'm—"

"And it's been my impression," she went on equably, "that the duty of your English peerage is to demonstrate those same virtues for the masses. Therefore, you're under double obligation here, sir."

She folded her hands in front of her.

"Miss Montgomery, you're carrying this idea of duty a bit too far—" He pulled a squashed cheroot from his pocket, leaned round her—coming perilously close to brushing her waist with his arm—and lit the cheroot on a taper.

The expression on her face as she waited for him to take a puff—half annoyed, half impatient—was surely going to ruin a good smoke.

Why was it that women tended to do that?

Sure enough, after one measly draw, her brow furrowed deeper, and his pleasure in the cheroot evaporated.

Thank God he wasn't married.

She put her hands on her slender hips. "Lord Lumley." Her tone was point-blank. "You're obviously a devoted grandson to have traveled such a long way on your grandmother's behalf. And I already know that when your purse isn't under lock and key, you're a wealthy viscount. But what kind of man are you? For the purposes of my project— the Restore-Castle-Vandemere-to-Its-Former-Glory project, I've just now dubbed it—that's what I'd like to know. What I *need* to know."

A beat of charged silence passed. He felt an odd thrill at her boldness of speech.

"Well?" She peered at him with genuine curiosity and not a little impatience.

He needed to think on the question a moment, so he inhaled on his cheroot. "I'm the sort of man who keeps his promises," he eventually said. "I told you I'd stay and see you through, and I shall."

"In that case, you'll need to become noble and useful immediately." She stared at his black eye. "*If* that's possible for a bachelor of your ilk."

"And what kind of ilk is that?"

"The naughty kind, of course."

"How astute of you to peg me so quickly," he countered, and took a step toward her, the way a cold man instinctively takes a step toward a fire. He felt the need for some feminine attention. But not from a tavern wench or a milkmaid with a wandering eye. He wanted it from a girl who wasn't so easy to land. A girl like this one. Then the notice would feel hard-won.

Nothing was hard-won in his world.

"I wouldn't mind kissing you," he said, "to prove to you that your suspicions about my ilk are founded. I should tell you that after I conclude my duties here, the very same ilk will travel the world with fancy women and get stinking drunk wherever it goes, while *your* ilk will stay bored in the north of Scotland."

She stood staring at him, completely unfazed by his shocking speech. And the number of times he'd said *ilk*.

"Meanwhile"—he came closer, lifting her chin—"I'd like to find out what an indignant maiden's lips taste like. Scones? Sugar? Or scorn?"

She attempted to swat his hand away smartly, but he caught it.

"I'm not one of your London playthings," she said boldly, and yanked her wrist free.

He couldn't help but be impressed.

She took a small cracked china bowl off a marble-topped side table and thrust the container at him. "Please put it out."

She angled her chin at the cheroot.

He studied her pouting lips and took another drag of smoke. He wanted to kiss her more than ever now.

"Did you hear me?" she asked in that honey-bee voice of hers and pushed the bowl at him once more.

"We've just washed the drapes. My stepmother wouldn't care for the smell of smoke in them. We get enough from the chimneys."

He narrowed his eyes even further and reluctantly complied, smashing the smoking stick into the bowl while her arm remained steady, her too-thin wrist strong, her demeanor unshaken.

Charlie was impressed again. Or irritated. It was too much trouble to discern which.

Plain though she was, she piqued his temper, which was a good thing as he had no desire ever to be happy again. His head hurt too much. He didn't have his lucky penny. And he didn't have anyone to love.

Not that he *wanted* someone to love.

Blast it all, he *did* need that poultice. And a rum punch. And a warm bed in which he wouldn't fear for his life as he slept. He was getting maudlin, perhaps hallucinating, imagining himself one of those men who suddenly found the bachelor lifestyle unpalatable.

She put the bowl back down on the table, and he noticed above her head a charming stained-glass window depicting a solemn man and woman, in medieval garb, holding hands.

"You're playing with another sort of fire," he told her. "You're brazen in your requests and your demands. Your behavior has been as outrageous as my own would have been—had I given you that kiss." He hooked her waist and pulled her close. "In short, you Highland girls are a handful."

Something hummed between them, but she didn't

even blink. "You're in Scotland now, my lord. Not England. Highland girls speak their minds."

"And London boys, dammit all, steal kisses. It's what we do. For good reason."

So he did. He stole a kiss and was surprised at how perfectly soft her lips were—

At how perfectly naturally their mouths and bodies fit together.

"Dai-*seee*!" A shrill voice interrupted the suddenly cozy tête-à-tête Charlie was having with Miss Montgomery.

She drew back.

He allowed his hand to slide off her waist.

"Well," she said. "I see your point about London boys."

Which was a perfectly amusing remark to make. It made it easier for him to forget the primal beat of the blood in his veins. He could focus on the fact that the girl before him had a certain wit and aplomb.

Never mind about the fire he'd sensed beneath that proper exterior. That was not to be an issue. He'd already been wayward enough. Grandmother wouldn't approve of his taking advantage of her charge.

Not that Miss Montgomery appeared easy to take advantage of . . . she was rather like a small battleship, the sneaky kind that can render great destruction if it so chooses—all cannon and harpoons and diabolical strategies and worn sails that needed replacing.

The worn sails . . . that came from the fact that

she could use a decent gown. It had character, but it didn't do her justice. Not that he admired her particularly and wanted to *see* her in a nicer gown.

No, he didn't. He was wary of her more than anything.

Of course, he wouldn't mind seeing her *out* of a gown, just for curiosity's sake.

Now Miss Montgomery looked over her shoulder, and when her gaze returned to his, her eyes were blue-black. "We'll have to make something up. At least until we get our plan solidly under way. Otherwise, my stepmother will sabotage it, even if what I'm after is in her best interests. She's stupid and cruel that way. Not only that, when she finds out your rank, she'll do her best to make my stepsister your viscountess. Are you engaged?"

"Good God, no."

"Well, for your own self-preservation, pretend you are."

Before he could agree, she turned her head toward the door just as it slammed open and three females tried to push their way through the entryway at the same time.

One young lady was quite beautiful, with masses of black curls and delicate features. Were she in London, she'd turn many a dandy's head at first glance. But Charlie saw right away that she knew she was striking, which led him to believe she probably had little else to recommend her. She was accompanied by another young woman who was taller than most men and as broad-shouldered as a dock worker. She had small eyes, a sour mouth, and a wide jaw, offset by tightly curled tresses of dull brown.

The oldest of the three, obviously the stepmother, was of average height and had a handsome enough face. Charlie surmised she'd probably been a beauty not too many years ago. Her hair was the same dull brown as the homely one, but a lock of white hair that started from her crown and descended in a bold line to her left ear gave her quite the dramatic look.

Unlike Miss Montgomery, the three of them appeared well fed. The beauty was a curvaceous pocket Venus. The other two had square torsos rounded by ample bosoms and large hips.

"Move," the matron snarled beneath her breath and made a motion to discreetly elbow her companions, but the movement was sloppy and obvious.

The pretty one moved, but only after gasping in real or supposed pain at the intended jab. The giantess stood aside, a surly expression on her face. It wasn't until all three locked gazes with him that their irritated expressions became cloyingly sweet.

And then irritated again, once they'd a chance to take in his shabby clothes.

"Who are *you*?" the stepmother demanded in a flat London accent.

"Yes, who *are* you?" The beauty looked him boldly up and down.

The large one said, "I've never seen such a handsome man, even if he *is* dirty."

At that, Charlie had a difficult time keeping his

face perfectly neutral. She sounded exactly like a man trying to sound like a woman in a play. Could she be a male dressed in women's clothing?

He peered closer at her. No. He didn't think so. That would be too odd. But he couldn't be entirely sure. The abundance of fabric and flounce she wore could camouflage a whole platoon.

He made no attempt at a jovial smile but, in a herculean effort, did lift up one corner of his mouth. "Good afternoon, ladies. I'm—"

"For all we know," the stepmother interrupted him, "you—with your black eye and your tattered but fine clothes—could be a crazy vagabond who's perhaps tied up or, God forbid, *murdered* a gentleman, stolen his breeches and coat, and arrived here intent on seducing the lady of the house into letting you stay."

Charlie made an immediate assumption: she was shrewd but eccentric, a dangerous combination. "Of course I'm not that sort of fellow," he said. "But if I were, I wouldn't tell you, would I?"

All three ladies gasped, but the stepmother appeared—

No. She couldn't be excited at the idea, could she?

"He's Viscount Lumley, Stepmother," explained Miss Montgomery.

"Viscount, indeed," the older woman said scornfully.

"I *am* a viscount," he said. "Why don't you check *DeBrett's Peerage*? My name's right there, and I'm rich as Croesus. Properties all over England. I've got a castle here in Scotland, too . . . somewhere near a glen."

"There are tens of thousands of glens!" Perdita said.

"Hundreds of glens," Miss Montgomery corrected her.

Lord Lumley shrugged. "I mean to visit it someday and shear some sheep as a lark. If I ever get around to it. Of course, it might be years . . . London's never dull."

"Where do you live in London?" the stepmother demanded to know.

"Mayfair. On Grosvenor Square. If you still don't believe me, write my good friend and neighbor, the Duke of Drummond. He'll tell you."

"I've heard of the Duke of Drummond," the older woman murmured.

By now her cunning expression also showed hints of ambition, as Miss Montgomery had predicted.

Miss Montgomery smiled pleasantly and looked him square in the eye. "The poor viscount has been set upon by footpads and lost his way. A kind soul in Glen Dewey sent him to us."

"Good thing," he said, "as my *fiancée*"—he made sure to emphasize the word—"would be terribly concerned, otherwise."

"You're engaged?" the stepmother demanded to know.

"Yes. I am." Charlie felt the full threat of her words and was vastly relieved to have a lie to tell. "To a lovely young lady."

He tried to think of a name. And then he tried to imagine what his imaginary fiancée looked like and couldn't decide if she were blond, dark, or chestnut haired. Tall or short. She was most definitely the belle of every ball she attended, which she went to alone—as balls bored him.

She was also a perfect virgin by day and a vixen by night.

Even though that was impossible.

But as she was only make-believe, he could make her anybody he wanted. She'd never speak of their impending nuptials, which somehow would never occur. And she certainly wouldn't make outrageous demands, the way Miss Montgomery did.

Of course, if she kissed the way Miss Montgomery did, that would be ideal. But in no other way would she be similar.

"What's your fiancée's name, Viscount?" the giantess yelled.

"W-would you like some tea?" Miss Montgomery asked him at the exact same time.

Thank God for the tea question because he was hoping to avoid answering the first.

But when he opened his mouth to say something, the pocket Venus interrupted. "I'll see that he's looked after, Daisy." She raked him with a shrewd glance. "Go prepare his bedchamber immediately, and don't dawdle."

"Bring us that tea first," the stepmother ordered Miss Montgomery.

"And don't forget the milk," the large one added in a booming voice. "You always do."

Charlie put aside for study later the discomfiting fact that the others were treating Miss Montgomery like a servant. Instead, he focused on her name.

Daisy.

He liked it.

It suited her.

Not that it mattered. It didn't matter at all.

But when she moved aside and the dark-haired siren took her place, he felt a lack—a lack he couldn't put his finger on.

Yet it was there, just the same.

CHAPTER FIVE

Daisy hadn't taken two steps when her stepmother repeated Perdita's question: "Who *is* your fiancée, Lord Lumley?"

Daisy stopped moving.

Lord Lumley stared intently at her.

She stared intently back.

Come on, she was thinking. *Think of a name!*

"Lord Lumley." Mona's demanding voice grated on Daisy's ears. "Who is your fiancée?"

Yes, who was she?

"She stands here before me," the viscount said in a rough voice.

Who? Who stood before him?

Daisy's palms began to sweat. He'd spoken as if he'd had to recite that line in a very bad school play when he was ten years old.

She locked gazes with the viscount's and prayed he'd come up with a convincing tale.

"She is Miss Montgomery," he went on in a rather sick voice.

Daisy looked over her shoulder, but there was no one there.

He couldn't mean—

Gasps were heard from every member of her stepfamily. Daisy wanted to gasp, too, but she felt if she opened her mouth, she might scream.

Swinging her gaze back to the viscount's, she saw the sheer, dogged determination on his face to lie through his teeth and knew she was in for trouble.

"Through letters," he practically whispered, "Miss Montgomery—*Daisy*—has consented to become my wife. Her godmother, after all, is my grandmother. So it seemed perfectly natural, when I realized my obligation as the heir, that we align the two families."

Good heavens!

Daisy felt a pinch on her arm.

"You've never spoken of this," Cassandra said through tight lips.

"No," Daisy whispered, rubbing her arm. "I haven't."

"You don't *act* engaged," Perdita said, her hands clenched into giant fists.

"Oh, but we are." Lord Lumley took two steps forward, leaned down, and kissed Daisy right on the lips.

It was her second kiss, and once again Daisy's mouth felt scorched. She wasn't sure if it was a bad or good feeling, but she took no time to wonder because she was furious at the viscount! So furious she could no longer breathe.

I have to learn how to breathe immediately, she thought, *because it's too late. This kiss is already happening, and unlike the last one, it's not stopping.*

She also had the fleeting thought, *I hate this man. What has he done?* But she had to give that thought up to concentrate.

The kiss was passionate one second and tender the next, so tender that she was aghast to realize she felt like weeping with the sheer wonder of it. Lord Lumley hugged her tighter, and she put her arms around his neck—his firm, solid man's neck. The kiss grew passionate again, hot and demanding on both sides, as if they were in a battle of wills.

Who could kiss better . . . and longer?

She couldn't help responding to the challenge, even though she knew it was in her best interests to stop. Mona, Cassandra, and Perdita were standing right there. They'd tease her mercilessly later; Mona would say hateful things about how she couldn't kiss worth two cents and would make a terrible hussy (Mona hated all competition).

But kissing the viscount was like being tickled against Daisy's will. Her mind screamed *no,* but her lips—her whole body—screamed *yes.*

"Stop it, both of you!" Perdita shrieked.

Which threw an immediate splash of proverbial cold water on the whole incident.

Daisy's and the viscount's lips came apart.

Whew. For once in her life, Daisy felt she should be grateful for her loud stepsister. But she wasn't.

She was frustrated. Kissing was the best thing she'd ever done. And she longed to try it a third time.

The viscount smiled down at her, although the smile didn't reach his eyes. "I'm the happiest man on earth."

He picked up Daisy's hand—which made her jump—and folded it tightly beneath his arm.

"There, there, dear," he said, as she tried to curl her fingers into a fist to better pull away, but he held her in an iron grip. "It's all right. You're supposed to find your future husband irresistible."

Perdita flapped her arms, which caused a waft of air to stir all her ruffles. "I hate you more than ever now, Daisy."

Mona tapped her foot. "How could you keep this a secret?"

Daisy was afraid to make eye contact with her stepmother, and so she stared at the floor to compose herself as her mind attempted to devise a lie and failed. "I—I was afraid to tell you," was all she could produce.

A most feeble story.

"She's being kind." The viscount patted her hand. "The truth is, I told her *not* to tell you until I was ready. I've been doing my best to complete some unfinished business so we can be together, but it's taken longer than I thought, and—"

"And what?" Mona asked.

Daisy's mind raced.

"And she missed me," Lord Lumley filled in. "She missed me so much she's been crying. Every night. And I had to come see her in person to prove my devotion."

Cassandra peered at her. "I *have* noticed how red and swollen her eyes are lately."

"Me, too," said Perdita.

God, Daisy hated her stepsisters sometimes!

Well, *all* the time, if she were honest.

"And *you* missed *me*, as well," Daisy said through gritted teeth to the viscount. "So much so that you—*you* cried every night, too."

Mona and Cassandra stared at each other and then back at him.

"He doesn't look the type," Cassandra said.

"No," Mona added speculatively.

"I didn't cry," the viscount insisted, completely unruffled and still gazing at Daisy adoringly. "I merely moaned. Once. In my sleep. I think it was indigestion."

"But you said it woke the neighbors," Daisy said, looking deep into his eyes. It was so difficult to appear besotted when you were aggravated. "And you told them that was the last straw. You had to come see me. You said something about how love was better than . . . petting a lamb with brown eyes. Or a pudding."

"Funny," he answered her, his eyes sparking with a message that she read loud and clear as: *You. Will. Pay. And it won't be pretty.* "I don't remember that part."

"I do," Daisy said, feeling nervous as a result of that threatening message of his, which he disguised well beneath his own cloying version of a besotted gaze. "We simply couldn't stay apart any longer.

He came here to win you over, Stepmother, despite his unfinished business." She sighed. "I'm sorry I didn't tell you sooner."

Oddly enough, a corner of Mona's mouth went up. "Don't be. Finally, you're showing some much-needed wiliness. A trait to be nurtured."

And then she laughed—a slow laugh that built into a crescendo that sent Jinx flying from the room, her tail cocked to the ceiling and puffy, like a thistle in full bloom.

"Very well," said Mona, seemingly satisfied with the explanations, thank God. "We'll adjust. But we don't have room for you in the castle, Viscount. We're already cramped. You'll have to sleep elsewhere."

"Don't tell me," he said with a weary sigh. "The byre?"

"Right." Mona wagged a finger at him. "And don't think you can hide there. If you want to become a member of this family, prepare to be worked to the bone. No man will be allowed to steal my stepdaughter's virtue without paying heavily for it, if not with gobs of money—which you apparently don't have at the moment but is my preferred method of restitution—then with arduous labor. In fact, I need you to move this sofa immediately. Closer to the east window."

She pointed to the extremely large sofa the viscount himself had lounged upon not a few minutes before.

"Very well," he gritted out, and sent Daisy another *you-will-pay-and-it-won't-be-pretty* look.

It's your *fault,* she sent back.

"Shall I tell you the story of my life, new brother?" Perdita yelled in his ear.

He winced. "I don't believe now's the time," he replied in grim tones, moving small tables and footrests out of the way of the sofa's path to its new resting place beneath the east window.

Nevertheless, just as he hoisted one end of the sofa with ease, Perdita began to regale him with a tremendous lie about her amazing ride on the back of a camel that she'd paid a nickel to ride down the Broad-Way when it had come to New York with a traveling circus.

She really ought to write books, Daisy thought, engrossed in the fantastical tale despite herself. *They'd never been to New York* or *seen a camel.*

But Daisy was even more engrossed in the way Lord Lumley's form was shown to perfection when he lifted that sofa.

He was a virile man. Shivers of awareness ran through her from head to toe. She was to pretend to be the viscount's fiancée? Eventually, Mona, Cassandra, and Perdita would find out she was not.

She was trapped.

Trapped.

But meanwhile, she was looking after her own best interests: hers, Hester's, and Joe's.

Even with that thought to comfort her, she still felt completely hemmed in by the situation, in more ways than one. Behind her was a solid low table beneath which Jinx had returned to splay herself, belly exposed hopefully, for potential scratches.

To her right, Cassandra glared at her. To her left stood Mona, who clapped her hands loudly, startling Daisy.

And then she saw why. Joe had entered the room, his cap doffed respectfully. "Pardon me, missus."

"Get out," Mona barked, and waved her hand toward the door.

"Can you not see we're busy?" Cassandra added.

Joe's face fell, and Daisy couldn't help blurting out: "He's here to tell us something important, Stepmother. He never comes in unless he needs help."

"Shut up, girl," Mona said. "Whatever it is, we'll take care of it later."

Girl.

Mona always called her that.

Joe, his face ashen with distress, hunched his shoulders and limped out the door again, not making eye contact with Daisy, even though she wished he would with all her heart.

Daisy hated her stepmother more than ever.

Mona immediately swept round the table, lowered herself upon the sofa in its new location, and patted the cushion next to her. "Do sit, Lumley. I must tell you about the drawbridge. It sags. You'll begin work on it tomorrow."

She raked her bold gaze over his tight, if a bit torn, buckskin breeches.

He stared at her. Then slowly came forward. But he didn't sit.

Daisy could hardly breathe.

Mona opened her mouth to speak again, but the viscount cut her off.

"I won't stand by and allow you to treat your servants and stepdaughter so cruelly." He exuded all the cold hauteur one would expect of a viscount.

"Yes," huffed Perdita. "She treats me like the veriest toad. Why, just yesterday—"

"Not you," Lumley interrupted her.

Perdita's mouth hung open for an appalling second, exposing a row of yellow teeth, and then shut. "Then whom?"

Daisy wanted to swat her for being so stupid!

"Your stepsister *Daisy*," the viscount explained to Perdita, his patience running thin, judging by the dangerous edge to his voice.

"You misunderstand me." Mona paused to indulge in a light yawn. "I have only Daisy's best interests at heart." She threw her arm over the back of the sofa and stared off into the distance, her overlarge bosom thrust out rudely.

"I think not," the viscount said. "And your lack of compassion to an elderly servant is equally reprehensible."

Mona turned and glared at him.

He glared right back.

"Mine is a family that doesn't tolerate cruelty." He addressed Mona in a low, threatening voice that sent tingles down Daisy's spine. "Have a care if you want to be received into it with any consideration for your own comforts. For soon your stepdaughter will be my wife, and I won't tolerate your viciousness."

Perdita whimpered.

Mona frowned at her. "Listen to him, and you'll lose the upper hand."

"Oh, right," said Perdita.

Daisy had to restrain an exasperated sigh. Perdita would never have the upper hand with anything, even if it were handed to her, much less the upper hand over someone as intimidating as the viscount.

He turned to Daisy, his eyes still snapping with fury. Mona's was such a nasty soul. But there was also something else in his gaze Daisy couldn't name. Perhaps it was a bit more comprehension of her situation than she'd let on in the letter to his grandmother.

There was no particular kindness in his eyes, she noted. Simply a better grasp of the magnitude of her problem.

"Miss Montgomery," he addressed her, "shall we go visit your servant and attend to his needs?"

"I'd love to." Daisy put her hand through his arm and, despite everything, felt a tiny bit happy and hopeful for the first time in a long time. The viscount might not be what she'd expected, but things were already changing. Just as she'd felt in her bones they would.

CHAPTER SIX

It had been a momentous day. Daisy had kissed the viscount. *Twice.* And now she was pretending to be engaged to him. He'd also captured an escaped lamb, who'd been bleating for its mother high on a rocky hillock Joe couldn't possibly climb. It was a minor feat of heroism for which she'd longed to kiss Lord Lumley again but didn't dare.

Hester had called everything a "shocking turn of events" even before Daisy had whispered in her ear that the engagement was a ruse. *After* she'd learned the truth, Hester had amended her description to a "shocking, scandalous turn of events."

And it had been scandalous!

All afternoon and early evening, Daisy couldn't help thinking back to her initial conversation with the viscount, to how she'd slapped away his hand, exchanged bold words with him, and been pulled into his arms. Of course, the next thing she knew, they'd shared that first kiss.

It had been short and sweet, even more delicious

and unexpected than turning a corner and seeing a rainbow ahead. Or waking up, sliding into your chair at the breakfast table, and seeing a lovely cup of chocolate when all you thought you had in the house was tea.

The second kiss defied description. Thinking about it brought on shortness of breath.

Now it was dinner, and Daisy gathered her courage. She must face the viscount and decide exactly what to do with him—other than kiss him, that is.

The gown she wore, a castoff from Cassandra, wasn't the prettiest in the world, but she'd added a bit of lace trim to the sleeves and neckline that gave her an extra boost of confidence.

"I don't know why I feel the need to impress him," she whispered to Hester, while the servant laced up the back of her dress. "But I do."

"It's because he's so handsome," Hester said, adjusting Daisy's curls. "Even though he's got Sassenach blood, he's the Golden Prince, all right. It's uncanny." She took Daisy by the shoulders and turned her toward the looking glass. "And you're the Golden Girl."

Daisy blushed. "His being handsome has naught to do with it," she tried to convince herself. "I must impress him for practical reasons. That's why. He's the key to keeping Castle Vandemere."

But she couldn't help but wonder what it would be like to be held in his arms again and kissed once more, without interruption.

Hester made an impatient noise. "We'll have none of that talk. Ye're going to enjoy yourself tonight."

She draped the bold family tartan sash over one of Daisy's shoulders. "Don't ye be worryin' about the *feu* duty. Not this evening."

Daisy stroked her hand over the sash that had belonged to her mother. "Yes. Who knows when I'll ever be engaged in truth? I'll do my best to enjoy it. And at the very least, if the viscount can help us keep possession of the castle, then I'll be happy."

Hester sighed. "Happy? How can we be with the Furies in residence?"

"We must endure them," Daisy said. "Perhaps they'll grow tired of Scotland and leave. They hate it so."

"I wish they would."

"Until they do, we'll work around them," Daisy said.

Mama had taught her that. In the old days, she'd brought Daisy with her to her little bungalow that Papa had built her, to sit at her feet while she painted. *"You have to work with the paint,"* she'd told Daisy, *"and work with whatever the day brings you. If it's a wee bit dreary out, you paint it. But paint it so it makes you glad to be inside near a cozy fire."*

"Just think how much better our nightly chats in the kitchen are because we know the Furies are too lazy and rude to join us," Daisy said.

"True," the housekeeper replied with a sigh.

Daisy grinned. "I vow if they weren't appallingly close, the shortbread and milk wouldn't taste half so fine. Nor would our jokes be as entertaining."

"I never thought of it that way." Hester patted Daisy's rear. "There must be enduring," she said, "but there must also be true *living*. Which includes men and women falling in love."

"Hester." Daisy felt her cheeks pinken, "You speak much too hastily."

Hester chuckled. "I dinnae say falling in love right away, although it can happen. I meant when the time is right, lass."

It won't ever be right, Daisy reminded herself.

And then went back to thinking about the viscount's mouth. When he spoke, his lips appeared hard and firm with a cynical curl to the upper edge of them. But when he'd kissed her, they'd turned soft and teasing.

His hand about her waist had been possessive, yes, which had almost riled her, but she'd also experienced the wonderful sensation of being held close as if she mattered.

As if she mattered.

She'd no idea how Lord Lumley had managed that, especially as the act had seemed rather selfish and immature.

But during both kisses, she felt as if he'd never let her go. And when they'd parted, he'd had a gleam in his eye that made her breathless.

Before today, she'd never kissed a man. In the old days in Glen Dewey, there'd been many a fine, strapping lad, Hester had told her, but many of them had emigrated or been killed in the Wars. The few that were left were friendly, but none made Daisy's heart race. None made her shy to look at them.

Earlier, when she'd brought the tea tray into the drawing room after the lamb-saving incident, she'd not wanted to meet Lord Lumley's gaze. She wasn't sure why, especially when she'd spoken so bluntly to him, shared kisses with him, and seen a piece of his flesh through a hole in the back of his filthy, travel-worn breeches when he was climbing that hillock.

He'd not been wearing drawers—

But perhaps she'd felt shy because around her stepmother and stepsisters, he'd seemed somehow different. He'd made an effort to be charming. Less brusque. As if he were giving Mona a chance to redeem herself. She didn't deserve it, but Daisy supposed that was the gentlemanly thing to do.

Mona had responded beautifully, not asking him any difficult questions the way Daisy had. And after tea, he'd taken a walk about the estate with Cassandra, of all people, who usually hated traipsing out-of-doors. While they'd been gone, Daisy had carried hot water to the byre, refusing to let Joe and Hester bear the burden.

Now, at dinner, Lord Lumley was bathed, rested, and apparently recovered from his sore head, although his black eye gleamed blue in the candle-light.

Mona presided over the head of the table. The viscount was in the place of honor to her right. Cassandra sat next to him, and Perdita sat across from them.

Even though she was now supposed to be his fiancée, Daisy was relegated to the bottom of the table. A large epergne filled with gorgeous red velvet rose blossoms in the middle made it impossible for her to see any further than Perdita's elbow on her left or Cassandra's top knot on her right. As for the viscount and Mona, they might as well have been invisible.

Daisy was sure they couldn't see her, either.

Mona had seated her this way at dinner ever since Papa had died, and it was laughable, really. Like something out of a farce, especially as Daisy was tasked with gathering all the flowers and greenery with which to hide her presence.

Hester thought it comical, too, usually.

But tonight was different. When Hester entered the room carrying the trout and potatoes, she made eye contact with Daisy—and Hester's were not dancing with their usual mirth but gleamed with frustration.

Daisy allowed herself to feel the pang she'd been suppressing: finally, she was missing something worthwhile. She wanted to see the viscount, to be part of the party! She was pretending to be engaged to him, after all!

You want to be the belle of the ball, the way your father intended you to be, a voice in her head said frankly. *But you can't. And even more, you shouldn't be.*

The truth wasn't easy to bear. Her heart knocked against her chest, so to recover her equilibrium, she pretended to look under the table for a missing hairpin—

And saw Cassandra putting her hand on the viscount's leg.

Then witnessed him just as quickly moving his leg out of reach.

When Daisy sat up again, she was almost glad no one could see her. She knew her eyes would be wide with shock and, if she were honest with herself, a bit of amusement.

Cassandra was not only devious and disloyal. She was acting like a tart. Daisy always knew she would if given half the chance.

The viscount immediately went up a notch in Daisy's estimation.

"So, my lord," Cassandra was saying now, as if the under-the-table maneuvers had never taken place, "you look comfortable in my late stepfather's clothing."

"I am, thank you," Daisy heard him say in equally smooth tones. "I'm very grateful to you all for providing me with them."

Daisy took a sip of wine. She'd caught a glimpse of him as she'd walked in. He'd cut a fine figure in her father's coat—although it was a trifle tight across the shoulders. She'd felt a brief combination of sorrow and happiness at seeing the garment, curious to get closer to it—to the viscount—to suss out whether he deserved to wear it. She wasn't sure anyone did.

Yet Mona had kept Lord Lumley trapped in conversation, so she hadn't been able to talk to him.

And now . . .

Now it was as if she didn't exist.

"You look like the Golden Prince," Perdita said.

Lord Lumley laid down his fork. "Why, thank you—I think. Who is he?"

Perdita was so overcome by his direct gaze, her lips clamped tight. She was holding her breath, Daisy knew.

"There's a legend that the owner of Castle Vandemere will find true love at the ball held on the final night of the great hunt," she explained on her stepsister's behalf.

The viscount swiveled to look at Daisy, and she heard Perdita release a great huff of air. Lord Lumley didn't even flinch. Instead, he leaned over, presumably to see Daisy better around Cassandra.

"Can you tell me more?" he asked her politely.

She could see only the right side of his face as Cassandra was blocking most of him. "Did you see that stained-glass window in the drawing room?"

She knew, of course, that he had. He'd kissed her right below it. He couldn't have missed it.

"Indeed, I did," he answered her.

She saw a spark of something flash in his eye. Was he remembering that kiss?

"That's the Golden Prince," Daisy explained, "holding hands with the Golden Girl. They're the first pair of many lovers who supposedly declared themselves here at the castle on the night of the hunt ball."

"But they no longer have a great hunt around here," Cassandra interrupted rudely, "or balls, or any eligible men, for that matter. It's dull as dishwater."

"It's a perfectly charming legend," Lord Lumley said helpfully.

"But legends are for dreamers," Mona said.

"Idiots, more like," Perdita added with a snort of laughter.

Mona cackled with her. Cassandra smiled into her wine.

Daisy felt a stab of hurt on behalf of her parents, who'd treasured the legend and the bit of stained glass that preserved it.

"Legends become legends for a reason," she said. "There *is* something special about Castle Vandemere. I feel it every time I look at the Golden Prince and the Golden Girl."

The laughter immediately ceased, and there was another uncomfortable silence. Daisy was grateful for the epergne. She could sense the disapproval emanating from the other three women.

The viscount's face—what she could see of it—wore an inscrutable expression. "Excuse me, Mrs. Montgomery," he said, "but I can't see all the members of our party. Might we move the centerpiece, as attractive as it is?"

Daisy's heart almost stopped. *She* was the only one he couldn't see!

Why would he want to see me? was her first thought. But then told herself—because Hester would be angry at her for thinking otherwise— that she was well worth seeing, even though she didn't believe it and her stepmother and stepsisters didn't believe it, either.

Of course, she must remember she was the viscount's supposed fiancée, as well. That should count for something.

"Perhaps we could move the thing," Mona said in desultory fashion. "Daisy, you take care of it. The old man, wherever he is at the moment, is useless. He might as well be dead for all the good he does us."

"His name is Joe, Stepmother," Daisy said through gritted teeth. "And he may be old, but please don't suggest he's better off dead. I care very much about him."

When Daisy stood, she could feel Cassandra's eyes boring into her, but she refused to look that way, which meant she also made no eye contact with the viscount.

"*I'll* do the honors," he said, and stood. "Please be seated, Miss Montgomery."

She did as he asked, her chest constricting when she saw the look Mona directed at her. It wasn't pleasant.

Nevertheless, she sat with her brow smoothed out and her hands clenched, unseen, in her lap. Lord Lumley lifted the bulky object, carefully avoiding the flaming candle tapers on either side, and put the epergne on the sideboard, where it had always sat when her father had been alive.

When the viscount returned to his seat, he turned to her, a half-smile tilting one corner of his mouth. "That's better, isn't it?"

In the candlelight, his brown eyes had warm golden tints. Her heart gave a little flutter. He was handsome.

He was the Golden Prince!

Hester, and now Perdita, had noticed the same uncanny resemblance.

Daisy allowed herself only a close-lipped smile. "It's much better, thank you."

Mona and Cassandra stared daggers at her, but that was nothing new, so Daisy's appetite wasn't affected in the least. She ate heartily of her trout and potatoes, which Hester dished out liberally to her, knowing Mona wouldn't object while the viscount was present. Mona and Cassandra dominated the conversation with their inane prattle. Perdita had a tendency to moan her appreciation of her dinner while she chewed, so for the most part, she said little. The viscount appeared to listen attentively to the one-sided conversation, but Daisy could swear she saw his jaw tighten as the minutes passed.

"So the village is quite dull," Mona was saying. She punctuated the statement with an enormous sigh, which caused her massive bosom to jiggle. She was wearing her most low-cut gown, a vulgar puce sheath, and her hair was topped with a matching turban sporting three dyed feathers.

Cassandra, arresting in a golden gown of Grecian design, lifted a lovely shoulder. "Mother's right." She made a delicate moue that Daisy had seen her practice in front of a looking glass a thousand times. "There's nothing to do up here in Scotland."

The viscount put down his glass. "Nothing?"

Perdita let out a particularly ill-timed moan— not that Daisy could blame her. Hester's trout and potatoes were excellent.

"There are many things," Daisy interjected hastily.

Everyone turned to her. Mona and Cassandra were stone-faced.

Oh, dear, Daisy thought. Perhaps she shouldn't have spoken. But it was too late now.

Gathering her courage, she cleared her throat. "There's trout and salmon fishing. And deer stalking. And every year, after a massive hunt, there used to be a competition in which men raced each other up Ben Fennon. And you should have seen them toss cabers, which are like large tree trunks. They even lifted enormous rocks in feats of strength. To conclude the festivities, there was a *ceilidh* . . . a dance."

"I knew all that, of course," Lord Lumley told her, merriment dancing in his eyes.

And then he smiled.

Perdita gasped out loud. Daisy nearly slid down her chair. When he smiled, he was—

Magnificent.

Handsome wasn't a big enough word.

She inhaled a discreet breath to compose herself. "Then why did you allow me to boast of our vast array of amusements, sir?" She grinned back, just a little. "Not that I'll allow myself to feel foolish. My boasting was completely justified."

"It was," he agreed, and looked round at the other women at the table. "Which is why I dared not interrupt. It appears some people here aren't aware of the exciting opportunities to be had in the Highlands."

"Not for me," Perdita said.

Daisy couldn't tell which was worse: the ugliness of Perdita's tone, or the completely flat expressions on the faces of Cassandra and Mona.

So into the awkward silence, she blurted out what came to her head at the moment: "No one has ever stopped me from fishing. Indeed, it's a favorite pastime."

She didn't mention that fishing was a very necessary pastime, as well, to help keep them fed. When Joe was too busy to fish, as often happened, it was up to her to sneak away from Mona when she was finished with her chores and cast a line in the nearby burn.

"Is it something you enjoy?" the viscount asked her as if he were shocked.

"Of course." Why should he be surprised? Did he think women were weak creatures?

Cassandra gave a dramatic shudder. "The very thought of hooking a flopping fish makes me ill."

Lord Lumley ignored her disgust.

"Perhaps you can show me your angler's tricks while I'm here," he said to Daisy. "I find I always learn something new about fishing from the locals. Especially the ones kind enough to tolerate my own attempts not only to catch something in their waters but to surpass their own catch. It's very rude of me. But if you can endure my competitive nature, I'd be much obliged."

There was that twinkle in his eye again.

"I'm happy to put up with your sporting ambitions," Daisy answered him, "and if I were a better hostess, I'd inform the fish they should attach themselves to your hook, not mine. Alas, I'm not so well mannered."

Cassandra skewered Daisy with a piercing look that resembled hatred.

"People can't speak to fish," Perdita said in self-important tones.

There was another blank silence that Daisy longed to cover up but she dared not, as Mona stabbed her trout viciously and glared at her, almost white-eyed.

"Speaking of sporting ambitions," the viscount said eventually, "the last leg of my trip here I was picked up by a bevy of glossy black coaches carrying a group of anglers, all international travelers of some means. They dropped me outside of Glen Dewey and continued up to Brawton."

"They've fine fishing in Brawton," said Daisy. "Most visitors don't know Glen Dewey has just as much. We're a bit off the beaten path."

"So I noticed. But I must say, those extra three miles I walked to get here were worth the effort."

"Yes," Daisy said, "there's something special about Glen Dewey. Something unspoiled."

"That's a kind way to say *tedious*," said Cassandra.

"I'm so sick of *tedious*," Mona said with a yawn.

"Me, too," said Perdita with a long, rude sigh. "I long for the dirty streets of Cheapside."

Daisy caught the viscount's eye and saw that he was amused—or perhaps, bemused—by her step-family.

"I like *tedious* if that's what you'd call this trout.

It's delectable." The viscount pierced a forkful, held it up, then popped it in his mouth.

Daisy smiled. The twinkle in his eye softened, then as his gaze lengthened, she had to look away. She wondered what he was thinking. Had he been remembering earlier today, when they'd been alone? When he'd kissed her?

At the meal's conclusion, he excused himself early to write letters rather than retire with them to the drawing room.

He hesitated at the door and gave a little chuckle. "Oh, never mind. I can't do that."

"Whyever not?" Mona asked him. "There's quill and paper on the desk in the library."

"Oh, it's nothing," he said cryptically. "Pardon me for thinking out loud. I do appreciate the quill and paper."

"The footpads," Daisy guessed. "They took what money you had. You can't post letters."

She could tell by his expression that she'd guessed right.

"We can post the letters for you," Mona said.

He hesitated the barest fraction of a moment. "That would involve your spending money on my behalf, and I'd rather not."

"Really, Viscount, it's no trouble," Mona insisted. "It's only a few pennies."

He smiled that glorious smile he had. "I appreciate your concern, but I'll decline your generous offer."

Daisy thought his behavior a little odd. But she supposed he was being polite.

"Thank you for a delightful evening." He swept them a low bow. "I shall see all of you in the morning."

Try as he might to appear jaunty, his eyes were rimmed with fatigue, and Daisy found herself feeling sorry for him. He was to sleep in the byre, after all. "Are you sure you wouldn't like that poultice?" she asked before he left the room.

He turned to her readily. "I'll be fine, thank you. Although I intend to have a glass of whisky before bed. Your housekeeper brought me some today, and it's truly the best I've ever had."

"Joe makes it," said Cassandra. "Though God knows how. He can't even do sums."

"Well, those sorts of skills obviously don't matter when it comes to making whisky," Lord Lumley said with spirit. "The Prince Regent himself can get no finer elixir than what's to be found here at Castle Vandemere."

"I'll be sure to tell Joe you like it," Daisy said.

"Please do." The viscount inclined his head. "Meanwhile, tomorrow morning . . . shall we attempt to gauge which hook the fish prefer—yours or mine?"

"Certainly." Daisy couldn't help feeling a bit warm every time he spoke to her.

So when she retired to the drawing room a moment later, she did her best to appear nonchalant. Reaching for her sewing basket, she began to thread a needle—to show everyone that she was completely unaffected by Lord Lumley's presence at the castle.

Just as she'd gotten the thread through the eye, Cassandra tossed aside her own needlework. "Stay away from him," she said to Daisy, her eyes narrowed.

Daisy's heart sank. She'd been dreading such a showdown. "How can I? We're engaged to be married." Her voice was firm, and she finished threading her needle with steady hands.

"You know exactly what she means." Mona dangled a glass of whisky from her hand. "It's not as if we get any eligible men up here. He's destined for Cassandra. You must show a disgust of him immediately, so he's free to pursue *her*."

Perdita lowered her bushy brows at Daisy. "I like his legs," she said in warning tones.

Daisy felt their united threat but refused to be cowed, especially as outside the great mullioned window, even at this late hour, in the eerie light of the Scottish summer night, she could see Joe checking on the mother pig who'd had her litter of piglets two days ago.

She must stay firm for Joe. And Hester.

"I refuse to act unengaged," she said.

Cassandra gave a huff. "Very well. Prepare to compete with me for his affections."

"Engaged doesn't mean married," Mona reassured Cassandra.

Daisy wasn't a bit surprised at their selfishness.

"He won't stay long enough for you to win him," she told Cassandra. "He'll probably leave in the next several days."

She knew very well he'd hang about longer than

that, but it was a good opportunity to convince the Furies that they were responsible for his staying.

"We can't let him leave." Mona's brow furrowed.

"No, we can't." Cassandra bit her plump lower lip.

"How do you plan on getting him to stay longer?" Daisy asked them.

Perdita chuckled. "I'll tie him to his bed."

"*I* make those decisions," said Mona, pinching Perdita's arm.

Perdita winced.

Daisy sent her awkward stepsister a sympathetic glance, which she returned with a glower.

"Cassandra will lure him," Mona said.

"How so?" replied Daisy.

Cassandra shrugged. "I'll tell him we haven't had a healthy young man around the house for so long, we have a few repairs that need doing. He'll feel he owes us something for assisting him in his time of need and will stay a solid month."

Daisy shrugged. "But he's a viscount. He doesn't *do* repairs."

The Furies exchanged alarmed glances.

Nobody said anything for a few minutes while Mona drank, Cassandra jabbed at her needlework, Perdita yawned, and Daisy tossed aside her threaded needle and drew a picture of Jinx in her sketchpad.

"You do know we're short the hundred pounds we need for the *feu* duty," she said out of the blue.

"Pshaw," said Mona. "As long as Mr. Beebs has his eye on Cassandra, we have no need to be concerned with that."

Mr. Beebs was their landlord. He was the over-seer at the Keep, an enormous castle nearby.

Cassandra got a smug gleam in her eye. "All it takes is a mere wave of my hand when he rides by for his jaw to drop and sweat to break out on his brow. He wouldn't dare remove us."

Mona made a satisfied grunt. "Exactly. What money we have will continue going to purchasing the girls' things."

Things meaning the fripperies, gowns, and boxes of chocolates Mona had sent over from Edinburgh each month, which she shared only with Perdita and Cassandra.

Daisy restrained a sigh. "How long do you think Mr. Beebs will be pacified?" she asked Mona in a pointed manner. "Soon he'll figure out that Cassandra is merely toying with him, especially if he gets word that she's after the viscount. And then where will we be?"

"You're jealous," her stepmother said, "you un-grateful girl."

Cassandra giggled.

Perdita snorted.

"I am *not* jealous," Daisy said. "I simply don't want us thrown out of our home."

"If your father had been a better provider, we wouldn't be in this position," Mona said.

Her cold lack of respect for Daisy's father's memory, and her distortion of the facts, infuriated Daisy. "But it was *you* who spent all our savings," she responded, heedless of the consequences.

"Silence!" Mona stood up and swayed ever so

slightly. "If you don't stay out of Cassandra's way with the viscount," she told Daisy, "I'll get rid of Hester and Joe."

Daisy felt a sickening pit in her middle. "You can't do that. The only place they could go is the poorhouse."

"I know," said Mona.

Daisy blinked her eyes rapidly. "I'd go, too, and I'd get them out. We'd live in a cottage."

"Oh, really?" Cassandra laughed. "Not around here you wouldn't. Not when everyone finds out you're responsible for your father's death."

Daisy felt all the blood drain from her face. "I've told you." She was horrified to hear her voice tremble. "That was an accident."

Perdita snorted. "How do we know?"

Cassandra tossed aside her stitching. "At the very least, you'll be sorely embarrassed if we tell the viscount—and the world—the circumstances. Especially when they find out about you and Cousin Roman."

"Be quiet, Cassandra." Daisy found herself half out of her chair, panicked at the thought that Hester or Joe might have overheard her.

Cassandra laughed. Mona and Perdita chuckled.

"Daisy's not a virgin," Perdita chanted.

"I'm going to tell the viscount," Cassandra said.

"I did not have relations with your cousin Roman!" Daisy hissed. "I woke up with him. God knows how, but nothing happened. He might have been handsome, but he was an absolute boor and the last man I'd tumble into bed with—"

"Don't you say that!" Mona looked completely insulted, but she always did, so her expression didn't even change.

"You woke up betwixt his sheets," Cassandra insisted. "And don't blame the whisky. You were flirting with him all evening—"

"Hush!" Daisy practically quivered. "It was a terrible time. Do you have no respect for my feelings?"

There was a split-second silence.

Daisy fell back in her seat, overwhelmed by shame—shame *and* grief—so much of both, she didn't know what to say.

You're human, Hester had told her over and over. *Mistakes happen. Candles are left burning. You're not the first to have set an accidental fire.*

But even Hester didn't know that when the fire had been detected and her father had come looking for her in her bedchamber and found her gone, Daisy had been in Cousin Roman's bed, drunk and half clothed.

Only the Furies knew.

And so her father had thought her lost in the fire. He'd presumed she was in the bungalow, working on a sewing project. He'd been so stricken with grief standing before the conflagration that his heart—

It had given out not long afterward.

He'd had a history of weak spells, but Daisy knew—everyone knew—that when he mortally collapsed at dinner a week later, it was the trauma of that evening's fire that had done him in.

Dear God.

She couldn't think of that fateful night without shaking! She'd escaped Roman's room with no one's being the wiser. She'd even come up with a likely story for her absence from her bedchamber—she'd repaired to the kitchens for a late-night snack.

But when Cousin Roman left for Australia, Cassandra came to Daisy and told her she knew the shameful fact of her true whereabouts that evening, and that was all it took . . .

She was now the Furies' fool.

Daisy sat up in her chair and kept her eyes on the floor, incapable of looking at the three women avidly staring at her. She could feel their scorn.

And then she released an audible sigh of despair, not caring that they heard her. Forgetting to blow out a candle was perhaps forgivable. But the rest?

Daisy would never forgive herself, and neither would anyone else, including Hester and the viscount, if they knew the extent of it. So she must cooperate with these three women she despised, at least until she found her four hundred pounds. After that, she'd work so hard to make the estate better, they'd either leave because their tauntings couldn't bother such a busy person as herself, or they'd stay and she'd—

Well, she'd have to continue enduring them. Because there was no way she was ever going to leave her home.

If that turned out to be the case, at least she'd be distracted. Creating and maintaining a thriving sheep herd would occupy her time, and she'd take satisfaction in knowing that she'd be providing a comfortable life for her, Hester, and Joe.

"Ladies," she said in a thin, calm voice, "I promise you I'll have as little to do with Viscount Lumley as possible, although I won't break off the engagement."

"You'd better!" Cassandra cried. "Or I'll tell him everything."

Daisy held up a hand. "If I break it off or if you tell him, he'll leave straightaway."

"He won't if he's in love with me." Cassandra arched a smug brow.

Daisy kept her patience. "Give yourself at least a week or two to allow that to happen," she said, her tone perfectly serious.

"Oh, right." Her vain stepsister nodded.

"He's probably already halfway in love with you," Mona assured her ebony-haired daughter, "but you'll want to clinch it."

"Yes," Perdita said. "You must clinch it." She made a giant fist.

At her mother's and sister's exhortations, Cassandra's eyes brightened and her mouth became a big O. But when she looked at Daisy, her expression turned surly. "You'd just better lie low until I clinch things. And then all bets are off. I'll tell him everything if you so much as blink in his direction."

"Right," Daisy replied dryly, ignoring the fact that all three women were nodding vigorously, pleased with their campaign to destroy Daisy's chance at marital bliss.

She turned her attention to Perdita. "I think it best if you prepare yourself to charm Mr. Beebs. Since we won't have the funds to pay the *feu* duty, and Cassandra will be occupied with attempting to win away my fiancé, someone has to persuade Mr. Beebs not to demand payment."

There was a silence.

Everyone knew Perdita couldn't charm anyone!

Which led to Daisy's next suggestion: "The other option is for you to give me permission to speak with Lord Lumley in a discreet manner about raising funds. If he's a peer of the realm, surely he understands estate matters. Perhaps we can produce the *feu* duty without having to make Perdita work her wiles on Mr. Beebs."

"Wiles?" Perdita gnashed her teeth. "What are wiles?"

"Charms," Daisy told her. "You must try. We wouldn't want to be removed from the castle before the viscount has the opportunity to propose to Cassandra."

She hoped her point would stick.

Cassandra, her eyes wider than usual, grabbed her mother's arm. "I've no time to waste on that little man, and Perdita's about as charming as an old mare put out to pasture."

Perdita merely sucked her teeth at the insult.

Mona's mouth became a stubborn, flat line and her eyes, more beady than ever. She swiveled her square body in Daisy's direction. "You may speak with the viscount when warranted. But only in a discreet manner."

The woman's tone was so threatening and low, Daisy felt the words vibrate in her breastbone.

"Don't you dare make wedding plans with him," Cassandra added, then poked Daisy's arm. "Or kiss him again. That's the most important thing."

"It was a shocking display." Mona shook her head. "Shocking."

"It was," Daisy said thoughtfully.

A moment went by in which Cassandra and Perdita hurled the expected infantile insults of her character and kissing performance, but as Daisy was prepared for them, she was completely unmoved. The kisses had been worth it. Nothing her stepsisters said would ever make her regret them.

"All right," she said quietly, masking her enjoyment at their obvious jealousy. "I'll do my best to avoid the viscount. Although you know I promised to go fishing with him in the morning. And I can't exactly avoid him entirely."

"But watch yourself," said Mona. "No flirting. No fawning. And find the *feu* duty without causing hardship to us. Or else."

Or else.

It was a phrase that Mona often bandied about with Daisy—and followed through upon, too— usually with forays into her bedchamber so she could rifle through her things and toss them out the window or into the fire. Other times, she'd lock her away with no supper. Several times, she'd made Daisy clean all the hearthstones with a tiny brush.

But this time, Mona's *or else* carried more weight. This time, Mona was looking out the window at

Joe, on his way back from visiting the sow and her piglets. He saw them inside staring at him, and he waved.

Daisy lifted a limp hand.

Poor Joe! And poor Hester!

Daisy would be nervous tonight drinking warm milk and sharing a nibble of shortbread with them near the kitchen fire.

Mona only laughed when she saw Joe.

Which made Daisy cringe. She knew very well what her stepmother's *or else* meant this time.

She watched until Joe's cap disappeared from view and girded herself mentally for the next few weeks. It promised to be a precarious journey.

CHAPTER SEVEN

"Pardon my bluntness, but what the deuce is going on in your household?" Charlie asked Miss Montgomery early the next morning. It was cold and damp, the dew still clinging to the heather. They stood at the edge of the swirling burn, their fishing rods in the water. "I feel as if I've stepped into some Gothic tale. Your stepmother and stepsisters are . . . unusual, to say the least."

Overnight, in the decidedly uncomfortable byre loft—away from the smiling Joe, the cheery Hester, and the mesmerizing force that was Miss Montgomery—he'd had the chance to replenish his waning stores of cynicism. He'd discovered the young miss was entirely kissable, which would have usually pleased him no end, but he couldn't bear to let this particularly brazen money-seeker know she'd affected him so strongly.

It had been a shock to feel her respond with such passion to their second kiss, but then he'd guessed she was putting on for her stepmother, so *he'd* put on, and then it had seemed like a competition—

One that he hadn't wanted to end.

"Of course," he reminded her now, "your stepmother and stepsisters will find out eventually this engagement of ours is all a ruse."

"Oh, well." She blew a curl off her forehead. "We'll have the money for the castle by then, won't we? I'll explain everything when the time is right. Stepmother will attribute the lie to my learning to be wily. Like her."

"It's convenient to have a dastardly relative at times, isn't it?"

"Yes. Terribly."

"But don't even think of trapping me into a real marriage—"

"Don't be ridiculous. I'd rather live in a hut than stand at the altar with a man who—"

"Won't allow his wife access to a farthing of his wealth," he warned her.

"No, whose ilk will get stinking—"

"I know the rest."

She flushed. "My point being, this is a temporary arrangement we must both endure." She looked with concern at his black eye. "You definitely need something on that."

He couldn't believe she would still consider helping him, after all the barbs they'd exchanged. Unless she were still hoping . . . hoping he had a secret pocket full of money.

"Women entrap men into marriage all the time," he reminded her. "And your stepmother is an obvious schemer. Am I supposed to believe you haven't taken on her tendencies?"

"I'm nothing like her," she lashed out. "Nor my stepsisters."

She said it with such passion, he found her nearly pretty again. Funny that, as she was wearing a coarse gray gown, hideous boots, a lumpy wool shawl, and her hair wound in a tight knot at the back of her head.

At dinner last evening, Miss Cassandra had looked breathtakingly lovely in her fashionable gown and her abundance of ebony curls. Yet she excited no interest in him whatsoever.

This woman, in her grim but serviceable attire, somehow did.

She indicated the flannel bag on the ground. "I suspect you need another worm."

"Oh?"

"Yes. A trout just took yours."

"I didn't notice." It was because he was taking too many glances at *her*.

"It takes a sensitive hand to pull in a large catch up here," she said with a chuckle, pulling in a trout even as she spoke. "The fish are wily. They take the bait and swim off."

He couldn't help wondering if she were describing what *she* planned to do in this outlandish scenario.

"I'll admit I need some practice," he said, taking the wriggling trout from her and putting it in a bag filled with ferns. "However, don't rest on your laurels. I still intend to best you."

"Oh?" She gave him a sideways glance. "Shall we bet on it?"

"I've no money to wager," he said.

"That shouldn't stop us," she insisted.

"I agree." He raised a brow. "I've the perfect bet."

"What is it?" Her wide blue eyes were full of excitement.

"A kiss," he said. "Whoever loses must bestow one on the other party."

She took a step away from him. "Lord Lumley," she said in the same cool, confident tone she'd employed the day before when she'd reminded him of his duty to help her. "I'm not in the market for flirtation. And you know that a wager like that is not only inappropriate but ridiculous. No matter what, both of us will be involved in the kiss. So there is no incentive to win."

"Yes," he said, "but initiating it will be awkward for the loser, don't you think?"

"I suspect you wouldn't feel awkward in the least. You're a rogue. You've said so yourself."

"I suppose I am," he said, tugging on his line. He'd caught his first trout. "But I can't help wanting to foist that awkwardness upon *you*. I'd quite like to see how you'd handle the matter."

She pursed her lips. "I don't approve of this wager. Move on to the next idea, please."

"I dare you," he said.

She kept ignoring him. In fact, she pulled in another fish. "I'm going to win, no matter what."

He liked how she wouldn't meet his gaze yet didn't seem coy in the least.

"You only *think* you will," he said back.

Another minute went by.

"I thought you Highland girls had more spunk." He yanked in another trout and put it in the bag. "Although who can blame you for backing down? I'm winning, after all."

"It's a go," she finally said, her profile stern, her brow furrowed. "And only because you can't challenge a Highland girl's spunk. When the sun rises over that branch"—she pointed to a beech tree—"the contest is over. But the kiss will be brief, and no one shall ever know."

"Done," he said.

Not a word passed between them as they cast their lines. She was concentrating. He could tell. She was anxious to best him.

He pulled in another fish.

She got two.

Within a half hour, they were neck and neck.

She sighed. "I suppose you can't fish *and* contemplate ideas for raising four hundred pounds, all at the same time?"

She looked at him with a spark of challenge in her eyes.

"You supposed wrong," he answered. "It's been on my mind since the first moment you mentioned it. It's why I'm here, after all."

The sun was baking the grass dry. Soon, it would rise above the beech tree's branch, which extended like a long arm over the water.

"What ideas have you?" She sounded anxious to know.

"The most important thing is to identify a source of the four hundred pounds," he said. "We're here in a remote corner of Scotland. Who here has that sort of money? The next question to ask is: why would they hand it over to us?"

Miss Montgomery attached another worm to her hook. "The villagers and farmers aren't well off in the least. Even if they pooled their resources, I'm sure they wouldn't have that amount. And then there's Mr. Beebs, the overseer at the Keep. He's been there for several years. He might as well be the owner himself. But he's not. So I don't think he has the funds."

"Who does own the Keep?"

"Mr. Beebs is very quiet and doesn't talk about them. Probably because absentee property owners aren't looked fondly upon by the locals. They became quite prolific after the Clearances, of course."

Charlie looked up at the fortress on the side of Ben Fennon. The Keep was a spectacular example of castle architecture. Its windows sparkled, the grounds were immaculate, and the building itself, with its scarlet pennants waving stiffly in the Highland breezes, had a general air of prosperity about it.

"Mr. Beebs's employers must spare no expense to keep it looking so fine," Charlie guessed.

"True, and it's why the village endures his presence. Occasionally, he employs local help to maintain the castle and its grounds, although many times he resorts to using craftsman and laborers from Edinburgh, Glasgow, or even England, depending on the project."

"Have you been inside?"

"No. But according to the villagers who've had that privilege, the interior's as lavish now as it was back then. Hester says it used to be a showpiece—the heart and soul of Glen Dewey. But since Mr. Beebs took up residence, no one visits anymore. The Highland games and the subsequent *ceilidh*—all held on the Keep's grounds—ceased, as well."

"That's a shame." And Charlie truly felt it was. "Can you not hold the festivities at Castle Vandemere?"

"I suppose we could, although it wouldn't be the same. We cling to the side of a cliff here, and our grounds aren't nearly as extensive as those at the Keep. Vandemere itself is small and snug, more charming than the Keep, in my opinion, but it's hardly adequate for a *ceilidh* grand enough for all of Glen Dewey to attend. But you're right. The Keep's inaccessibility is all the more reason to keep Vandemere from crumbling. The locals need some reminder of our history and a recollection of the traditions that bind us. It's no accident that since Mr. Beebs has been in residence, village morale is the lowest it's ever been."

While she was speaking, she caught another trout.

She was now in the lead.

Charlie attended to his own line, baiting it with the largest worm he could find in the flannel bag. "All right, then. No one here has four hundred pounds. We'll have to go outside Glen Dewey to find it, perhaps to wealthy folk who don't know about its treasures. People like those travelers at Brawton who dropped me nearby."

"Yes," said Miss Montgomery.

"Do they stalk deer in Brawton?" He pulled in two more trout. He was winning now.

Miss Montgomery shook her head. "It has only fishing to recommend it."

"They certainly don't have Joe's whisky, either." Just remembering how good it was made Charlie happy.

"Nor has Brawton ever had a Highland games," Miss Montgomery said.

"Do they have any castles there?" Suddenly, Charlie was praying they didn't.

"No."

He saw Miss Montgomery's eyes gleam with something . . . he hoped something along the lines of what he was thinking. "You said yourself at dinner last night—Glen Dewey has all that's best about the Highlands."

She nodded vigorously. "But we've no inn. We're not set up to host visitors, especially lots of them at once."

"But that's what you need—many visitors at once. Rich ones. People who'll pay to stay somewhere in style. People who want . . . the Highland experience."

"I like that," she said. "The Highland experience. Perhaps they could stay with us at Castle Vandemere."

"It's too small."

She winced. "And it's not very grand. Not at the moment."

Something zinged between them. A flash of understanding.

"We need a place like the Keep," Charlie said.

Miss Montgomery said it, too, at the very same time.

And then he noticed that the sun was over the branch of the beech tree.

"I won," the viscount said, a slow grin spreading over his face.

Daisy was so excited about the idea forming in her head, she didn't know what he was talking about.

"I won the bet," he explained further, and held up the sack of trout.

"Oh, that." She whirled away from him to stare at the Keep. Was it the solution to her money woes? "We'll worry about the bet later. Let's think about the Keep. Can we borrow it?"

It was an outrageous idea.

"You can always ask." Lord Lumley grabbed her wrist. "And we won't think about the bet later. Now's more like it."

She looked over her shoulder at him. "But the bet's not important—not in the least."

"Which is why we need to get it out of the way. I won't be able to fully concentrate on the task at hand while it's hanging in the air between us."

"I don't feel it hanging in the air at all." She huffed.

"That's because you're all business. It's time you had some fun."

"This is an inopportune moment." She flapped her hands at her sides. "We have an idea. A *marvelous* idea."

"It's never the wrong time."

Never?

"Not even during church?" she demanded to know.

"That's the best time." His voice was like silk.

"Are you saying you've kissed someone during church?"

"*Behind* the church. Does that count?"

"Yes. And it's very bad of you."

"Don't criticize until you try it." He stood at the ready.

She leaned up and then—

She pulled back. "I can't. What if someone sees?"

"No one will observe us," he said, "especially if we retreat here." He pulled her behind the beech tree.

She bit her lip. "I have to do this fast. Cassandra would be furious if she knew. And I can't risk that."

"What do you mean?"

"She and my stepmother have threatened to get rid of Hester and Joe if I spend too much time with you. And that can't happen. They mean more to me than anyone in this world. So please—don't push me."

Concern lit his eyes. "They'd do that?"

Daisy nodded. "Even though I'm supposed to be your fiancée, Cassandra still plans to be your viscountess."

"Have they made any other threats to you?"

Daisy hesitated. She could never tell him about the other. "No," she lied. "But that one is enough."

"I should say so."

"I'm warning you now," she said, "to be prepared in case I appear standoffish in their presence."

"I see. But you're standoffish now, too."

"No I'm not. You're used to flirts in London. I've no interest in flirting."

"Why not?"

The viscount's was a face that had probably caused many a virgin to consider leaping into bed with him.

"Because I have responsibilities," she enunciated clearly, more for her own benefit than his. She wished she were one of those badly behaved virgins—it wasn't as if she'd ever get married, here in a remote village with a dearth of young men. She wished she didn't have to rebuff him. But it was true. She *did* have responsibilities.

Besides, you don't deserve what your parents had. Never. Ever.

She closed her eyes against an image of Cousin Roman with his glib smile and open shirt and wished she didn't have to say such cruel things to herself.

But she did.

She must.

"Are you all right?" Lord Lumley's words, rich and rough, penetrated her thoughts.

She opened her eyes again.

His gaze was intense, worried, his face mere

inches from her own. "Surely even a young lady with responsibilities can find some time for amusement."

She shook her head. "Not until Castle Vandemere is safely back in my possession."

And not even then, she thought, although she'd never tell him.

"Then I am more committed than ever to securing those funds," he said, oblivious to her inner turmoil, so unaware how deep it went, how unchangeable her position was.

After Mama died, Papa used to call her his North Star. It was a loving observation—his whole world revolved around her, he'd said. But now she felt she must be pinned to the sky like a fixed point, reaching and shining . . . but never blurring her borders.

Never touching.

Never connecting.

"I'd like to see you lighthearted, Miss Montgomery," the viscount said. "I'd like to see you bat your lashes at me and beg me with your eyes to kiss you behind a rhododendron bush, after a picnic. Do you go to picnics?"

"No." She couldn't help it. Despite her dark thoughts, she laughed. "You're impossible, Lord Lumley."

"So some people say." His mouth tipped up, but he said it as if he were very lonely. And as if she were the only person in the world who could make him happy again.

He was a roué.

She knew it, but even so, something propelled her out of her darkness. It urged her to lift up on her tippy toes and kiss him. Full on the mouth.

He kissed her back.

Then she wrapped her arms around his neck and kept kissing him, all the while feeling like a tree with loving branches enveloping a needy boy-turned-man who'd come to sit among her leaves and admire her.

Which made no sense, but for some reason, she felt as if she'd known him for a lifetime—and that this branchy-tree feeling she had when she was kissing him was natural.

Perfectly natural.

Like the eddies on the burn. And the snap of grass drying in the sun. And the sigh of the wind brushing the mountainside.

I must be dreaming, Daisy thought.

I'm a hussy, she realized.

And rather liked the idea.

A few weak-kneed moments later, the viscount released her.

"I can think again now," he said. "And the first thing I'm thinking is that we will never do that again."

"Right." She felt vastly disappointed and concerned that perhaps she was a very bad kisser. But he was good to remind her they shouldn't. They couldn't risk it.

"At least not anywhere your stepmother and step-sisters can see," Lord Lumley continued. "I wouldn't dare put your Hester and Joe in peril."

"No. Never." She felt vaguely hopeful again. And guilty. Nothing could ever imperil Joe and Hester.

"So have no fear," the viscount said. "Next time, we'll be completely secluded, so you can enjoy yourself."

Her head was still spinning, and her lips were tingling. "But I did enjoy myself."

"Not as much as you could," he said.

"There will *be* no next time," she reminded him, because she did have fear—those fears about Hester and Joe. And the other fear, the one the Furies had taunted her with last night. But she was also angry that things had gotten to this point—that her stepfamily had made her so afraid that she couldn't live without worrying about people she loved.

"What strategy will you employ with Mr. Beebs to get him to agree to our using the Keep?" asked the viscount.

Not only had he completely changed the subject, he appeared to be thinking clearly, while she was still blinking, trying to forget the feel of his hand caressing her back and his lips teasing her own.

"Mr. Beebs doesn't mix with the neighborhood," she said, "but it appears he has a fondness for Cassandra. Perhaps he'll say yes for that reason alone."

But inside, she was thinking that the viscount's lips had done magic, had cast her under a spell in which she couldn't concentrate on anything but getting another kiss.

"Then Cassandra should ask him," he said.

"Ask him what?"

"If we can borrow the Keep." Lord Lumley squinted at her. "Are you listening?"

"Of course." Daisy blushed and gave a nervous shrug. "I wouldn't recommend that. Cassandra's so rude, Mr. Beebs might catch on she doesn't like him. No, I think I'd better. Let's go. Right away." She began the walk to the Keep, hugging herself as she stumbled along, wondering if their idea was so preposterous that Mr. Beebs would laugh it off or call the constable.

But she was also thinking about how she'd kissed the viscount.

Three times now.

Lord Lumley joined her with all their fishing gear and the bag of trout. "If Mr. Beebs says yes, we'll have to make a plan."

Her hand swung close to his side, the side with the trout. But she was thinking about how she'd seen that hole in the back of his breeches the day before and how sad it was that he wasn't wearing the same pair any longer.

"Mr. Beebs has a skeleton staff at the Keep," she managed to say. "But we'll need extra maids, cooks, and footmen."

"Will the men from the village be willing to lead a hunt and pull together a small Highland games?"

"I hope so." Daisy was actually a bit worried about that. "They don't get along the way they used to. All the village's problems used to be resolved during the games and the hunt. Now differences simmer."

"Is it the same with the women?"

"Yes. They've become quite catty, mainly because their husbands are testy with each other. But we'll need them, as well, to do the cooking for the hunt and the games."

"What about the *ceilidh*?"

"We'll need everyone to dance. And we must have fiddlers and pipers."

They were halfway to the Keep now.

The viscount's nearness was still affecting her.

"Even if only half of the anglers come back to Glen Dewey," he said, "we could make your four hundred pounds. They were rich. They spent vast sums freely. They were also fascinated by the idea of kilts and clans and all the things that Sir Walter Raleigh writes about. I must admit, I am, too. If I had access to my usual wealth, I'd be the first to jump at the chance to stay at the Keep and play Highland warrior."

"That's wonderful to know." Daisy allowed herself the luxury of imagining him in a kilt for a fleeting second before returning to matters at hand. "But what's even better is that this will be a boost to Glen Dewey. We need some excitement. And an infusion of money. If Mr. Beebs says yes and the venture goes well, perhaps we can repeat it. The village will take on new life."

They were at the door of the Keep. She was just about to knock when the massive castle door opened.

It was Mr. Beebs himself, dressed in walking clothes and carrying a pair of opera glasses. He was of medium height and medium build, somewhere in his late thirties, and was distinguished by a high-spirited air and his prematurely snow-white hair, which he wore cut straight across his forehead.

"Oh!" he cried. "I was about to go on a hike."

Daisy made the introductions.

He apologized right away for employing no butler as no one came to visit. "It's awfully quiet at the Keep. But it's a fine family you're staying with, Lord Lumley, full of lovely ladies."

Daisy was sorry he didn't often visit Castle Vandemere because he was really a very nice gentleman.

She smiled back. "Yes, Miss Cassandra is busy today."

"Is she?" Mr. Beebs squinted at a bird that flew overhead.

"She's so clever," said Daisy, hoping he was listening. "She's . . . making candles right now."

Which was a lie.

"She's awfully clever," echoed the viscount.

Mr. Beebs cocked his head. "Clever girl."

A silence came over them, and then Daisy let out a sigh and folded her hands. "We were wondering, Mr. Beebs—"

"Yes?" His curious gray eyes bored into hers.

"We were wondering if—" Daisy bit her lip. How would she put it?

And then she simply laid out everything. Not in any particular order. She noticed Mr. Beebs slowly nodding his head occasionally as if he didn't quite understand what she was getting at, but eventually, he nodded his head at a faster tempo—much faster—and said, "Right, *I* see," over and over.

"Well?" She tried not to hold her breath.

The overseer winced. "I don't know about that. It's quite a hefty proposition."

"But—"

"No, I'm sorry, Miss Montgomery. It won't work."

"If we give you a portion of the profits?" Charlie suggested.

Mr. Beebs shook his head. "I don't need any money."

Daisy bit her lip. "I'm so sorry to hear this, Mr. Beebs. I—I was looking forward to the men's dance competition, especially the sword dance. Rumor has it you were once a champion sword dancer yourself, where you grew up, near Aberdeen. Of course, that's probably a silly story—"

"No." Mr. Beebs drew in his chin. "I *was* a champion sword dancer, as a matter of fact. But I haven't danced in years—"

"What a pity the younger generation won't have the same opportunity." Daisy released a wistful sigh and turned to look down the glen at the village. "I've never seen a Highland games in Glen Dewey. I suppose I never shall. Neither shall my stepsisters. I know Cassandra, in particular, was looking forward to it."

When Mr. Beebs cleared his throat, Daisy turned back around with a flare of hope in her heart.

"When would this event take place?" he asked her.

"As soon as we can find people to come."

"Well, now," he said gruffly, "perhaps we can work this out, after all."

Daisy exchanged a secret smile with Charlie.

"I've a standing invitation to stay with a bird-watching friend of mine near Edinburgh," Mr. Beebs explained. "And if I go now, I can combine business with pleasure. Last month I received a letter from one of the magistrates in London who handle the Keep's affairs. He asked if I'd be in Edinburgh at all this summer—he's there for several months and would like to discuss estate matters in more detail than letter-writing permits. You see, the Keep's only recently changed hands, about five years ago."

"That's considered recent?" Charlie asked.

"Yes," said Mr. Beebs, "in terms of longevity of possession. Some of these properties stay in a family for generations."

"Like Vandemere," Daisy said.

"Exactly," Mr. Beebs concurred.

"You appear to have a perfectly lovely reason to vacate the Keep." Daisy grinned.

Mr. Beebs chuckled. "I suppose it is. So *do* hold your hunt party here, and enjoy yourselves. I would quite like a bird-watching holiday as it is. I'll be back in less than two weeks' time. In fact"—he looked around at the beautiful vista—"I'll leave right after this walk. There's a black-throated diver I'd like to find first." He looked upward at the tops of the trees, then gave a small, elegant bow. "Your servant, Miss Montgomery. Lord Lumley."

And he began to traipse off.

"Shall we tell Miss Cassandra you said good-bye?" she called after him.

He turned and swallowed rather hard. "I suppose you could."

He took a few steps.

"So may we work with what servants you have here and bring our own, as well?" Daisy added.

"Indeed." He inclined his head graciously. "We've plenty of room in the stables, too, for at least a dozen horses."

"Very good," Daisy said.

How generous of him!

She got a grand idea.

"Mr. Beebs"—she screwed up her nerve—"you've been so kind. Perhaps you'll find it in your heart not to require a *feu* duty this year? Or any year, really, as my family has been paying it for nearly a hundred years? That way we can use all the money we make from our Highland adventure to fix up Castle Vandemere. Wouldn't it be nice if when people arrive at the village, they'll look up Ben Fennon and see both castles looking marvelous?"

"Sorry, Miss Montgomery," Mr. Beebs said in jolly fashion. "The *feu* duty is due, as always, on the first of July, and not a day later. I don't want to have to throw you out."

"No," she said weakly.

"There are plenty of people standing in line who'd love to take possession of Castle Vandemere," he called back to her.

"Are there?" She could barely speak.

"Oh, yes," he said. "At least three that I know of. Lady Brompton of Nob, Mr. Finch of Trickle Top, and Baron van Bunting, of Lower Cross Junction—none of them as interesting as Vandemere's current occupants."

"Damn the feudal system and feudal lairds," Daisy said under her breath to the viscount. "The castle should belong outright to our family by now."

"Oh," Mr. Beebs went on, "and if you're looking for wealthy travelers to stay here, a few of my bird-watcher friends are in Lower Cross Junction. They're here for the bird-watching symposium, but it ends tomorrow, so they'll be at loose ends, all with money in their pockets and seeking diversion. Some are thinking about staying for the theater festival. Others are going to a big society wedding in Inverness. But loads of them will be twiddling their thumbs, dreading their trips back home and seeking ways to delay them."

"How—how do you know all this?" Daisy couldn't help asking.

"I write the social column for the *Royal Society Bird-watching Journal,* of course. I'll stop by Lower Cross Junction on my way out. I'll bring you back a half-dozen well-heeled visitors. What will you be charging?"

"Thirty pounds each for a ten-day stay at the Keep, a complete Highland experience," said Daisy.

That was an exorbitant amount!

The viscount stood with his legs apart and his hands on his hips. "How rich are these people?" he asked Mr. Beebs.

"Very." Mr. Beebs scratched his ear. "A few will bring bodyguards. They carry that many valuables."

"Let's make it fifty pounds each, then," said the viscount.

Fifty pounds?

"Right." Mr. Beebs chuckled. "I've no doubt I'll be able to get it, too."

"Are you sure?" Daisy plucked at her skirt. "The viscount was going to head to Brawton to invite some anglers he knows are there."

"Don't bother. Brawton's on my way. I'll stop for you myself."

"Thank you," Charlie said. "Another half-dozen guests would be quite welcome and, I believe, easy to come by. The party's twenty strong and can't be missed. They're throwing money about the local shops and pubs when they're not casting their lines."

Mr. Beebs slung the ribbon holding the opera glasses over his head. "Very well. Expect your visitors tomorrow at four o'clock, or my name isn't Ebenezer Hiram Beebs."

And then he left, striding briskly around a copse of rowan trees.

The viscount stared after the retreating figure. "He's been here five years, and has no one attempted to befriend him?"

Daisy bit her lip. "Hester did once or twice, but he appears to shy away from visits. She says she made him some bannocks, then once sent over a jug of Joe's whisky. But he's all about birds, business—and now Cassandra, I suppose. Did you see his reaction when I mentioned her name?"

"Yes." The viscount shook his head. "I can't fathom his interest in her. But he lives alone, and—"

"There's really no reasonable explanation," Daisy said, "other than the fact that she's beautiful." She paused. "Of course, she could have hidden depths

I haven't discovered. Mr. Beebs doesn't strike me as a fool."

"Nor me." Charlie cocked his head, as if he were listening for distant music or sensed something out of the ordinary. "It's strange country up here in the Highlands," he said quietly. "It seems anything could happen."

He looked at her again, and she felt it, too . . . something tantalizing. Something just out of reach. But whatever it was, she would find it someday. And when she did, she would hold it close and never let it go. Because whatever it was, it would help her stay in her castle. She just knew it.

CHAPTER EIGHT

"Oh, no," Charlie heard a little while later from Miss Cassandra. "Not trout *again*."

Miss Montgomery's stepfamily had roused themselves out of bed in time to partake of the midday meal, which Hester had made with the assistance of Miss Montgomery *and* Charlie, who'd never cooked a fish before, much less a fish over an open fire that he'd had to build himself on the side of a mountain. Hester said everything tasted better that way.

Old Joe, the shepherd, had been recruited to pull out all their chairs in the dining room, and now that they were seated, he stood to the side of the door, beaming at Miss Montgomery.

"It's a *braw, bricht* day," he whispered loudly to her.

"Indeed, it is," she replied with a smile that made Charlie feel more trapped than ever in his seat between Miss Cassandra on his left and Mrs. Montgomery at the head of the table.

Charlie knew he was likely never to marry. His lifestyle didn't sit well with his mother or his sisters, and he didn't look forward to the prospect of disappointing a wife. Not only that, his wealth made it so he distrusted almost all women, with the exception of his mother, sisters, and the wives of his best friends.

But he liked Daisy Montgomery. He especially liked her version of standoffishness, which involved kisses behind beech trees.

Which was why he didn't mind the repeat of last night's meal in the least—because he'd caught the trout with a delightful companion in the most delightful fishing expedition he'd ever had.

He felt a little nudge of worry that he was feeling so delightful about everything . . . he'd become used to being the cynic, the jaded man about town.

Yet at the moment, he was happy. The little man, Joe, made him happy. Hester, the cook and housekeeper, who was eyeing him with a gleam of speculation in her eye, made him happy. Most of all, Miss Montgomery made him happy.

After their success speaking to Mr. Beebs at the Keep, they'd made huge plans all the way back to Castle Vandemere, stopping only once to look at the amazing view of the village perched prettily below them, the pristine loch to its side, the verdant green of the mountainside, splashed with purple, white, and pink, and the overarching blue sky that reminded him of Miss Montgomery's eyes.

When she spoke to him on that walk, she conversed as if she didn't care in the least that he was a wealthy viscount from London. And he'd forgotten, too. He'd felt like a man who had a job to do, a job that would require sharp wits, perhaps some hard labor—and no money.

No money at all. It felt quite freeing and exhilarating to confront this challenge without having any money to fund it.

Funny how he hadn't felt free and exhilarated coming north with no money.

Perhaps because he'd had no one with whom to share the challenge. If he'd had Miss Montgomery with him—which never would have happened, of course, but a man could dream—they could have slept in stables together. Run into fields and stolen apples from trees when no one was looking— together. Been miserable on cold, rainy hikes down miles of muddy roads—together.

No matter what the impoverished scenario, he couldn't see himself being miserable with her. He could see himself being naked with her . . . laughing with her . . . all right, perhaps fighting with her and making up and then becoming naked with her *again*—but miserable?

No.

Now he watched her as she told the other occupants of Castle Vandemere about their plans to host a hunt party at the Keep, which included an excursion to the village of Glen Dewey that very afternoon to recruit the natives' help.

Charlie could sense her nerves.

Of course, the widow dropped her fork on her plate and interrupted her stepdaughter mid-sentence.

"Outrageous," she said, staring down the table at Miss Montgomery's pale face. "This was your idea, wasn't it?"

"It was both of ours," Charlie interjected before Miss Montgomery could defend herself. He fixed his gaze on his sour-faced hostess. "I'm grateful for your understanding concerning our engagement. I'm only here thanks to your largesse. Your very *large* largesse. This moneymaking scheme is my way of repaying you."

Mrs. Montgomery preened, her bosom sticking out farther than ever.

Charlie dared to exchange a brief glance with Miss Montgomery. Her eyes were dancing, although her expression was serious.

"But we don't live at the Keep." Miss Perdita expressed the obvious in a loud voice.

"True, but the Keep has been made available to us," Charlie said. "And if all goes well, you should have no more financial worries in the interim. However, as time goes on, you'll need to consider a repeat performance, if Mr. Beebs is willing to perpetuate the idea."

"Of course he will," said Miss Cassandra, adjusting a long curl over her shoulder. "I shall see to it that he does. Not that I will live here much longer," she said meaningfully. "I plan to marry well and leave Mr. Beebs and the Keep behind me. London calls . . . London is where I belong."

"You belong in a peer's bed," said her mother.

A peer's bed?

Charlie set down his wine. "Naked ambition can

take many forms," he murmured, only for Miss Montgomery's ears.

She appeared to choke but recovered after a sip of water.

Perdita sat squinting at nothing, apparently lost in her attempts to crunch through a fish bone.

Charlie took a swig of his own wine. "It would be ideal, of course, if Mr. Beebs could get the permission of the property holder. His backing would lend a greater sense of propriety and importance to the venture. Perhaps he could encourage his wealthy friends to participate."

Mrs. Montgomery drained her glass of wine. "Very well, Viscount. You may proceed, but whatever money you accrue above the *feu* duty comes straight back to me. I intend to take my girls on a tour of Italy, unless Cassandra is married off by then. If so, Perdita will accompany me." She lowered her chin at her stepdaughter. "You don't need to go. I've bestowed an honor upon you that will occupy you while we're away."

"You have?" There was a small quiver in Miss Montgomery's voice.

Charlie braced himself.

"Yes." Mrs. Montgomery frowned. "I've decided you're to be my companion for life."

"That's impossible," Charlie said. "She's to marry me."

Of course she wasn't to marry him, but he'd had to say *something*.

"*If* you ever come up to scratch," Mrs. Montgomery told him rudely. "She might very well change her mind if you can't make something of yourself. Or you might discover you don't want *her* anymore. There are many more fish in the sea, Viscount, more elegant, beautiful fish who'll look so good on your arm, the business deals will come fast and furious."

Miss Cassandra did an excellent impression of a fish by sucking in her cheeks and pursing her lips at him.

"I don't want another fish," he said. "And as for my prospects, they're very good."

Miss Montgomery sat blinking furiously.

Mona turned to her again. "Companions stay home to answer correspondence and see to the general upkeep of the estate. It's quite a responsibility."

"I—I don't know what to say," Miss Montgomery stammered.

"Left you speechless, have I?" Mrs. Montgomery cocked an eyebrow, her mouth pursed in a smirk.

"Er, yes," Miss Montgomery replied, "but Stepmother, I'll need the profits from the Highland venture to see to the estate's upkeep. Without it, how can I fix the drawbridge or increase the size of our sheep herd? Or get a new suit of armor? Not to mention repair the crumbling chimneys—"

"Those things can wait," Mrs. Montgomery said, "for the *next* Highland venture."

"I care only about the first one," Miss Cassandra said, her nose in the air. "Viscount, I'm going with you to the village."

"Sheer genius." Mrs. Montgomery looked at Charlie with small, beady eyes. "Cassandra will help recruit the men there to your cause."

The trout suddenly tasted dry as dust. Charlie twisted his neck in the cravat he'd borrowed.

In a generous act he'd never forget, he watched Joe hasten to the sideboard and pour him a finger of the finest whisky in the land, made by his own hands.

Charlie slugged it down. "Thank you," he told the servant.

Joe bowed, grinned, and limped his way out of the room.

"You're welcome," Cassandra answered Charlie, even though he hadn't been thanking *her*.

Mrs. Montgomery smiled at her ebony-haired daughter. "You'll be queen of the hunt and the sportsmen's lucky talisman at the games."

"In that case, I'll need special sashes." Cassandra turned to Miss Montgomery. "That's your job," she said flatly. "I prefer white satin with gold and scarlet embellishments."

Miss Montgomery bit her lip. "But I'm much too busy—"

"You'll do it, and you'll do it well," the stepmother informed her stepdaughter in bright tones. But the expression in her gaze was anything but friendly. "Otherwise, I shall ask Hester."

The servant had gone back to the kitchen to put on the kettle, she'd said, and to pull some more shortbread out of the oven. One thing Charlie had come to love already about Castle Vandemere . . . there was always shortbread.

And fine whisky.

Miss Montgomery's brow furrowed. "The sewing will strain Hester's eyes, and then she'll feel miserable if she doesn't do it well." She looked down at her plate. "Of course I'll make the sashes."

Charlie didn't like seeing her capitulate so readily to her bullying stepmother. But he knew now that Miss Montgomery had her two servants' welfare uppermost on her mind, so he understood.

"When do we leave, Viscount?" Miss Cassandra asked him.

Charlie was annoyed. He liked having a job. He'd never had one before (investing money didn't seem to count). So it was imperative that he do this job right, especially because Grandmother would be asking.

He didn't need the whiny beauty tagging along to Glen Dewey.

"Soon," he told Miss Cassandra, "but you needn't bother coming."

"I insist." She licked her lips after swallowing her wine and looked at him with wide eyes.

"And I'm going with *you*." Mrs. Montgomery pointed her fork at Miss Montgomery. "Those women of Glen Dewey need to hear what's what."

Miss Montgomery kept her expression neutral, but Charlie could tell she was most concerned. She'd told him that it would take a great deal of finesse to bring the village women together and gain their cooperation. It was apparent that Mrs.

Montgomery didn't have an ounce of finesse in her body.

"You really don't need to—" Miss Montgomery began.

"I'm coming," her stepmother said.

Perdita stopping chewing long enough to say, "If there's to be a Highland experience at the Keep, I want to be there."

"But you really should stay here," Miss Montgomery told her. "This will be a gathering of sportsmen. And perhaps bird-watchers. You wouldn't enjoy yourself."

"No," said Perdita, scarfing down a glass of wine. "There. *There* is where I'll be."

"We're going to the Keep, and that's that," her mother said.

The woman was full of vague threats, Charlie noted.

What's what. That's that.

What next?

Miss Montgomery stood. "I'm off to the village." Apparently, she'd decided a change in subject was best. "I plan on walking there now."

"And I'm accompanying her." Charlie also stood and turned to Miss Cassandra. "Miss Montgomery is much too busy to make sashes. They're completely unnecessary."

Miss Cassandra sucked in a breath.

"Nor will we need a queen of the hunt or a female posing as a lucky talisman at the games," Charlie told her mother.

Mrs. Montgomery scowled and opened her

mouth, no doubt to berate him, but Charlie put up a hand.

"What we'll need," he said firmly, "are beautiful ladies to impress our guests, ladies who don't appear fatigued in the least. I suggest you lounge about today, playing cards, reading, eating bonbons. Miss Montgomery can pack your trunks when she returns from her thankless errand to Glen Dewey."

He leaned forward. Stepmother and daughters bent toward him, almost as if they were under a spell.

"You don't want to have to mingle with the villagers," he whispered to the spoiled trio. "Leave that sort of drudgery to the workhorses."

He cast a discreet glance at Miss Montgomery, then turned back to the rest of the company and winked.

"You're a man after my own heart, Viscount." Mrs. Montgomery chortled and pushed her chair back. "I'm off to take a nap. Cassandra and Perdita, eat the remaining chocolates from the basket and be sure to lounge about as much as possible. You mustn't appear fatigued tomorrow."

And she left.

Cassandra and Perdita jumped up, anxious to be indolent.

"I get the chair by the front window," Perdita called, and practically raced her sister out of the room.

Only Charlie and Miss Montgomery were left.

He ignored the odd glimmer in her eyes. "We'll repair to the Keep tomorrow morning. If all goes as planned, we'll have guests in place there by to-morrow afternoon."

She didn't say a word, only sent him a basilisk stare.

"I had to do it," he said. "At least they won't be coming with us now. You've got to admit it was genius."

"Genius? I'll be up all night packing their trunks. Enduring their tantrums."

God, yes. She would be, wouldn't she? "But you'd be doing that anyway," he dared to say. "Correct?"

She didn't say a word.

"I'll make it up to you," he promised her. "I'll do anything. Anything you ask."

"Anything?" Her gaze was speculative.

"Yes. I'm supposed to, anyway. Godmother's orders."

"Huh." She kept observing him.

He couldn't help it. He put on his best peer-of-the realm expression: intimidating, cold. In control. He always did that when he was in trouble.

But she wasn't cowed in the least. Instead, the corner of her mouth turned up. "I'm going to hold you to that promise, Lord Lumley," she finally said.

And swept out of the room.

CHAPTER NINE

Glen Dewey should be charming, Charlie thought that afternoon. It had all the ingredients to make it so: a quaint, colorful high street; chapped, smiling faces at every door, each person ready to greet you and invite you to linger; smells that would make a full man hungry again—roasting lamb, baking bread, simmering pudding.

But something was lacking. To be charming, one had to be free of worry. If one looked closer, the houses of Glen Dewey had been repaired umpteen times. The puddings were thin. The smiling faces were strained.

The village was clearly in trouble.

"Nothing's happened here for the past five years," Miss Montgomery told him on the way down Ben Fennon's slope. "I hope we can do something."

They parted ways, each on their own mission.

Two hours later, Charlie saw Miss Montgomery through the window at the village shop, speaking with all the local ladies. He waved, and she came running out to meet him.

"Success?" Miss Montgomery's expression was hopeful.

"What do you think?" He grinned.

"Same here!" She clasped her hands together. "It's going to be wonderful."

"We're on target," he affirmed.

On the way back up the hill to Castle Vandemere, she scampered up the narrow road ahead of him.

"Joe will be so pleased his shinty sticks finally saw some use," she said over her shoulder. "He's made so many over the years, and they've been sitting in a small closet off the kitchen, going to waste."

Charlie liked seeing the extra skip in her step. "He told me he'd watch the game from one of the fields below the castle."

"Oh, that makes me glad for him." Miss Montgomery threw Charlie a grateful smile. "But what gave you the idea that shinty would bring the men together?"

He gave a little laugh. "No man can resist an opportunity to compete. I knew when Joe showed me the sticks, along with a ball to hit, that nothing would be able to prevent the men from playing. And by the end of it, all their differences seemed puny. They agreed to hold the hunt." He paused, reflecting on his success. "Not that the gathering was trouble-free at first. They were leery, and a few unfriendly remarks were exchanged that I managed into jokes. But Joe's whisky was also an irresistible lure and made it easier for the men to get past their awkwardness with each other."

"You're quite the diplomat." Miss Montgomery said it as if she truly admired him.

"Do you really think so?"

"I *know* so."

Her confidence in him was flattering. "Tell me more about what happened with you and your ladies."

She sidestepped a pothole in the road, and Charlie followed her lead. "They almost walked out on me, saying they didn't have time to waste," she said. "Their daily work is hard and unforgiving. But then I told them about the *ceilidh* at the conclusion of the ten days, and they forgot to be wary around each other. They grew excited at the idea of dressing up for it. Everyone loves a good dance. They're even willing to cook and clean for the visitors—I think a bit of pride in the village began to come out by the end of the visit."

"You sound like quite a diplomat yourself. Or perhaps it's your dimples. I know they've charmed me."

She slanted her gaze back at him. "That's enough of that, my lord." Her voice was a bit breathless, and he didn't think it was from the climb.

She resumed her forward stride, her hips angling right and left as she picked her way over the rough road. "The best thing of all," she said without looking back at him, "is that Mrs. Gordon gave the women everything they'd need to look lovely for the *ceilidh*."

"You're a clever girl." He meant it, too. "How did you get Mrs. Gordon to donate all the fripperies?"

Miss Montgomery paused in her hiking and turned to look back at him. "I had to give her the only inheritance from Papa that I've been able to hide from my stepmother, a beautiful ring with lovely stones that was more a precious memento than anything of great value. Nonetheless, it was enough for Mrs. Gordon. I . . . I hope Papa would have understood."

She looked as though she really weren't quite sure. Traces of guilt lingered around her eyes.

The wind picked up and blew mournfully around them, at odds with the sunny day.

"No doubt he'd have given you his blessing completely," Charlie reassured her.

He saw her brow soften a little at that, which made him glad. But the truth was, he hated that she'd given away her cherished keepsake. Although he wouldn't tell her—no need to make her feel the absence of her ring even more.

"Did you pick out a dress for yourself?" he asked her, and wished with all his heart that he could have paid for the gowns.

"No," she said, her voice light. "I have one with which I can make do very well."

"You should spoil yourself, too."

"What I wear that night won't matter," she said with a stiff shrug. "I'll have more important things to think about, such as how the visitors and villagers are enjoying themselves."

It was no use arguing with her. The woman was

stubborn. And perhaps she needed a little more convincing that she deserved to don a beautiful gown.

That was *his* secret project.

He put down the bag of shinty sticks. "How about a break to take in the glorious view?"

And before she could answer, he turned his back to her, made great fists, and stretched his arms above his head as high as they could go. He was mildly sore from the shinty, had even taken a hit to his lower back that still stung.

But the stretch felt good. *He* felt good. He dropped his arms and sighed. In spite of the soreness, he felt brimming with vitality.

And there was a certain young lady behind him who quickened his blood to fever pitch.

She arrived at his elbow, put her hands on her hips, and took in the vista of mountains, loch, and sky. "It *is* magnificent, isn't it? I could stay here all day and gaze."

"Aye," he said softly.

The word came naturally to him up here in the Highlands. It was such a pleasant, easy utterance, and he certainly felt a hundred times more relaxed in this corner of the world than he did in London.

Who couldn't forget their worries when they were surrounded by such beauty? Including the unspoiled beauty of the woman at his side, a woman who didn't believe she deserved a pretty dress.

But she did. He only wished she knew.

"I think what you're doing to save Castle Vandemere is grand," he said. "But what you're doing for the ladies of Glen Dewey is equally as generous."

She shook her head. "Anybody would do as much."

"Not really. I know plenty of people who don't think any further than themselves. Myself included."

She laughed. "You *are* a rather self-centered viscount. Although today in the village, you were simply—"

"What?"

"A good man."

"Is that so?" He pulled her close. "I've known you but a day. Why does it seem longer?"

"I wonder that myself," she said. "I feel like I've known you forever."

Forever.

She pulled away from him, grinning. She clutched her skirt in her hands and took small steps backward, up the slope.

"Where are you going?" he asked, climbing after her.

"Nowhere," she whispered, a teasing lilt to her voice.

She kept backing away.

He kept following.

And then she stood still. "I didn't know it would be like this." She released the hold she had on her skirt. Her expression was serious, yet there was also a gleam of something happy in her gaze.

She was so beautiful then, he could hardly bear to blink. "You didn't know what would be like this?"

"Meeting a man. Feeling as if I know him already." She hitched her shoulders.

"I'm honored." He allowed himself a grin. "I think."

Her mouth curved in a small smile, and she pulled a lock of hair out of her eye. "But I also feel that I'm a bit in danger around you. A pleasing danger."

He grabbed her waist. "There's nothing to fear."

"I think there is," she whispered, and moved a fraction of an inch closer to him.

He was touched. When one was in danger, one usually moved away.

"I'm afraid my stepsister will find out," she said. "And she can't. I'm frightened for Hester and Joe. And I'm afraid that I'm selfish."

She bewitched him with her honesty.

With her vulnerability.

"I won't let your stepsister find out," he assured her. "Joe and Hester will be fine. And you're the opposite of selfish."

He held on to her, and they stood still for a moment, listening to the sough of the wind through the glen.

She looked up at him with her fairy blue eyes.

And he saw trust.

Trust.

Funny how that twisted his heart.

Funny how it made him almost speechless.

Almost.

"All I can think about right now is kissing you," he confessed, his voice hoarse with longing.

He wouldn't apologize or pretend to be a cool, sophisticated London bachelor. With her, he couldn't.

He'd tried, in the dining room. But it was stupid. And false.

He wasn't that man.

Beneath his expensive clothes and behind his illustrious name, he was like any other man. And that was a good thing. A relief.

He'd felt different for so long. Left out. Bound by his family's expectations and society's rules.

But in that moment, standing on the slope of Ben Fennon, he felt closer to what being a man is all about than he ever had before. He still wasn't sure what it meant to be one entirely, but here in the Highlands, with Miss Montgomery keeping him on his toes—and trusting him at the same time—he felt the stirrings of understanding.

She peeked at him from beneath her lashes. "You've kissed a lot of women."

He nodded. "That's what Impossible Bachelors do."

"What's an Impossible Bachelor?"

"A silly title given me by Prinny himself. It means I'm adept at charming women *and* avoiding legshackles."

She put her hands on his chest. "Prinny named you this?"

"Yes, His Royal Highness himself. It was a lark, of course. He lives for amusement. As I have always done."

Until now, he wanted to add. But he didn't want her to know he was enjoying the newfound sense of responsibility he felt as a stand-in for his grandmother.

God forbid anyone knew.

Miss Montgomery tilted her head. "So why should I let you kiss *me*?"

"Because I think you're beautiful." His hands were splayed across her back, and he felt her rib cage still.

She wasn't even breathing.

"I'm not just saying that," he reassured her.

She started breathing again. "You're not?"

"No." How could he get her to believe what he said was true? "Don't get me wrong. A lot of men say that to . . . to get women to kiss them, but I mean it. You *are* beautiful. You're full of fire, and your eyes get to be a stormy blue when—"

"Sssh." She stood on tiptoe and kissed him.

It was exactly the tonic he needed!

The kiss went on . . .

And on.

The sun warmed the back of his neck, and the smell of the heather mixed with the scent of her skin tantalized him. He couldn't get enough of her sweet mouth.

Finally, after endlessly frustrating but glorious kisses, he picked her up.

She laughed. "Where are you going with me?"

"Over there." He angled his chin at a fine patch of soft grass off the road. Above it a slab of rock jutted out toward Glen Dewey. It looked like a set of stairs. Below it was a grouping of three larch trees, standing sentinel on the mountain.

"No one can see us from above or below," he said, "and if someone decides to come up or down the road, we'll hear them well before they get here."

"You've brought me to the Stone Steps," she said, and kissed that vulnerable place beneath his chin. It was rough from lack of shaving. "It's the best place to be to get a view of Glen Dewey, and the mountains behind form a marvelous backdrop. But a warning to the newcomer."

"Yes?"

"Right next to the steps is the worst place to be." She pointed to a copse of trees to their left. "Binney's Bog lurks behind those pines. Stay far away. You'll sink and never be found if you accidentally land in it. And that's not a barmy Scots legend—it's the truth. Mr. Binney was the first on record to have lost his life there, some four hundred years ago."

"Thanks for the cautionary tale. I'll heed it well."

She kissed him beneath his chin again, lingering as he walked with her.

They'd arrived at the perfect spot.

"Here," he said, and lowered her to the grass.

He took the pins out of her hair one by one, until the tight bun was released and her long golden locks lay across her shoulders and down her back.

When he fell down beside her, she immediately turned to kiss him. Her eagerness made him so heady, he pulled back. "Miss Montgomery—"

"Can't you call me Daisy?"

"Daisy." He bent and kissed her, luxuriating in the feel of her satiny-soft lips against his own. Their tongues collided and played, and she sighed when he caressed her waist and moved to her breast.

By sheer strength of will, he stopped and pulled her close, so close her face was buried in his chest.

"I want you desperately," he said to a small boulder and a stalk of wintergreen behind her. "But I respect your honor. You're my charge, too, so I can't—I mean to say, in a moment, after a few more of these lovely kisses, we're going to stand. And then we're going to head up the road to the castle. After we fix your hair, of course. I couldn't resist letting it down." He reveled in the silkiness of her hair against his palm and the feel of her lithe body against his own. "Oh, and you must call me Charlie."

"Charlie!" Her muffled voice tickled his chest. "I can't breathe."

He immediately pulled back. When she looked up at him, she had the faint impression of one of his jacket buttons on her cheek and that vaguely smashed look people get when they've been sleeping on a pillow in one position too long.

"Goodness," she said with a chuckle, and pulled a piece of her own hair out of her mouth.

"I'm sorry." He was sorely embarrassed.

"It's all right. I liked being so close. Your skin is . . ."

"What?"

"I don't know. But I like it. Very much." She ran a hand over his chest.

He closed his eyes against the sensation. "I'm trying to do the right thing. But you're impossible to resist."

"I hope so." She kissed his mouth.

A moment later, he lowered his own mouth to the line of pale flesh above her bodice. Cupping one of her breasts in his hand, he pushed it up and kissed the exposed mound. Then he moved to the small cleft between her breasts and nuzzled it with his mouth. Her skin smelled sweet, like clover and honeysuckle.

She gave another little whimper of pleasure deep in her throat. "You've made me feel very beautiful, indeed."

He lifted his head. "I can make you feel even more beautiful."

"Can you?" The bees-and-honey voice had never been more alluring.

He heaved a great sigh, wishing he could show her and also dreading what he must say next. "I can, but it's time to go." He stood up and offered her his hand.

"Not again," she said.

"I'm afraid so."

"Oh, my." She didn't move. Her gaze was focused on his breeches.

He looked down, where proof of his arousal was plain as day. "My apologies," he said.

"Please don't apologize," she murmured, and allowed him to pull her up. Her face took on an obstinate expression. "I'm not ready to leave. You said you could make me feel even more beautiful."

He forced himself to laugh. "I was boasting. You shouldn't listen when a man says outrageous things—"

"*You're* beautiful," she said out of the blue.

He inhaled a breath. "*Daisy*. It's time to leave."

"Viscount." She pulled his head down by wrapping both hands around his neck. "You're at my beck and call, remember?" She paused. "I know you won't dishonor me. And you promised me anything. *Anything*."

He'd never seen her so solemn.

Or entrancing.

He put his hands on her rounded bottom and pulled her firmly against his hips. "You're right. I would never dishonor you, or allow anyone else to. And I did make that promise."

She gripped his neck. "Show me how beautiful I am," she whispered. "Please. Before I have to go back tonight and pack the trunks of three harridans."

And that was all it took.

He picked her up again, lifting her high in his arms and wrapping her legs around his waist. She clung to him, enjoying the sensation of her most intimate place pressed firmly against his hard belly as he strode a few feet up the slope, onto the Stone Steps themselves. She could hardly bear to part her lips from his when he set her down, as gently as he could, on the third step from the bottom.

The sun had baked the steps a warm temperature. Daisy basked in its rays as Charlie sat beside her and kissed her again, one hand around her waist, the other cupping her breast.

When his thumb caressed her nipple, she relished the new sensation.

He made her feel so alive, Charlie did! Alive and wanting more pleasure. More closeness.

"I want to untie your laces," he whispered in her ear.

She murmured a sound of acquiescence, shrugging out of her bodice and letting him fumble with her stays.

Free. That's how she felt when he released her stays, especially with the sun and wind on her bare flesh. Charlie's obvious appreciation made her lose all concern that she didn't compare favorably to women he'd seen before.

"God, you're gorgeous," he said, and bent low to kiss her.

She sucked in a breath at the wonder of his tongue laving her nipple, and when he took it in his mouth and suckled, a sharp dart of pleasure between her legs made her lift her lower belly toward the sky. He grabbed her bottom with his free hand and rubbed a slow circle around it, his mouth still dancing across both her breasts, causing them to pucker and tingle with such sweet pleasure, she moaned out loud.

"Don't stop," she said.

"Never fear," he replied, and gently plucked a nipple with his teeth. "I'm not going to stop until you've had enough."

"Oh, thank God," she whispered, her hands clinging to his hair. "But I don't know when that will be."

He looked up then, his pupils dark. "Is that a kind way to say I'm at your beck and call again?"

She nodded. Then giggled.

"That's a special sound," he whispered.

"It is?"

"Yes. The first giggle I've heard from you."

She felt bashful of a sudden.

He tilted her chin up. "Don't be shy to do it again," he whispered. "It was a gift. Thank you."

She bit her lip. "You're welcome. I—I didn't—"

"I'll relive that sound," he interrupted her, his tone serious. "I'll play it over and over again in my head."

She blinked, touched at his words and yet a bit confused. "You're sweet," she said.

"There's nothing sweet about me," he said, and came up to plunder her mouth with his own.

But he *was* sweet. Generous with his body and his words. Carefree like a boy—but strong like a man.

"Shall I stop?" he asked her.

She shook her head. "If you stop now"—he kissed her right below her ear—"I'll never forgive you."

"All right." He dipped down to lay kisses along her jaw. "But I don't want to rush you. Perhaps it's too soon."

"*No.* It's not. Show me, Charlie. Please."

He showed her, all right, caressing her intimately with the palm of his hand, making her arch and ache for more.

She clutched his circling hand with her own. "More," she said against his mouth, and was delighted when his fingers worked into her drawers to tease the nub of her softest flesh.

The feeling was so tantalizing, she threw her hands out on either side to grasp the edge of the step, her mouth connected to Charlie's in a ribald, frantic kiss.

And when his fingers slid inside her—oh, glorious feeling!—she felt herself clench hard around him, pulses of pleasure urging her hips to thrust upward.

"Charlie," she said in wonder.

He kissed her while moving his fingers in and out, mingling with her hot, damp curls. She arched, waves of pleasure taking her over the edge of bliss as she cried his name into his mouth, and then as she sank back down.

"Charlie," she whispered, her head fallen back, her gaze filled with the bowl of Highland sky and nothing else.

She wilted onto him, his hand buffering her spine against the hard edge of the stair behind them.

When she blinked again, she opened her eyes to a whole new world. And Charlie's satisfied smile.

"Oh," she said.

He gave a short laugh. "Really?"

She let out a long breath. "That was more than I ever imagined."

He stared at her seriously then. "I'm glad."

A bee went buzzing by, and they both watched it go.

"But what about you?" she asked, caressing Charlie's shoulder. He sat next to her on the steps and pulled her onto his lap. "I want you to achieve such a blissful state, too. It hardly seems fair that only I do."

They were nose to nose. His legs were hard, his belly was hard, and he gripped her hard, but in his arms she felt like a fragile china teacup, the most exquisite one in a person's possession . . . or a petal-soft flower much adored.

"Believe me, I can," he said with a grin. "On my own. Although it's not nearly as much fun alone."

"Let me," she said, and pressed herself into him so she could feel the hard length of him through his breeches.

He pressed back, like a lion preening. "I want you to. More than anything. But today's about you."

"Why?"

He squeezed her close. "Because everyone needs to have a day about them, other than their birthday. Didn't you know that?"

"No. When's *your* special day?"

"I think it falls in April sometime."

"I think you're making this up." He had the most beautiful eyes, brown with golden glints, especially when he was being playful.

"I'm not." He touched her nose with a finger. "Your day is today. In fact, some people get more than one day. Some people get *every* day."

"Every day?"

"Every day. And since you have me here, you're one of those lucky people. Every day we can do . . . whatever you like."

"No." She was utterly shocked and delighted at

his fancy. "I realize you're still making this up, but wouldn't it be nice if it could be true?"

"It can be." He said it as if he felt sorry for her for not believing him.

She grew serious. "I think you're amusing. And this . . . this has been incredible. But in real life, people can't do whatever they want when they want."

Charlie bit his lip. "You're right, I suppose. But who gets to make the rules?"

She shrugged. "I don't know."

He gave her a slow, languorous kiss. "When it comes to you and me, *we* make the rules. Let's establish that right now."

Daisy nodded. "I like that."

"You'll like what I'm about to do, too," he whispered in her ear.

"Charlie—"

"And don't stop me," he said. "Remember, today's your day."

She felt a great thrill of anticipation and nerves, but his kisses, even as they aroused her, calmed her in a way nothing ever had. Feeling spoiled, she barely noticed that somehow he'd managed to deftly maneuver himself around her so that she was sitting back on the steps. He knelt two steps below, his broad chest between her legs. In fact, she was forced to spread them to accommodate his hard, lean body.

Next thing she knew, he was raising her gown: first, above her ankles. Then her shins, knees, thighs, and gracious goodness, above her waist! And he was removing her drawers, shimmying them off her—

one moment they were there, and then they were gone—and gently pushing her knees even farther outward.

She had no time to be shy about basking in the sun with her legs spread wide on the Stone Steps. How could she when she was forced to endure the exquisite pleasure of his warm mouth upon her inner thighs, while she admired the curve of his back, the top of his curly head, and the large muscles bunched at his shoulders?

And then she was fully immersed in the sweetest pleasure she could ever imagine. Charlie's mouth nuzzled her womanly core, gently at first, but her moans drove him to licking and sucking and loving her with great abandon.

She'd never felt so wanton, so beautiful, so in touch with life as she did at the moment she cried his name over and over, his fingers and his mouth sheer poetry upon her as she alternated between grinding her rear end into the warm stone and arching upward, hoping to get closer and closer to him—

Her viscount.

CHAPTER TEN

Charlie woke the next morning from a fitful slumber, and it wasn't only the poor sleeping accommodations and the extraordinary light that had kept him awake. Images of Daisy naked and inviting his caresses at the Stone Steps pervaded every aspect of his dreams. And as warmly sensual as those imaginings had been, he'd awakened with an uneasy feeling.

Of course, in the true light of day, he knew why. He didn't like to admit it, but he was walking a risky road with Daisy. A dalliance in London was one thing, with a knowing widow or a kept mistress . . . but Daisy wasn't made for dalliances.

And he wasn't made for marriage.

Looking up at the crude beams above his head, he vowed to keep his distance from her, as difficult as it would be. First chance he got, he'd tell her there were to be no more kisses of such an intimate nature, as much as he craved holding her in his arms again and lavishing her with kisses from head to toe.

As much as he longed to make every day for her a special day.

"Lord Lumley!" The hiss came from the ground outside the byre, from the other side of the rotting shutters.

He peered through a crack in them.

Daisy stood below, bright-eyed and apparently well rested. Dreams of *him* obviously hadn't kept her tossing and turning all night.

She wore the plainest gown he'd ever seen, and her hair was once more tightly bound. Even so, when he pushed the shutters open, he couldn't help thinking how feminine she always was, especially in the throes of passion.

"You're up awfully early," he managed to say, trying to ignore his desire for her.

She put a hand to her eyes and squinted up at him. "I had to come see you. Before all the visitors arrive at the Keep and we don't have a chance to speak."

"Hold on a moment, and I'll be right out."

"No," she said, and sounded rather embarrassed. "Please don't bother."

"But there's something I need to talk to *you* about—" He was already standing and tucking his shirt into his breeches.

"Very well." She sounded a trifle uneasy. "But first, I have to tell you I've had a chance to think over what happened yesterday, and as memorable as it was, we can't do it again. I've too much at stake here with winning the castle back. I can't afford to be distracted. And—and you're a man of a certain ilk. We both know what that means."

"*Ilk* again? Are we always going to come back to that?"

She shrugged in pixieish fashion. "You told me yourself you're an Impossible Bachelor, wise in the ways of the world. So let me speak frankly. You helped satisfy my curiosity about certain things, and it was very nice. Thank you, but now it's over. We'll continue our ruse of being engaged, but it certainly won't displease my stepmother to see us apart."

He ceased in his dressing. "You *used* me yesterday afternoon?" he called out to her.

"I didn't mean to. I couldn't help it. You looked very . . . appealing, having just come from shinty. And the way you held the bag of shinty sticks, I could see all your muscles to perfection."

"Wait a minute. Are you describing me the same way I'd describe a horse I admire?"

"I don't mean to. I've never bought a horse. Is that how men talk about them?"

"Never mind that. Did you say my lovemaking is very *nice*?"

She nodded. "Perfectly agreeable."

"*That's* all you can say about it?"

"Yes, and I'm sorry if that disappoints you, my lord." She didn't look sorry. She looked annoyed and impatient, the way she was throwing her arms about to add weight to her words one minute and pushing her hair behind her ears the next. "No doubt plenty of women in your future will be more ebullient in their assessment of your—your *skills* because they're not very busy, are they, those London ladies? Riding about on their horses in Hyde Park, lolling on sofas with glasses of ratafia—"

He shook his head. "You were *assessing* me?"

She waved a hand at him and turned partially away. "I've got to go. One last thing—I know at the Keep, you'll do your best to treat me the way you would any other woman there."

He saw her stride away, toward the castle, and he hurriedly finished tucking in his shirt, climbed down the ladder he'd taken to the loft, and strode after her.

"Miss Montgomery," he called to her retreating back. *"Daisy."*

She kept going. "I really must go." When he caught up with her and took her arm, her eyes were stormy. "Which part of our conversation did you not understand, my lord?"

"First of all, it was *your* conversation," he said. "I barely got a word in."

"But—"

"And secondly, I must tell you that at the Keep, we'll still need to work together to ensure that the visit goes off without a hitch."

She let out an impatient breath. "Of course. But the Keep is vast. We probably won't see much of each other, except at meals. By the way, I gave you the largest suite, the Blue Room. I'm up the stairs and down another corridor entirely."

She took off again.

"Wait a minute—"

"I can't," she said, her back to him. "I promised Mrs. Skene and Mrs. MacAdoo Hester's receipt for her special apricot brandy pudding. They volunteered to take charge of the kitchen at the Keep all ten days of the Highland venture." But then she stopped and turned around. "You do know you won't be able to participate in the hunt, don't you?"

He couldn't help scowling. "But that was the part I was looking forward to most. Stalking red deer, eating around a campfire . . ."

She shook her head. "You have responsibilities here. You can't just disappear for a couple of days in the mountains."

"But—"

"The men of Glen Dewey will take care of our guests on the hunt. What if some of the travelers prefer to stay back at the Keep? Perhaps there'll be a few crotchety old men who like to play whist, or some who'd rather go fishing. You'll need to bait their hooks."

"*Me?*"

He was used to having people bait *his* hooks!

"Oh, and I must remind you. Joe said he's going to need help shearing the sheep here at Castle Vandemere. It will fall right in line with showing the visitors what the Highlands are about. To a large extent, we're about those stubborn, woolly beasts. The guests will enjoy traipsing over to watch."

She sounded quite pleased at the idea.

He huffed. "I'll do my best to shear the sheep for Joe's sake but not in front of any guests. I've never done it before, and I'll look like a fool."

"They'll love it. Just remember"—she grabbed her index finger—"pleasing the guests. It's our first priority. And then"—she held on to her middle finger and wiggled it—"winning the castle back, priority number two." She then grabbed her thumb. "Keeping as much money out of my stepmother's hands as possible. Those are the three subjects uppermost in my mind, as they should be in yours, as you're a stand-in for my godmother, Lady Pinckney."

So their kissing wasn't uppermost in her mind, eh? His pleasuring her until she cried his name was already forgotten, too?

She looked over the rail on the shady side of the byre at the sow and her piglets—said a few words of encouragement to the sow—then headed toward the castle kitchen without either a backward glance or a farewell.

Although she did stop and admire a potted lemon tree on the steps before she disappeared through the door.

He put his fists on his hips and turned in a slow circle, taking in the castle, the byre, the chicken yard, the sheep huddled on a nearby hill next to a crumbling stone wall that needed repair, and the sagging drawbridge that needed fixing.

Then he remembered those sharp shears he'd seen hanging in the byre. And the obstinate look he'd seen in the eyes of sheep the few times in his life he'd bothered to notice them.

"Bloody hell," he said.

London felt a long, long way off.

Daisy inhaled a great breath when she got inside the kitchen of Castle Vandemere.

Heavens, her little showdown with Charlie had been difficult to pull off. She was far from indifferent to him—remembering that hour late yesterday afternoon on the mountainside still made her heart beat faster and her limbs weak. But she could hardly afford to indulge in romantic feelings for a man who lived far away, had no intentions of ever settling down, and who could have any woman he wanted if he merely snapped his fingers.

She was a temporary amusement.

A false fiancée.

She'd be amused herself if she didn't feel so afraid of her own feelings. Charlie had made her feel beautiful. He'd made her laugh. He'd also brought her great pleasure. She'd like to be so pleasured every day for the rest of her life.

He was the perfect companion, friend, and lover.

But she wouldn't think about that. She'd think instead of the viscount's incredulous face as she'd stormed past him just now, thrust those menial jobs his way, and ruined his hopes of going on the hunt.

He'd been so generous with her on those Stone Steps, but she couldn't allow him to think she'd not be able to live without his attentions—and he also didn't need any more spoiling.

"Poor man," she muttered as she sifted through

Hester's receipts, which she found in a little wooden box.

Although she must take that back. He was *not* a poor man. She shouldn't and wouldn't feel sorry for him. He'd made a promise to assist her, and he was a gentleman. Supposedly, gentlemen ached to fulfill promises. So she was only helping him do his duty.

"What was that you said, dearie?" Hester was bustling about, making cups of tea, a small frown on her face.

"Oh, nothing," said Daisy. "Is something wrong?"

"No, not really." The housekeeper gave a small sigh. "It's just that Jinx hasn't come round for her morning saucer of milk. She's like clockwork."

"Maybe she's out on the prowl."

"That's what I'm supposing." Hester chuckled. "That's the thing about cats. They're independent. They come when they want to." She eyed Daisy over her spectacles. "But back to you. Who are you calling a poor man? I presume you mean Joe? I've good news. His limp's improving in this warm weather. He's already off herding the sheep to the east pasture."

"You read me right." Daisy threw her a nervous smile. "I was thinking of Joe."

"Of course." Hester whistled as she poured the tea.

Which meant she thought something wasn't quite as it should be. She was worried about Jinx, but had she noticed something about Daisy, too?

"All right," Daisy confessed. "I was fibbing. I

wasn't referring to Joe. I called the viscount a poor man. He's not used to doing chores and missing out on amusements. But he will over the next ten days. He'll have to. It's why he came up here, after all."

She waited for Hester to react.

The older woman took her time, putting the kettle back on the hob and wiping her hands on her apron. "I think he's a lovely lad," she said. "And I'd call him a poor man, too, if he didn't need this whole experience the way a thirsty man needs water."

"Do you think so?" Daisy brightened.

Hester chuckled. "Of course! Every man needs to be challenged. I doot he's ever been." She wagged her finger at Daisy. "So behind his back, you may call him a poor man, but to his face, stay strong, my girl. Don't give him an inch. He'll be better for it."

"That's a fine idea," Daisy agreed, and renewed her vow once more to stay far away from Lord Lumley.

"Even though he's verra kissable," Hester said lightly, and immediately turned her back to pull out a crock of flour.

Daisy felt heat creep up her neck.

Hester put her crock on the counter and came over to lay a hand over Daisy's own. "Remember, lass, your heart is a precious thing. When you choose to give it away, make sure you give it to the right man. Sometimes you'll meet him at the wrong time. He or you—or both of you—might need a little growin.' Or you could meet the wrong man at the right time . . . someone who comes along at the moment you're ready to soar like a bird—and then he goes and clips your wings."

Daisy bit her lip. "It all sounds scary. And very confusing."

"Not if you pay attention to your own heart, dear." Hester gave Daisy a tremulous smile and patted her cheek. "You'll know."

Daisy gave her a big hug. "You're the best lady in the world."

At which moment the most wretched woman Daisy knew came into the kitchen. "Get back to work," Mona hissed at them both. "It's time we're off to the Keep."

Hester's cheeks were bright spots of pink. "Do ye not want to break your fast?"

"No, old woman," Mona said, "and don't you dare ask me any more questions without a decent curtsy."

Daisy met Hester's eyes.

Ignore her, Daisy said with her own.

Hester had terrible aches in her bones, but somehow she managed to make a respectable curtsy.

Slowly.

But she did it.

"Would you care for anything from the kitchen to take with you, missus?" Hester asked when she stood straight again.

"No." Mona curled her lip. "Where's the tea?"

"Soon to boil," Hester said placidly, but she cast a comically long-suffering eye Daisy's way, which served to calm her desire to throttle her stepmother.

At that moment, Cassandra and Perdita appeared,

freshly bathed and dressed in their best walking gowns, which Daisy had pressed for them.

"We're looking for Lord Lumley," Cassandra said without greeting anyone.

Perdita nodded enthusiastically.

They acted as if going to see Lord Lumley were incredibly exciting. It *was*, but who were they—or Daisy—to indulge themselves in daydreaming about his good looks and charismatic charm?

Lord Lumley was off limits. A creature of pleasure. An emissary merely following his grandmother's orders. A man with no interest in the residents of Castle Vandemere beyond a superficial interest, which he'd maintain until he could leave the glen forever.

"I'll go, too," Daisy said.

"Why?" asked Cassandra. "Have you forgotten what I told you? You don't need to be around the viscount unless it's strictly necessary."

She angled her head at Hester and mouthed the words *poor house*.

Daisy wished she could narrow her eyes at her stepsister. But she dared not.

"He's to carry your trunks," she said instead. "If you want them to arrive at the Keep when you do, he'll need to know where the wheelbarrow and ropes are kept. I was about to show him, but if you'd rather—"

"I wouldn't dare set a foot in that byre," Cassandra said in a surly manner.

"Nor I," Perdita added. "Although I like a nice wheelbarrow ride."

"Shut up, Perdita," said her mother. "We've no time for wheelbarrow rides."

"I'd like a ride of another sort," Cassandra said under her breath, and flung a challenging look at Daisy. "I intend to get one, too."

Daisy knew exactly what she meant.

Wicked girl.

But if Cassandra thought she'd bed a certain viscount, she'd thought wrong.

Once outside, Daisy let go of her aggravation. The air was as peppery fresh as it had ever been on a sunny summer morning. It was a perfect day for visitors to arrive and experience the Highlands.

And she needn't worry about Charlie. He wasn't stupid. Cassandra's charms were only skin-deep.

Even so, a memory of the Stone Steps rushed back. *He's my viscount,* Daisy thought. *And I won't give him up to any other woman.*

Which was silly of her, as she'd already told him there could be nothing between them.

She cast a glance back at the kitchen window, where Hester stood watching them. The older woman pulled on her ear—which signified, *Damned Furies*!—then touched her fingertips to her lips and gently blew a kiss toward Daisy.

Daisy smiled back, but inside, she was pensive. Hester and Joe meant everything to her. She couldn't veer off course. Saving Castle Vandemere for them was paramount.

Worrying a bit about Jinx, too, she scanned the grounds for a sign of the cat, and even called for her, but she didn't come. Cassandra and Perdita made no effort to help, and Daisy put aside her own vague worries. It was much too soon to be concerned, she told herself. Surely Jinx was fine and was merely ignoring her call.

So when she caught sight of Joe and the viscount, both of them looking down the mountainside, she allowed herself to feel a surge of happiness as she strolled toward them.

But Cassandra stepped right in her path, forcing her aside.

"Hello, Lord Lumley." Cassandra batted her eyes at him.

"Your coat is exquisite," said Perdita in a plodding manner.

She'd obviously practiced her words.

"Good morning, ladies," the viscount answered in a gallant fashion but didn't bother to glance at Daisy.

Well, what could she expect after their earlier conversation?

Cassandra sent a gloating look her way.

It took everything Daisy had in her to ignore it and appear completely at ease.

"The visitors have arrived even sooner than we expected," Charlie said. "We saw them pull into the village. They'll need to rest the horses before they dare attempt the slope."

"Five coaches and six outriders," Joe announced.

"How exciting," Daisy said.

"I can't wait," Cassandra said.

"Nor I," said Perdita.

For a moment, they were all united in their excitement, their differences forgotten.

But that bad feeling dogged Daisy. She was sure it had everything to do with the fact that she and Charlie were not ever to be together again. But something in her prompted her to say: "Have you seen Jinx?"

"She lives in the kitchen," said Joe right away.

"I know," Daisy said, "but she's not there. She hasn't even come in for her dish of goat's milk."

Perdita snorted.

Daisy whirled around and looked at her. Perdita scratched her nose in an offhand manner, but her eyes glinted with glee when she exchanged glances with her sister.

Perdita had done something to Jinx. Daisy just knew it. And Cassandra had helped.

The witches.

CHAPTER ELEVEN

Charlie was shocked to see the fierce look on Daisy's face, and even more surprised to see her stand toe to toe with her large stepsister. "Where is she? What have you done with Jinx?"

Miss Perdita whimpered. "I don't know. I haven't done anything to her."

"You're lying." Daisy turned to Miss Cassandra. "If you were cruel to that cat in any way—"

"I don't like your threatening tone." Miss Cassandra managed to look angelic. "You have a tendency to be impulsive—"

"Oh, bother with that." Daisy put her hands on her hips. "Where's Jinx?"

"If either of you knows, out with it," Charlie urged the two girls. He was disgusted with their obvious guilt.

Miss Cassandra drew herself up and looked at him with wide eyes. "Of course we didn't harm Hester's cat." She put her chin in the air. "I'm horribly hurt, Daisy, that you think we're capable of cruelty to an innocent animal. You're embarrassing the entire family in front of the viscount. You're volatile, careless—"

"Careless?" Daisy's face flared red. "How have I been careless? I care enough to look for her—"

Miss Cassandra put on a patient look and swiveled to face him. "You do know about the tragedy, don't you?"

Charlie felt vastly uncomfortable. Something was terribly wrong here. "No," he said, and wished he could walk away. This was a family squabble. Private business. He didn't belong.

But Daisy was obviously outnumbered and outflanked, and damned if he was going to let her stepsisters hide the truth about the cat. He already had a soft spot for Hester, and he wanted answers, too.

"Now is not the time," Daisy said to Miss Cassandra.

Charlie couldn't agree more.

The charged atmosphere sent Joe limping away.

Miss Cassandra crossed her arms over her chest and locked gazes with Charlie. "She burned down the bungalow." She wore a distasteful smirk.

The words made no sense at first. It took several seconds for Charlie to understand.

Daisy looked at him with steel in her expression. "It was an accident."

"Yes," said Miss Cassandra, "but you were careless." She looked at Charlie. "Sadly, her father—my stepfather—was so traumatized by the incident, he died a week later."

Miss Perdita began to tremble.

A sheen of tears appeared in Daisy's eyes. "You *are* cruel, Cassandra. How could you bring that up now?"

"I wasn't trying to be cruel!" Miss Perdita roared, and put her hands over her ears.

"Enough." Miss Cassandra laid a hand on Perdita's shoulder. "Jinx is fine."

"Then where is she?" Daisy demanded to know, but her voice was thin with worry.

"Be quick and tell us," Charlie interjected.

Miss Perdita merely stared goggle eyed at all of them, her hands still over her ears.

"She's locked in Perdita's wardrobe," Miss Cassandra said quietly.

"We put her in," Miss Perdita boomed. "And I turned the key."

"How could you?" Daisy's voice trembled with fury. "The two of you should be ashamed of yourselves."

Miss Cassandra lifted her chin. "Perdita did it and told me afterward. I was on my way to getting the cat out when we were diverted by news of the visitors."

"No you weren't," Daisy said. "You strolled into the kitchen, and—"

She felt a restraining hand on her arm. It was Charlie, and she couldn't help but take comfort from it.

"Just go let the poor animal out of the wardrobe," he said quietly to Miss Cassandra, who blinked at him once and turned on her heel.

"Follow me, Perdita," she said in injured tones. "As usual, I am being blamed for your folly."

Miss Perdita finally dropped her hands from her ears and lumbered after her sister, shaking her head all the while. "I'm going to tell Mother, and Daisy will get in trouble. Not me. How dare she say I did anything wrong?"

Charlie watched Joe limp after them. He'd see to it that Jinx's release was complete.

When they all disappeared into the house, Charlie looked at Daisy. "What's going on?"

She had a hollow look about her. "You heard them."

"Yes," he said. There was a moment's silence. "I'm sorry about your father."

He could see her jaw working.

"We don't have to talk about it," he assured her.

She looked at the ground but cocked her head to her right. "Do you see that empty spot, over by the oak and rowan trees? It looks as if something was once there?"

He nodded.

She wouldn't look at the site herself. "That was where my mother's bungalow stood. Papa built it for her. She painted there. It was the perfect spot, she said. She could see everything—all the way down the glen to the village, and up to the top of Ben Fennon."

"I see." He waited for her to go on.

"I used to go there, too, to sew at Mama's feet. And after she died, I continued. It was my haven. I did almost all my sewing there. Papa would come in, too, and sit and write occasionally. The place reminded us both of my mother." She took a breath. "One night, I was sewing late, and I must have left a candle burning—"

She hesitated again, and he saw her jaw work even more.

"It's all right," he said. "You don't need to talk about it. And you mustn't blame yourself. It was an accident."

She looked up at him then with the most mournful eyes he'd ever seen. "I know," she whispered. "It was a terrible accident."

He wanted to take her into his arms then and assuage her grief. But he daren't. No doubt Cassandra and Perdita were watching them from the castle windows. And she didn't want him to get close, did she?

Not an hour before, she'd let him know very clearly that their intimacy couldn't continue.

"At least Jinx is safe," he reminded her.

She gave him a wobbly smile. "Yes, that's true. It would have broken Hester's heart if she'd been hurt. Mine, too."

They began a slow walk toward the sheep pasture.

Daisy allowed her mouth to quirk up on one side. "I long for the day when Castle Vandemere is ours again."

Her home had slipped out of sight. They were beyond the byre now, with only fields before them and the long, curving road that wended its way down the slope of Ben Fennon to the village below.

"Ours?" he asked.

"Mine, Hester's, and Joe's." She bit her lip and was silent a moment. "That's the way it needs to be," she said eventually. "The castle will be ours. Not my stepmother's nor my stepsisters'. Because unless a miracle occurs and they change in the near future, I'm—I'm going to kick them out." She looked up at Charlie, almost as if she were fearful. Or would faint.

He took her upper arms and braced her. "It's all right."

"I never thought I'd say that," she whispered, staring at his chest. "But today is the last straw. I can't wait to see them go." Her voice gained more strength. "I don't even care where. My stepmother will land on her feet, without a doubt." She took a deep breath. "I'm not just saying this, either. I mean it."

Her gaze was unwavering.

"I believe you." He sensed she needed reassurance, and he had it for her. In spades.

"Do you?" Her expression was more determined than he'd ever seen it, yet he saw a bit of desperation there, as well.

"I think it's a very good thing." He longed to caress her. "You deserve better treatment than what you receive from your stepmother and your stepsisters."

"I never really thought about what I deserve." She began to pace in a tight circle. "I've always thought about what I *wanted,* however. I wanted freedom from Stepmother's vitriol and Cassandra's disrespect—Perdita's, too—but I've been so busy trying to survive their lobs, jabs, and outright attacks, it simply didn't occur to me that I don't have to live with it. With *them*."

She stood still a moment. "I can cut them loose. Not only in my imagination, either. In real life. I used to dream of their moving back to London, far away from me. But I never thought it could actually happen. Maybe I can make it happen. Or at the very least, push them in that direction."

She turned to look at him, and he was gratified by her keen interest in his response.

"Yes, you can," he said. "Trouble is, will they go? Or will they hang on by their claws?" He tossed her a small grin. This was serious business, but he wanted to bolster her spirits.

She managed a weak grin back. "I don't know." There was a frustrated edge to her honey-bee voice. "But we *will* get to that point, after these visitors leave and we get our money. And I can't tell you how much I look forward to it."

It was a miserable hour later, and they still hadn't arrived at the Keep. Castle Vandemere was without a wagon or a horse, so Charlie had had to strap Mrs. Montgomery's and her daughters' trunks onto the wheelbarrow to get them there.

It was rough going.

Daisy carried her own things in a bag. It was light, she said, and not bulky. It was also about a third of the size of the trunks.

Along the way, Perdita pouted, still shaken by

that morning's events. Cassandra kept up a steady stream of chatter, as if she'd not been involved in a cruel prank at all. Mrs. Montgomery strode ahead of all of them, her dark cape swirling out behind her.

Daisy said very little. It was obvious to Charlie that she, too, was still affected by the incident of Jinx's incarceration and her subsequent decision to rid herself of her stepfamily as soon as possible.

And no doubt she was sad to say a temporary farewell to Hester and Joe.

"Although I'll be down every day if I can," he'd heard her whisper to them before she'd left, and kissed both their cheeks.

When they arrived at the bottom of the impressive front steps of the Keep, neither Mrs. Montgomery nor her daughters offered Charlie a word of thanks for carrying their trunks over rough terrain.

Daisy, still in a brown study, lifted her gown with one hand and walked with great purpose up the steps to the grand entrance to the Keep. Charlie couldn't keep his eyes off her ankles, so dainty and fine they were. He remembered seeing her whole leg bared—indeed, her whole self bared—to him on the Stone Steps, and the memory caused a surge of heat in his loins that he knew would plague him all day.

To his left, Mrs. Montgomery waved away the four crofters' sons who were doing a fine job at playing footmen, offering to help the residents of Vandemere with their trunks. "Don't you dare touch my precious things. You're thieves, all of you!" she cried.

The young men managed to race back up the stone steps and go back through the gigantic front door of the Keep as fast as they could, disappearing long before Charlie could call them back.

And no wonder. Mrs. Montgomery was terrifying, especially in her swirling black cape.

Not that Cassandra and Perdita seemed terribly concerned about their mother's fit of pique. They rushed up the steps after the footmen, giggling the whole way. Charlie had no doubt that they were off to introduce themselves to all the males in the house.

"Lumley," Mrs. Montgomery called to him. "Take the trunks to our rooms straightaway."

He wondered what particular sin he'd committed that caused him to have to endure this particular widow. With a weary sigh, he hoisted her trunk onto his shoulder and regretted every moral lapse of his youth and childhood.

"And don't dally," she told him, her tone curt. "Daisy's gone on ahead, the impertinent girl, so I need you to empty them and—"

"Put all your shoes in perfect rows," he finished for her.

"Right," she said.

He'd been *joking*.

Poor Daisy, to have to perform such menial chores for the ungrateful harridan on a regular basis!

The weighty trunk dug into his shoulder. When

he circled around Mrs. Montgomery, he resisted the perfectly natural urge he had to knock her over like a bowling pin with the end of the trunk—"by accident," of course.

He heaved a sigh and carried the bulky chest up the front steps of the Keep, wondering how far in the bowels of the castle he must walk to find the woman's bedchamber.

He ran into a maid who said she knew the way, so he followed her.

It was hard work, carrying that massive trunk, but it felt good to exert himself. Charlie thought of the myriad times he'd allowed other men to pick up his bags, shine his shoes, deliver him his horse, fix his wobbly chair legs, feed him meals while on the hunt, tie his cravat, carry his dead birds, balance his accounts, clean his guns, wipe down his saddle, pour his whisky, shine his cuff links, build his homes, remove his dishes from the table, bury his faithful hunting dogs, escort women he'd slept with from his home, take his coat, his hat, his coat, his hat, his coat—

His damned hat.

His coat.

How many times?

How many *thousands* of times?

His throat tightened.

What kind of a man are you? Daisy's words echoed through his mind.

The only exertion he'd ever made had been artificial work—in the boxing ring and at D'Angelo's, fencing.

The trunk dug into his neck now, and he was sweating. God help him, he was sweating. He straightened his back, felt his spine align with his hips and shoulders, and adjusted the trunk.

He was going to be the best damned trunk carrier there ever was.

At least it was a start.

By the time he'd turned back around to carry in the other trunks, as well, he'd even convinced himself he'd be the best damned sheep shearer there ever was for the visitors. And then when he got back to London, he'd be the best damned . . .

He had no idea.

It would be something substantial—something beyond the contrived world of high society and the advantages that had been bestowed on him because of his wealth and birth.

It would be something . . . real. And he couldn't wait to tell Daisy. She'd be excited for him. She'd take an interest. He just knew it.

Perdita rushed through the great front hall and stopped in front of him.

She was patting her frizzy brown hair. "Excuse me, Lord Lumley. They're here—the visitors are here! I saw them out a window, many carriages pulling up to the drive. And there's a man—"

She stopped talking and went running past him.

He inhaled a breath to recover from her onslaught when Daisy came around the front door of the castle into the great hall. She was all aglow. Those were the only words for it.

A gentleman appeared behind her, obviously the

one that had left Perdita speechless. He looked like Apollo, and he carried himself as if he were the Keep's owner. Perdita's trunk sat lightly on his broad shoulder.

"Where should I put this, Miss Montgomery?" he asked Daisy in an American accent.

"You really didn't have to carry that," she said warmly. "You should have stayed outside with your colleagues to admire the view."

He halted in his tracks. "It's my great honor."

"How kind." She gave a nervous chuckle. "Please put it down here, Mr. King, and we'll get a footman to take it."

Charlie had never seen Daisy so discombobulated.

Mr. King shook his head. "I insist on delivering it to its proper place."

"Follow me, then," Charlie chimed in.

Mr. King made a quarter turn and locked gazes with him.

In that instant, Charlie assessed him as being a man who was used to getting his way, was familiar with power and success, and had more ability to charm women in his little finger than most men had in their whole bodies.

In other words, he was very much like Charlie.

Mr. King grinned. "Lead on, sir," he said with jaunty confidence.

"My lord," Daisy stammered to Charlie, "may I present to you Mr. Matthew King, of Smithfield, Virginia? Mr. King, this is Charles Thorpe, Viscount Lumley."

"It's a pleasure to welcome you to the Keep." Charlie inclined his head while Mr. King stood unmoving.

Granted, the trunk made it difficult to do anything else.

"I'm most grateful to be here," the handsome visitor replied with enthusiasm. "It must be quite something to be master of such a place. I envy you, Lord Lumley."

Daisy's eyes widened at him. *Play along,* they said.

Charlie decided it was becoming rather a thing with them, this role-playing. He stood tall and cleared his throat. "Thank you, sir. It's a great privilege. I hope my fiancée—"

"I usually reside at the neighboring castle," Daisy interjected, as if she were afraid of scandal.

"Yes." Charlie smiled patiently. "I hope Miss Montgomery's informed you that the Keep is yours to explore for the next ten days. We want you to have the full Highland experience."

"Indeed, she did," said Mr. King in the warmest of tones. "And I intend to take full advantage."

He looked directly at Daisy when he said so, and she appeared delighted, clasping her hands together and giving one little hop, as if she were a child in front of a window full of sweets.

She'd never hopped for Charlie before.

And in exactly what quarter did Mr. King plan to take full advantage?

"Mr. King is not only an avid bird-watcher," Daisy told Charlie, "he's a self-made man."

Mr. King chuckled. "Yes, we Americans have to start from scratch, as they say."

"He's invented several important agricultural tools that have saved innumerable farmers from bankruptcy and thousands from starvation," Daisy went on.

"How . . . inventive of you," Charlie said.

He hated the man already.

"He also designed and built his own home," Daisy waxed on, "a three-story Elizabethan-style mansion on a large plantation on the James River."

And she'd learned all this in the one or two minutes since they'd met?

"I didn't hammer in every nail or lay every brick," their esteemed guest said. "But I certainly did my fair share. I enjoy that sort of thing."

"Do you?" Charlie asked politely.

"Oh, yes. A life of leisure bores me. Bird-watching is only one of my hobbies."

Oh, right. Mr. Beebs had collected not only Charlie's anglers from Brawton but some bird-watchers staying at Lower Cross Junction.

"My newest passion," Mr. King prosed on, "is working with wrought iron. I'm still a beginner, but I made a lovely balcony railing for whoever is going to be my bride." He grinned, his white teeth sparkling like jewels. "I like to think ahead."

"It sounds lovely, Mr. King." Daisy's admiration appeared sincere, although Charlie felt it was misplaced.

She should be admiring *him*. Of course, he'd never built a house or designed a wrought-iron balcony, but he had skills. Skills she'd assessed as being *nice*. Surely that counted for something.

"I'll not hold you up, Mr. King," said Charlie. "Let me show you where to put that trunk. No doubt the footmen are itching to take it from you. You're our guest, after all."

"I'm in no hurry," Mr. King replied. "And I've little need of servants. I find they hamper my independence."

Was he going to stand there all day with that bloody trunk on his shoulder and wax on about how marvelous and independent he was?

Charlie knew exactly how much Miss Perdita's trunk weighed—as much as Mrs. Montgomery's, which surely meant the man's back was aching by now.

"Oh, but we'd like you trunk-free so we can show you about the grounds," Charlie said in the amiable way a good host should.

"Yes," Daisy piped up. "I'd like to take him around myself. I'll wait right here until you come back, Mr. King."

"Fantastic." Their guest bestowed a charming smile on her. "I'd love a private tour with you, Miss Montgomery, while my traveling companions settle in."

"We'll be happy to provide that for you," Charlie responded smoothly.

Emphasis on *we*.

"Excellent," the man said just as smoothly back.

Oh, he was good!

"Shall we?" Charlie gritted his teeth and began

the circuitous route to Miss Perdita's room, Mr. King following easily along beside him with that blasted trunk.

They chatted about what wealthy, powerful men usually do: the state of international affairs, horses—"We keep very few up here," said Charlie, "although the stable is large and will accommodate yours quite well"—and the condition of his wine cellar and his library, both of which he said were in fine shape, although he really had no idea.

By some miracle, they avoided Miss Perdita and Miss Cassandra.

In the bedchamber, Mr. King refused to let Charlie take the trunk from his shoulder and, in one swift, graceful movement, placed it at the foot of the bed. When he stood again, he smiled cheerfully.

"Miss Montgomery has a piquant face and an expansive personality, doesn't she? I can see why you're attached to her, even though she dresses as if she comes from little wealth. She has other charms, eh? I wouldn't mind a little flirtation with a Scottish lass myself."

Charlie's expression turned to stone. "I don't discuss my personal business with strangers," he said, "particularly my relationship with Miss Montgomery. She, by the way, shall be treated with all the respect due one of your hostesses and my future wife."

A slight shift occurred in Mr. King's eyes, but his expression remained affable. "Of course, Lumley. No offense meant."

Charlie refused to say *none taken*. "I'm rather busy overseeing things, so I'll leave you to find your way back," he said gruffly. "If you get lost, consider it that private tour you wanted."

And he left without a backward glance, torn between wanting to evict the man immediately and needing to keep him on for the money.

The money Daisy needs, he reminded himself sternly.

But it wasn't enough to make him turn around and escort Mr. King back to the front hall. Nor, he determined, would he ever treat the man with anything but common civility. Even that, he knew, would tax him.

The truth was, Mr. King's careless remark—revealing his obvious lack of respect for Daisy—had made Charlie eager to pummel him until his patrician American nose bled profusely.

Why was that? All men made careless remarks about comely females.

Ah, but this was different—just as Daisy was different. Different from any girl he'd ever known. She was a danger to his Impossible Bachelor's heart.

CHAPTER TWELVE

To Daisy, the afternoon had been a blur of activities: situating very important gentlemen in their bedchambers; reminding Perdita to stand up straight; on Mona's orders, hiding her secret stash of chocolates beneath her bed (Mona couldn't bend that far); and allowing the travelers some time to rest—all except Mr. King, who'd insisted on seeing the castle from top to bottom with her.

Daisy didn't know why, but Charlie had put on his worst viscount expression and accompanied them. Not only was his bearing aloof, his expression was more than a bit condescending.

Mr. King appeared unfazed. In fact, he was so well versed in Scottish castle architecture he'd been able to tell her and Charlie more about the castle than she'd ever known.

And when Mr. King asked Charlie what tidbits of information he'd picked up about the Keep since owning it, he'd said, "Nothing. I'm from England, so what do you expect?"

There'd been a great silence because all three of them realized Mr. King was from America, which was much farther away from Scotland than England, and look how much *he* knew about Scottish castle architecture!

God, Daisy had thought the man remarkable.

Remarkably *annoying,* that was.

At first, she'd been thrilled to meet him for two reasons: he was an American (she'd never met one before), and he was accomplished. But on the castle tour, his talk about himself began to wear thin, especially as in every room with a mirror, he found a way to stop and look at himself while pretending to admire a piece of furniture, or the view. And when he laughed, he brayed like a donkey, which came as quite a shock. A man of consequence should have a fine, rich laugh, like Charlie's.

Now as the third course of a delicious Highland dinner was about to be served, Daisy—who was wearing Perdita's emerald shot silk, cut down and with all the ruffles ripped off—felt a deep calm beneath her outer excitement, which she must admit was mixed with a bit of nerves.

It was really happening. The plan to raise money to save Castle Vandemere was under way.

She was terrified. Absolutely terrified. It was her one chance, this Highland experience—her one chance to earn that money. Which was why she drank two glasses of wine in short order, even though she'd thought she didn't particularly care for wine.

But this wine came from the Keep's cellars, and

it was fine, very fine. And she noticed that the more wine she drank, the more she understood that nothing was coincidence. Nothing.

She wished she could sing about it. Or write a poem.

Immediately.

But at that moment, the roasted pheasant arrived, so she had to content herself with knowing that she had nothing to worry about. The signs were clear. The ten days would be a raging success, and she'd make her money to pay the *feu* duty on the castle.

But that was only part of the reason she was so happy.

She'd figured out a way to rid herself of the Furies.

Oh, Mr. King!

She could weep for looking at him. He was perfect for Cassandra—

Simply perfect.

Daisy wouldn't feel a bit of guilt foisting her selfish stepsister on him. Cassandra would be that bride at his wrought-iron balcony at his plantation house on the James River in Virginia.

And she'd take her mother and sister to America with her.

Just as Daisy lifted her wine glass to her mouth to celebrate again, she caught Charlie's eye. He was glaring at her, in that understated way that only *she* was meant to understand. She had no idea why he was glaring at her, so she glared back in her secret way that only *he* would comprehend.

She felt a bit smug as she swallowed a gulp of

wine. As she matured, she found she was becoming increasingly more sophisticated. Especially about men. She was now a woman who could give hidden signals.

She never thought the day would come.

"Is something wrong?" Mr. King asked her from across the table. "You're glaring, Miss Montgomery."

She gave a nervous chuckle. "Not at all. It was a piece of dust in my eye." And to cover her embarrassment, she held up her nearly empty wine glass to make a toast.

What would she say? The only thing on her mind was Mr. King and Cassandra. Cassandra King. Matthew and Cassandra King. The King family. Mrs. Matthew King.

Well, that and the way Charlie's throat was tanned and extremely kissable at the moment, even if he was still glaring at her. She had a mad fantasy to pull up her skirt and part her legs right now and let him come to her under the table and—

God, she must stop her silly daydreaming.

But just as she opened her mouth to toast the cooks, who were hovering outside the door and peeking in, a Mr. Woo, an impossibly short angler at the other end of the table, said loudly, "Where's the son of the son of a Highland chief?"

Oh, no.

Daisy put down her wine glass and looked at Charlie.

What was Mr. Woo talking about?

"Mr. Beebs told us we'd have the son of a son of a Highland chief here," the diminutive sportsman explained. "I refused to come, otherwise. The fish were biting well at Brawton."

Oh, God. They should have thought to have the descendant of a Highland chief. It would have made the experience so much more authentic.

Yesterday, if Daisy had only spent less time allowing Charlie to suckle her breasts while he teased her softest flesh with his fingers, she would have thought of—

What would she have thought of?

Besides Charlie's mouth?

And his manhood straining against his breeches?

She wished she'd seen it. She'd never seen a man's privates before, and she longed to see Charlie's!

Daisy was losing her breath *and* her train of thought.

Charlie cleared his throat. "I'm so sorry, Mr. Woo. The chief's grandson is delayed tonight."

Oh, right. The son of a son of a Highland chief.

"Actually," Daisy added with a shrug, "he said he couldn't be bothered."

Mr. Woo's eyes widened. "Surely he intends to come eventually."

"Yes," Daisy replied. "Probably tomorrow. But no one can tell him what to do. He works on his own schedule, and woe to anyone who pushes him."

Mr. Woo's face drooped. "I am most disappointed."

"Just don't tell him that," Daisy said, "or he'll leave. He's very sensitive and proud. All descendants of Highland chiefs are."

"We can't have him upset," Mr. Woo said hurriedly.

She sent Charlie a subtle message: *I really wish we'd thought about this sooner, and we'll have to talk about it in the library after dinner, and you look very handsome tonight, especially with Papa's tartan pin stuck in your cravat.*

But amazingly, Charlie didn't seem to get the message. He angled his head at her and squinted as if he had no idea *what* she'd been trying to say!

Men.

They weren't nearly as perceptive as women—women other than Perdita and Cassandra, that is, who were about as perceptive as logs. Daisy had to grant that her stepmother would be perceptive if she weren't always focused on hating people and devising plans to make them miserable.

Indeed, at that very moment Mona was telling the man to her left some of the best ways to make someone deathly ill without getting caught, all of which she'd learned in the lurid novels of which she was overly fond.

Perdita, meanwhile, was staring lovelorn at Mr. King. Daisy had made her much more attractive with her hair sleekly pulled back. She'd also made Perdita don a plain white muslin gown that used to be one of the girl's older night rails. It still had a flounce, but it wasn't nearly as bad as her usual. Daisy had pinned a lovely brooch at the vee of the neckline and flung a simple paisley shawl over her stepsister's broad shoulders.

The most clever thing Daisy had done was tell her not to speak.

Perdita had "lost" her voice.

A bucktoothed marquis from Spain was leaning over to look down Perdita's décolletage, which was good news, as far as Daisy was concerned.

"Miss Montgomery?" Mr. King called to her across the table.

"Yes?"

"Tell us about your home."

Her heart warmed to him. "Castle Vandemere has its own special charm."

"Why do you find it so?" Mr. King's dark eyes were focused only on her.

Daisy wasn't used to being the center of attention, particularly at a large gathering. "Its great beauty lies in its simplicity," she said.

"I like that answer." The visitor from Virginia smiled at her.

Daisy found herself blushing once more. She couldn't help thinking that someday, if she had her way, he'd become her brother-in-law—her *step*brother-in-law—who would live far, far away. So far away, in fact, she'd never visit. And never have to see Cassandra (along with Mona and Perdita) again.

But enough of Mr. King. At the moment, Charlie was handsomer than she had ever seen him. She couldn't help thinking that she was a beginner in the art of making love. So it was

Charlie's duty—wasn't it?—to be at her beck and call and teach her everything he knew.

Everything.

She found she'd parted her lips and was rubbing the top one over the rim of her wine glass.

Charlie stared at her. So did Mr. King.

And so did everyone else.

"Excuse me," she said to the table. "I felt faint for a moment. I was gasping for tea and . . . and I had only wine."

"I see," said Mr. King.

Daisy ignored the uncomfortable pause and went back to her new favorite subject—Cassandra. "You really should meet my stepsister," she said to Mr. King. "She's a beauty. And according to her mother, she belongs in a peer's bed."

Charlie nudged her knee under the table with his own knee and gave her a pointed look.

Oh, no! She'd forgotten. Mr. King wasn't a peer at all, poor man.

"Pardon me, no doubt she belongs in the bed of *any* man who's powerful," Daisy said. "And rich."

She noticed Cassandra making a horrible face at her.

Dear God, the girl was sitting only two seats down on the other side, to Mr. King's right. Which meant she could hear everything Daisy had said about her.

"I'd like to go with you to Castle Vandemere," said Mr. King to Charlie in a change of subject.

"Every day that I'm in residence. Whatever interests you, interests me."

Charlie inhaled a breath. "What did Mr. Beebs tell you?"

Mr. King slapped Charlie on the back. "He says you're not some lofty lord—you like to do chores over at Miss Montgomery's castle. He said you'll get down in the dirt and work if you must. Nothing worse than a man in his prime going to seed because he's too important to do the things that make life worth living, right?"

"Right," said Charlie.

"Beebs also said the one thing you've never attempted is shearing sheep. Neither have I. Since we're on level playing ground there, perhaps I can challenge you to a sheep-shearing contest for a lark. When shall we take each other on?"

Daisy noticed Charlie had a small tic in his jaw. He was *not* happy, and she couldn't help but wonder why.

"Tomorrow, perhaps?" Charlie said woodenly, and drained his glass of wine.

"It's very good wine," Daisy whispered to him. "Isn't it?"

The meal finished without incident, and the men repaired to the library for cheroots and their choice of brandy or Joe's whisky while the four ladies at the table gathered in the drawing room with their various sewing projects.

The effects of the wine were beginning to wear off, Daisy thought thankfully. Or maybe it wasn't such a good thing. She dreaded confronting Cassandra.

"How could you?" Cassandra said accusingly to her from an elaborate blue velvet sofa.

Daisy was seated on a hard, Egyptian-style chair herself. "What did I do?"

Cassandra huffed. "You made it sound as if I would simply jump into Mr. King's bed. Or that I was a cow at market, ready to be bought."

Mona had begun work on a pillow. Her tongue stuck out of her mouth at the most awful angle as she attempted to jab the thread through the needle. But then she skewered Daisy with a knowing look. "I suspect I know why you're fobbing Cassandra off on the Virginian."

"Oh?" Daisy longed for more wine.

Mona narrowed her eyes. "*You* want the viscount. We told you to stay away from him."

Cassandra twirled a curl. "I care nothing for the American bird-watcher."

"Perhaps you should," said Daisy. "He might be more wealthy than the viscount. And he does have that house with the balcony."

Cassandra furrowed her brow. "I don't care. Lord Lumley is a far better catch, and if you continue to interfere with my getting him, Daisy, I'll tell him everything I know."

Daisy bit her lip. "You already told him about the fire."

"I'll tell him the rest," Cassandra insisted. "I'll tell him about Cousin Roman. You drank too much with him that night, too."

"No I didn't," Daisy protested. "I had one glass of sour wine with Roman, no more than you had. This is the very first time I've ever drunk more than one glass. And no wonder. Tonight's was a fine vintage."

The others snickered, and Daisy's heart sank. She would never win. Ever.

Drinking wine tonight hadn't helped her in the least. Her fuzzy glow was now gone.

Everything was bleak.

Perdita sighed, oblivious to the tension. "I like Mr. King. In fact, I'd like to make him"—she gazed round the company to see if they were paying attention—"the king of my heart."

Daisy couldn't help being a bit scornful of her stepsister's attempt at rendering the mushy feelings she felt toward Mr. King into something poetic.

But Charlie's the king of your *heart, Daisy,* a ridiculous voice inside her head told her.

Right, she told it back. *And I'm a beautiful, wealthy heiress with a large bosom and a saint for a stepmother.*

She did *not* have a *tendre* for Lord Lumley, not in the least. She only wanted to kiss him sometimes. And lie with him naked.

And receive great pleasure from him—give it to him, too, if she only knew how—although that was neither here nor there.

None of that had anything to do with love.

Of course, she was still clueless as to what love actually was, but at least she knew what love *wasn't.* That was almost as helpful.

She knew tingly feelings all over your body when you looked at someone didn't necessarily mean that you were in love.

Nor did the odd daydream wondering how a certain man must appear with no clothes on signify you were in love.

And looking forward to private time so you could discuss a money-raising project you were working on together—a project that was a bit dicey and could fail and that might get one kicked out of one's home, fear of which only a warm, naked hug and perhaps a few hot kisses could alleviate—well, *that* didn't mean one was in love, either.

She was sure she was becoming very wise, in her own way, about love.

"Well, Perdita," she said, "you barely know Mr. King, so it would be prudent not to get your hopes up in that direction. Did you notice how much the Spanish marquis liked you?"

Perdita glared at her. "*He* is not the king of my heart."

"I hear the castles in Spain, particularly those along the coast in southern Spain, are much warmer than the ones up here," Daisy said nonchalantly.

"I don't care," Perdita said. "Wait a minute. Is that my old gown you're wearing?"

Daisy shrugged. "What if it is? You put it in the rag basket ages ago. I merely altered it."

"It has no frills anymore."

"Precisely," said Daisy. "As you've proven tonight with your new sense of style, frills and flounces are all well and good in moderation, but too many of them mask a lady's true beauty. You are more beautiful tonight than I've ever seen you, Perdita."

Which was still a long way from beauty, but it wasn't a lie. Perdita had inched closer to being acceptable in appearance, and Daisy wanted to give her every bit of encouragement she could to stay on a less flouncy, frilly path.

"You're just complimenting me because you took my gown without asking." Perdita roared.

"Ssshh!" Daisy held her finger to her mouth.

"Besides," Perdita whispered loudly, "what would someone as plain as you know about true beauty?"

Daisy threw down her needlework and stood. "That's enough. I don't have to listen to your insults. I'm your stepsister, Perdita, or have you forgotten?"

Perdita made a disgusting scoffing noise that sounded as if she were sick to her stomach.

Daisy flinched. "Do you have *any* love for me at all?" she asked her.

Mona snorted. "Are you going to let her get by with spouting that nonsense, Perdy?" She always enjoyed a good sparring match between Daisy and Perdita and made no secret of the fact that she always wanted Perdita to win.

Perdita ignored Daisy's question. "Your future is over. Mine has only begun."

"Why do you say that?" Daisy felt hot anger rising through her body.

Perdita shrugged. "I don't know. But it's true."

Daisy's anger burst from her in a torrent of words: "Don't be so sure. I've had it with all three of you.

I don't intend to endure your lack of feeling much longer."

Mona sucked in her cheeks. "Exactly what do you mean by that, young lady?"

Daisy instantly regretted speaking. "I won't tolerate your cruelties."

Mona was as still as a cat in the seconds before it catches its prey. "Don't think you can fob me off. You speak as if you plan to leave us. But you wouldn't leave Hester or Joe. And you certainly couldn't support them if you took them with you. So I'm left to conclude that you're suggesting that *we* shall be the ones leaving, Perdita, Cassandra, and I."

There was a beat of silence. Daisy had no idea what to say. A deep-seated fear of her stepmother gripped her throat like a chokehold.

Cassandra sat up straighter. "Why, you're wicked!"

"No," said Daisy. "I never said that. And I'm *not* wicked. You are, not me. All three of you are." That great anger was threatening to overwhelm her again.

"You're up to something," Mona said in menacing tones, "and I intend to find out what it is. And when I do, you'd best be prepared. Because a stepmother betrayed is a stepmother who will make you pay. Until it hurts. Oh, excuse me." She put a finger to her mouth and reconsidered. "Until it hurts very *badly*."

Perdita and Cassandra laughed. Thank God the Keep was so large and that the library was far enough away that the gentlemen couldn't hear.

Shivers of disgust and fear ran down Daisy's

spine. "What have I ever done to you, except try to be a good sister and daughter? Why do all of you hate me so much?"

Mona merely arched one eyebrow.

Perdita stuffed a chocolate in her mouth and chomped in Daisy's general direction.

Cassandra wore an awful smirk on her beautiful face.

"I'll leave you to yourselves," Daisy told them, sick to her stomach that they hadn't bothered to answer.

Their mocking laughter followed her out. She'd never felt so miserable and alone in her life.

But even worse, she felt afraid. Mona had caught on that Daisy didn't want her at Castle Vandemere.

CHAPTER THIRTEEN

Surrounded by a dozen gentlemen as wealthy or more than he and whose interests somewhat overlapped (Charlie had never claimed to be a bird-watcher), he decided he'd never felt so miserable and alone in his life. The whisky and brandy had made the travelers talkative, but eventually, even they grew tired. So it was with much relief that he stood when the men eventually called it a night a little after midnight.

"Sleep well, gentlemen," he told them as they filed past him at the door to the library.

"I thought I saw a buxom maid or two about the premises," said Mr. Woo in a leading fashion.

A few of the others made suggestive remarks about the maids, as well.

"Yes, well, even buxom maids need their sleep, don't they?" Charlie said.

Mr. Woo lowered his brow. "The Highland experience doesn't include Highland lasses?"

"No. It doesn't." Charlie couldn't care less if the

man were offended. He saw how hard the villagers had worked today. He'd seen the pride on their faces when he'd complimented their cleaning and cooking.

Obviously, Mr. Woo assumed Charlie was to provide opportunities for bedroom activities as part of their arrangement. Charlie knew the upper classes were used to getting what they wanted. But he refused to acknowledge the men's more unseemly expectations.

Their bedchambers were situated on one long, candlelit corridor that turned at a right angle in the middle. As the first two visitors went to their rooms, escorted by footmen, Charlie couldn't help wondering where Daisy was situated.

He knew she was on the floor above theirs. Was her room directly above his own? He'd like to imagine it was. He was sure she was fast asleep.

But there she was, striding confidently toward him. He should have known she'd yet be awake for one reason or another. She carried a sputtering candle in her hand and was still dressed for dinner. But now she wore a gorgeous pink blossom over one ear.

She looked breathtakingly lovely.

"Miss Montgomery!" Mr. King hailed her heartily. "You've not retired for the evening?"

"Of course not, Mr. King." She smiled at him, completely alert, all signs of imbibing too much wine erased. "A hostess doesn't sleep until her guests are down for the night. I've spent the last several hours outdoors, walking and reading in the gardens.

Lasting daylight is one benefit of living in the Highlands in the summer. I feel quite refreshed."

She looked round the group. "Does anyone require a small bite to eat from the kitchens?"

A chorus of *no*s rang out—they'd had plenty for dinner, they all claimed in a most hospitable manner. With the presence of Daisy, the men seemed to have perked up and become mannerly again.

Mr. King held out his arm. "Please join us on a midnight stroll down the corridor."

She laughed. "I'll be glad to." Catching Charlie's eye, she bestowed a small, close-lipped smile upon him.

He recognized that smile. It was her shy one. He'd have liked her on *his* arm, but he wouldn't make a fuss this time. Mr. King was on his best behavior. He was the last of the guests to reach his bedchamber door. Once there, he bent low over Daisy's hand and kissed it.

"Thank you," he said, "for an extraordinary beginning to our Highland adventure. It will be a most interesting ten days."

"You're welcome," she said, blushing.

Charlie couldn't help feeling jealous.

Mr. King also exchanged a cordial good-night with him, but it was obvious their American guest much preferred the company of his hostess.

Alone at last in the corridor, Daisy hooked her arm through Charlie's.

He relished the contact.

"Only nine days to go," she whispered.

"Nine *long* days," he whispered back.

She stifled a laugh. "We'll make it."

It was a brief moment of camaraderie, and he had a sudden, mad desire to make love to her right there, against the cold, stone walls of the corridor.

She drew in a small breath and turned to look at an elaborate tapestry.

Hah.

So she must have sensed the tension, too. Of course, it was still there. Their afternoon on the Stone Steps had done nothing but whet his appetite for her.

He didn't know how he'd ever thought her plain.

"Good night, Charlie," she said, suddenly stopping. "It's past midnight, and it's still light. Isn't that amazing?"

"Yes."

"I've got to go," she said.

"Wait—"

But she strode quickly away, around the corner, and then he heard the pat of her slippers on the stairs to her bedchamber.

On the third step, he found the flower that had been in her hair.

CHAPTER FOURTEEN

The Keep's walls loomed over him after Daisy ran off. Charlie heard nothing. It was lonely after midnight in a strange castle, even with the eerie summer light. He felt an ache near his heart as he stared at the flower in his hand and bent to sniff it. The sweet, musky odor was pleasing, but it didn't satisfy him nearly as much as the scent of Daisy's skin.

He would bring it to her. The flower.

He knew he was being stupid. Daisy was a maiden. She was in his charge. He shouldn't seek her out. Besides, he had no idea which room was hers. And many other people slumbered in nearby rooms. What if they discovered him where he shouldn't be?

What would it mean for Daisy?

She'd be ruined. That's what.

He knew if he walked up the stairs with this flower and found her that he would enter her bedchamber and close the door, and—

He closed his eyes.

Why was he torturing himself so?

Turn around, Charlie.

With every bit of will he had, he turned himself around. Walked back to his own bedchamber, turned the knob, and—

A door next to his creaked open. "Lumley! Is that you?"

It was Mr. Woo.

"Yes," Charlie answered, a bit annoyed.

"I want a midnight snack, after all." Mr. Woo looked at him expectantly.

"Uh, I suppose I could walk with you—"

"I was hoping you'd get it for me. I'm sure all the servants are asleep."

Charlie clenched his jaw. He was the host. He would have to comply with his guests' wishes. "You're right," he said, and forced himself to smile. "What could I bring you?"

"A piece of bread and butter," said Mr. Woo. "And a glass of wine. Cheese would be nice, too."

Charlie nodded. "I'll do my best. Just give me a few minutes."

He walked down the corridor, made a few turns, crossed the great hall, and eventually came to the rear of the castle, where a fairly modern kitchen had been set up in the last decade. He found all that he needed for Mr. Woo and brought it back to him.

Mr. Woo nodded his thanks when Charlie entered his room and placed the goblet of wine and a plate of bread and cheese on a small table.

"Good night," said Charlie.

"Good night," Mr. Woo answered him. At the door, he added, "I see you got the smugglers' bedchamber."

Charlie turned back to him. "What's that?"

"A servant told me today that your bedchamber has a secret stairway to the upstairs hall, at the end of which is a balcony over the gardens. In the old days, smugglers could make a quick escape."

"Interesting," said Charlie.

He wasn't terribly excited about the news. The usual stairs were near his bedchamber and would carry him up to the next floor almost as quickly, which meant he was unlikely to be discovered by prying eyes either way if he ever went looking for Daisy.

Nevertheless, he was curious.

In his bedchamber, he felt the walls for the secret stairway and found it almost immediately near the fireplace. It was rather spacious, actually, and easy to ascend. When he came to the top, he opened the door and peeked out, entertained in spite of his rather dour mood.

The hallway was quiet.

Daisy was here somewhere, which made it a special corridor.

He looked to his right. There were the stairs that she'd rushed up—the stairs he'd almost decided to go up himself.

Good thing he hadn't.

Good thing he'd been honorable and stalwart and mindful of his responsibilities.

He began to pull the door shut when he saw a

scrap of something pink on the floor. A petal. A petal outside a bedchamber door.

"Dammit," he whispered.

It could mean only one thing. She wanted him to come. She'd been hoping he'd come. She'd left the flower on the staircase for a reason.

A few minutes later, Charlie scratched at Daisy's door, flower in hand, and felt a genuine stirring of happiness—combined with a bit of trepidation—when the door opened on silent hinges.

She stood looking at him with large eyes, her arms crossed protectively over her chest. "Oh, dear," was all she said, her voice a mere whisper. "You *did* come."

He entered, shut the door gently behind him, and placed the flower in her hair once more. "Did you not want me to?"

She bit her lip and looked away, then turned back to him. "No, I did want you here. But I figured I'd leave the decision up to you. If you came, then . . . good. If you didn't, then—"

"Then what?"

"I would have been miserable." She blinked up at him, her heart in her eyes.

"Of course I'd come." He hugged her close.

"This is very bad." She wrapped her arms tighter around his waist. "And I know that." She pulled back. "But Charlie, I'll never get married. I can tell you that right now."

"You won't? Why not?"

"It's a long story." She sighed. "I'd rather not go into it."

"Does it have anything to do with your father?"

She nodded.

He pulled her close again and squeezed her tight. "You shouldn't blame yourself. It was an accident."

"I know," she said against his chest. "But I can't help my feelings, however complicated they are. At this point, I don't want to wait for the future to reveal itself to me. I just want to feel what it's like to be with a man I'm comfortable with, someone I trust. Right now."

She looked up at him. Her words moved him. But the truth was, he was also already imagining her with no clothes.

She might have guessed because she slipped away from him to toy with a few figurines on a shelf. "Are you happy you're here?" she asked him over her shoulder.

He was bewitched by her coyness.

"Of course." He gave in to her obvious need for space, threw himself on the bed, and propped himself up on an elbow to watch her from afar. "I've been dreaming about being with you alone."

She finished her nervous fiddling with the figurines and began to pace about the room. "Perdita is next door."

"Good God."

She stopped and looked at him. "She snores. Very loudly."

He chuckled. "I've never been more glad to be next to a snorer."

She sighed. "I'm nervous."

He got up and went to her. "I'm not a wolf," he assured her, his hands wrapped around her waist.

"I know." She leaned again on his chest.

They stood there for a moment, breathing. He loved the feel of her warm palms pressed so trustingly against him.

"Can I—"

"Will you—"

They both spoke at once.

She pulled back and grinned. "I was going to ask you if you'd like to read with me."

"And I was just going to ask if I could do anything to help you feel more at ease." He allowed his mouth to tip up.

She picked up her skirts and practically raced to the bookshelf on the far side of the room. Scanning the titles, she pulled out a tome and held it aloft. "This," she said. "And if you don't like it as much as I do, I'll be quite put out."

"What will you do if I don't—and you are?"

"I don't know yet. But it won't be pretty." Her smile made the whole aggravating day worth it.

She headed to the bed with the book and paused. "I forgot. I need to put on my night rail. I'll feel cozier."

"I'll get it," he said, and pulled open several drawers before he found one.

She put her beloved book aside and took the garment. Then looked at him and bit her lip.

"I won't look." He turned his back and crossed his arms.

"Thank you," she said.

It took a good few minutes for her to prepare herself—it seemed like a lifetime to him. He was tempted—sorely tempted—to turn around and peek.

"Done," she eventually said.

She was already tucked in beneath the covers. The lamp on the bedside table sent a lovely glow over her features.

She held the book open. "I'm waiting for you."

Oh. He'd been caught doing absolutely nothing but staring and admiring. He felt as if he were a student who'd been reprimanded by a schoolteacher. A very tempting schoolteacher.

"Please," she said. "Make yourself more comfortable."

"I've no modest way to disrobe," he told her, and yanked his shirt over his head, exposing his chest and belly.

He had to restrain a laugh when he saw her eyes widen.

"You *will* keep your breeches on, won't you?" she asked.

"Of course." He strolled around the bed to the far side, lifted the quilt, and got into bed with her.

Immediately, there was delicious tension. She tried her best to hold on to the book and pretend that everything was all business, but he knew better. Her cheeks had flushed a lovely rose color, and she wouldn't quite look at him.

"Daisy?" he whispered.

She turned to look at him. "Yes?"

"Read to me," he said.

Her eyes lit with both relief and anticipation. "You're going to like this. Poems by Robert Burns. He's beloved by all of Scotland."

"Is that so?" Charlie settled himself back on his pillow, his hands folded behind his head, and listened to her read a poem called "To a Mouse":

> *Wee, sleekit, cow'rin', tim'rous beastie,*
> *O what a panic's in thy breastie,*
> *Thou need na start awa sae hasty,*
> *   Wi' bickering brattle!*
> *I wad be laith to rin an' chase thee,*
> *   Wi' murd'ring pattle!*

She took a breath, but he interrupted her before she could go on. "I'm sorry," he said, "but . . . I have no idea what you just said."

"Oh!" She leaned closer so he could see the words. "It's about a mouse turned up by a plow—"

"Really." He was enjoying the closeness, her shoulder propped against his.

"And the farmer is feeling awfully guilty for destroying its home," she went on.

"Is that so?" He lifted a lock of hair off her shoulder and put it behind her ear.

"And—" She looked at him, and her brows lowered. "You're not really listening, are you?"

"Oh, I am," he said. "Please go on."

He lay back on his pillows again and didn't interrupt her once. He already knew the poem by heart. So when she got to the last verse, he recited along with her, his eyes on the ceiling.

When they both said the last word together, she slammed the book shut.

He looked over at her and enjoyed seeing her mouth a big O. "You already *knew* it?"

"Yes," he replied in his driest manner. "And I hated it. I hated it with a passion."

"Did you." She narrowed her eyes at him.

"Yes. So you're going to have to punish me."

She closed the book with a sigh. "I adore that poem. I'd like to meet that farmer. He seems so wise and kind."

"What about the punishment? Are you a woman of your word or not?"

She merely scooted away from him. "I wonder if Robert Burns really did turn up a mouse—"

"'The best-laid schemes o' mice and men gang aft a-gley,'" said Charlie with a sigh. "No matter how well you plan, something can go wrong. Leave it to a poet to couch a harsh truth in such a lyrical way."

"Exactly." Daisy scooted back in his direction and turned on her side to face him. "But he's right. You just never know what's around the corner."

"It's what makes life exciting."

"Yes," she said. "I've always felt my life was meant to be exciting. Even though I live here, far away from everything."

"I'll bet you look out the window of your little turret in Castle Vandemere and dream big dreams."

"I do. How did you know?"

He smiled. "I know you, Daisy Montgomery. And I like who I see."

There was a beat of silence. Her fairy blue eyes gleamed with something soft and vulnerable. Something hopeful. And something inviting.

Charlie felt as if he were being pulled by some inexorable force toward her. She moved an inch toward him, and then their lips met.

"Charlie," she whispered. "I like you, too. Very much."

He lifted himself up, scooped her in his arms, and gazed down at her.

She gifted him with a shy smile.

And then he kissed her—madly, passionately.

It was better than being at the finest opera with the chorus going and the big drums booming, violins flying up and down the scale, the lead tenor singing his heart out to the lead soprano, and the lead soprano singing back—and the whole audience struck dumb with wonder and anticipation, the applause surging . . . surging into a great crescendo with cymbals crashing.

And that was only the kissing part. Charlie had never, ever felt so exhilarated by mere kissing.

But he was kissing *her*.

Daisy.

The girl who'd made everything different. And not because she was a Highland lass. Not because her voice was like buzzing bumblebees. Nor was it because she had an outlandish sense of adventure.

It was because of how she looked at him. It was

as if she could see deep into his soul, past the bad Charlie to the real Charlie—

And the real Charlie she saw wasn't a shining knight, thank God.

No, the real Charlie was the same as the bad Charlie.

But she liked him anyway.

It was such a relief . . . he didn't have to pretend to be someone else. Not that he ever thought that was what he'd been doing, but now he saw that he had. Hiding from his parents his title of Impossible Bachelor. Earning loads of money to impress the world with his business acumen since he'd not been able to go to the Wars—thanks to being the heir who wasn't allowed to die.

With Daisy, he could let go.

"Let go with me," he said into her ear.

"I want to," she murmured against his jaw.

He closed his eyes, wishing with all his heart he could bed her. But he couldn't.

How was he to let go?

He decided not to think about it, and to focus on her, the delightful, sweet-smelling young lady melding her body to his.

Heaven on earth . . . merely sliding his hand down her arm, over every swell and valley, until their fingers clashed and clung.

"This time it's your day," Daisy said.

They were side by side.

"No," he insisted. "It's yours."

She shook her head and got that very obstinate look in her eye that he well recognized.

And next thing he knew, she was pressing her hand on his hard length, caressing him through his breeches, all the while kissing his neck and then his chest. He groaned at the sensations coursing through him when she mouthed his nipple, sucking tenderly.

But then she stopped. "I want to take off your breeches," she said.

"Well, then." He was amused by her forthright manner. "Go right ahead."

She got to work, fumbling with the flap. He did his best to help her, but she kept shooing his hands away. She was so busy that when she finally had success, the effects of what she'd accomplished appeared to hit her like a ton of bricks.

"Oh, dear," she said, and looked from his privates to his face and back again to his nether regions.

He shrugged.

"You're magnificent," she said. "Like David."

"The statue?"

"No, David the baker's son." She giggled. "Of course I meant David the statue. I've seen illustrations."

"Ah. Well, it's your turn to look like Bernini's Daphne."

Without a word, she pulled off her night rail, exposing her beautiful naked body to the lamplight. "Was she naked?" she whispered.

"Uh-huh," Charlie said back, and pulled her on top of him.

Daisy closed her eyes and clung to him.

"Are you all right?" he asked her.

She nodded.

He lifted her chin. "Are you sure?"

She nodded again. "It feels so . . . perfect."

"It can feel even more perfect, as you know. But now's a good time to remind ourselves of something."

"What?"

"It can feel even more perfect than the perfect you felt on the Stone Steps."

She groaned as if she couldn't bear to hear it. "Really?"

"This is good news," he said, "usually. But not for us. We can't go to that particularly perfect place. It would mean I'd compromised you so completely, there would be no turning back. We'd have to marry."

"Gad," she said.

"It's how babies are made, and I'm afraid neither of us is ready for that."

"No, indeed."

"But we can still enjoy ourselves, and each other."

"The other perfects suit me very well," she said gamely.

"Good," he said. "Because I'm going to make you feel perfect again, but this time you won't be sitting up on some stone steps, you'll be flung back against some lovely pillows."

And before she could protest, he'd pleasured her that way. Twice, as a matter of fact. But the second time, he'd been beneath her, his tongue flicking in and out of her sweetest spot while she clung to the headboard and whimpered above him.

God, he was happy.

But she made him even happier in the next few moments, with no instruction at all.

"I'll explore," she said, and did just that . . . with her fingers and her mouth.

It was exquisite torture for him.

When she dared to kiss the length of him, he almost stopped her.

But she insisted on continuing.

"Messy," he croaked out. "It. Will. Be."

"I don't care," she flung back.

Resigned to his fate—and oh, what a fate it would be!—he lay back against the pillows himself and watched her graceful body and generous mouth pleasure him almost to the point of no return. But he didn't crash over the edge until she locked gazes with him and he read in her eyes her own happiness.

He closed his eyes and let the feeling of complete and utter perfectness overwhelm him then.

And the cymbals crashed louder than he ever knew they could.

CHAPTER FIFTEEN

The next morning, Daisy did all she could to find a man to take on the role of son of a son of a Highland chief for the remainder of the travelers' visit. But she'd no luck in Glen Dewey.

Those men were preoccupied with truly being fierce and readying themselves for the hunt and the subsequent games. All they cared about was preparing their weapons and their own bodies for competition.

"We're all descendants of chiefs in one way or another, lass," said one man, sharpening a hunting knife. "We don't want to be bothered, and no one wants to sit in a silly chair and pass out ribbons to the winners of the games. We want to be *in* them."

Except for one shy young man, a scholar who was the actual grandson of a Highland chief. He said he'd love to play the role, but he gave no impression of strength, despite his impressive height, sturdy body, and trunklike legs. He held up a magnificent old kilt—the kind with a sash that goes over the shoulder—and all the imposing accessories that went with it.

"It's not often I wear the great kilt of my ancestors, miss." His voice didn't match his body. It was thin, modest, and all too agreeable. "But for you and your project, I'll be happy to put them on and come stay at the castle and tell stories about my grandfather."

She didn't know how to tell him that he wouldn't do. He wouldn't do at all. The foreigners expected a Highland chief who'd make them tremble in their shoes with his fierceness.

She sat there racking her brain, but then he said, "I know you're disappointed in me. I don't seem particularly ferocious and brave, do I?"

How could she answer that?

She gulped. "I—I'm sure you are," she told him. "And you're an impressive scholar, too. It's just that—"

He waved a hand at her. "Never you mind, Miss Montgomery. I know what the guests must be expecting, and it's certainly not me. Take my kilt if you must. I wish you luck finding someone worthy of donning it."

She brightened. "Really?"

"Aye," he said. "Now, would you like some tea? And a bite to eat?"

A question that only proved he was entirely too thoughtful to be the man she needed.

She gave a sigh of relief. "I'd love that. Thank you, sir."

*   *   *

Back at the castle, Daisy didn't know what to do. She brought the kilt, which she'd hidden in a burlap sack, into her bedchamber and dumped it out on the bed that she and Charlie had slept in the previous night.

Well. If you could call it sleep.

She blushed at the memories. Last night had been spectacular . . .

She almost became dreamy about it, but the sight of the kilt and its matching sash, as well as the sporran and the scabbard gleaming with richness, evoked an amazing history of which Castle Vandemere and her ancestors were a part.

They must have the son of a son of a Highland chief by the midday meal, or it would be difficult to keep fobbing off Mr. Woo and the rest of the visitors.

She couldn't afford to have them upset in any way.

Castle Vandemere was at stake.

And Mr. King must remain long enough to discover how perfect Cassandra was for him.

"Dai-*seee*!" The shriek came from down the hall.

She rolled her eyes and went to see what her stepmother wanted.

"Perdy's all thumbs, as usual," Mona said with a scowl. "Come tie my laces."

Perdita flopped into a chair and pouted.

"She also broke my favorite brooch, trying to open the clasp," Mona complained.

Daisy stole a glance at Perdita. As much as she despised her, it must be difficult to be so clumsy.

"I've the perfect substitute pin for you," Daisy told Mona. "Perdita, would you mind going to my room and getting it, please? It's on my dresser, the small silver thistle."

"That old thing," Mona said rudely.

Which Hester had very lovingly given Daisy last Christmas! It meant the world to her. She pressed her lips together, refusing to rise to the bait.

"Tell Daisy to get her own pin," Perdita said, her voice practically rattling the windows.

"Do as you're told," Mona barked almost as loudly.

Perdita roused herself to stand and slouched out of the room, her hands clenched into fists.

Daisy finished tying her stepmother's laces and was desperate to leave. Being alone with her was *not* fun.

"Since we're waiting," Mona said, "massage my feet." She strode to her bed, threw herself back on it, and wiggled her toes.

God, no. The last thing Daisy wanted to do was touch her stepmother's feet, much less squeeze them. Mona would wince and yell and perhaps kick out at her if she didn't do an excellent job.

"I—I'll be right back," Daisy said. "Maybe Perdita can't find the pin."

Before Mona could answer, she ran to her own bedchamber.

And found Perdita there, holding the kilt up to herself before the looking glass.

"It's the most magnificent skirt I've ever seen." Perdita's words, as usual, came out almost like the growl of an angry bear.

"You know it's not a skirt, Perdita," Daisy admonished her. "Scotsmen will take huge offense at that. It's a kilt. They used to wear them to cross rivers and to hunt, to live the rough life."

Perdita sighed. "Men have all the fun."

And then she looked over at Daisy: square jaw, fierce eyes, booming voice.

Heavens. The answer had been here all along.

Perdita was Daisy's Highland chief!

Charlie was at Castle Vandemere doing chores around the byre with the ever-willing Mr. King, who was currently with Joe, learning about the sheep, when Daisy came over from the Keep, her cheeks bright from the exertion and the crisp Highland air.

"Has he spoken to Cassandra this morning?" she asked, looking breathless and beautiful.

"I've no idea." Charlie wanted to get his hands and mouth on her and make her feel perfect again. "We got down here earlier than I expected we would. Mr. King, I'm not surprised to find out, is an early riser. I think Cassandra was still asleep when we left."

Daisy bit her lip.

"Is something on your mind?"

"Actually, yes." And she proceeded to tell him about Miss Perdita's new role.

"That's absurd," he said. "She can't play the son of a son of a Highland chief."

"But the guests only saw her last night at dinner, and she didn't speak. I'm going to tell them the female Perdita is indisposed."

"She can't carry this off." It was an obvious

fact: she was a woman, although even Charlie had had his doubts when he'd first met her.

"You wouldn't believe how different she looks in the kilt," Daisy went on. "It was easy enough to strap down her, um—"

"I know what you mean."

Daisy's cheeks reddened further. "And since it's the old-fashioned kind, she has a massive tartan sash up there, too. It . . ." She trailed off.

"It disguises her femininity even more," Charlie said.

"Exactly." Daisy chuckled. "As for her hair, it's frizzy and easy to shove into a hat. I've got her a lovely hunting cap—she's itching to test her skill, you know, so the guests will believe she's entirely dedicated to the sport."

"But she's English!"

"She's only allowed to say a few words: *aye, nay,* and *slainte.* We practiced. She'll sound completely brutish and fierce and Scottish. She's thrilled to be able to drink whisky and smoke a cheroot. The visitors will be in awe."

"I suppose that small mustache she has helps, as well," Charlie muttered.

Daisy put her hand to her mouth and giggled. "I think it does. Even so, I burned a cork and rubbed it into her jaw to make her a bit swarthier."

She stopped giggling rather abruptly, Charlie thought, and her eyes were suddenly bright. "What is it?" he asked her.

Daisy shook her head. "Just that I've never seen Perdita so . . . happy. She was proud to be in that kilt. And she couldn't stop talking about Mr. King and how she couldn't wait to hunt with him. She wondered if maybe he'd talk to her more when she was dressed like a man." She sighed. "It's a shame she can't dress like that all the time. She was a delight. She even hugged me at the end. And it felt . . . genuine."

"Interesting." Charlie chuckled. "So you've discovered something nice about her."

"I really don't know what to think," Daisy said.

"About what?"

"About getting rid of her along with Mona and Cassandra."

"Play it by ear," Charlie said. "Imagine what she'll be like after the men depart and she has to get back into a gown."

"You're right," Daisy said with a sigh. "I won't get my hopes up."

"You always get your hopes up."

"I can't help it. She's my stepsister."

"And that's very kind of you. How did your stepmother take the change in her appearance?"

"Mona merely sneered. Which means she doesn't care one way or the other. She's too preoccupied attempting to win over Mr. Woo."

"Mr. Woo?"

"Yes, she fancies him."

"Poor fellow."

"She's heard he's the richest of the lot. And free to marry."

"Is he?"

"I've no idea. I made it up."

"You minx!"

"I needed to distract her from Perdy's situation. And it certainly worked."

"You don't feel guilty about subjecting Mr. Woo to your stepmother's increased attentions?"

"Not in the least. He can hold his own."

Charlie circled her waist with his hands. "I'm not even sure you went to sleep last night. How miserable for us both that the secret corridor makes it extremely easy for me to get to your room unseen. I might have to join you in bed again tonight and every night until the whole damned Highland experience is over."

She pushed his hands off her waist. "Oh, and one other thing. Perdita certainly can't have Mr. King."

"So you've nothing to say about our bedding down together?"

"Yes." Her cheeks reddened, and she looked at him with serious eyes. "I'm sorry. But we can't do what we did last night every night."

"You said that once before and changed your mind."

"You and I both know we can't keep playing with fire." Her tone was more pert than stern. "Because Cassandra and my stepmother can never find out."

"They won't. Did you hear all the snoring going on last night? It's not just Perdita."

"I know. All three of them do. But as you've already said, what we did could lead to other things."

"And as I've told you before, I would never, ever take such liberties, even with your permission, which"—he whispered into her ear—"I'd be able to get in less than thirty seconds, if you'd only let me try. I'm good, darling. Very good."

"Listen closely." She glowered at him. "Tonight, we're not touching each other. Is that clear? Last night was an accident. I was so exhausted I wasn't prepared to resist your, um, dubious charms."

"Dubious? Are you sure you didn't mean to say *countless*?"

She bit her lip and glanced away from him, refusing to answer.

"I know I wasn't prepared to resist *your* charms, either," he said, "which aren't dubious in the least. Especially now." He took a secret peek down her bodice.

"Somehow I wonder if you're taking me seriously."

"Oh, I am."

She stared at him a few seconds longer.

He stared fixedly back.

"I saw that," she said.

"What?"

"You looking down my bodice." Whenever her honey-bee voice grew thicker, he knew exactly what she was thinking of, and it delighted him no end. "Now what were we talking about before?"

She was adept at switching subjects.

"Perdita." He'd play along. Flirting with Daisy and not being able to follow through was taking a toll on him. "I hate to say this, but her chances of winning Mr. King's admiration are even lower now than they were before she donned the kilt. And her chances then were zero, so . . ."

"Oh," Daisy replied, as if she had a very big secret to reveal, "I meant that she can't have him because— even if she were the most beautiful woman in the world—"

She hesitated.

He'd play along again. "What?"

"I'm saving him for Cassandra."

"*You're* saving him? For Cassandra?"

She sighed. "Can't you see? They're perfect together. Both vain. Both of them good-looking and selfish."

So that's why she'd been so attentive to Mr. King! The little jealous part of Charlie that he'd been ignoring came roaring to the surface, like a quail beat out of the bush, and he was glad to shoot it down. "Are you sure you want him for Cassandra?"

Daisy made an astonished face. "Why, it's obvious they're an ideal match."

"Good. Did you know the braggart and I get along very well? I've even forgiven him his unduly high shirt points and the intricate way he ties his cravats, as if he's a mummy bound to escape unless he's restrained."

Daisy rolled her eyes. "I hope you do, Charlie, because I can't afford for him to be upset about anything."

Mr. King himself strolled up then, his shirt sleeves rolled to his elbows. "Are you ready for our competition, Lord Lumley? We're to pick out our sheep and sharpen the shears. Your shepherd said that'll get our nerves properly frayed."

"What competition?" Daisy asked him.

"Sheep shearing, of course, in front of all the company," said Mr. King. "Joe explained to me in great detail how to go about it."

"Of course, he also reminded us that one learns best by doing," Charlie said, "and that no amount of instruction can prepare us for shearing an actual sheep. Which should keep the match interesting. And perhaps comical."

"I think that might be Joe's intention," Mr. King said dryly. "He's a simple man, isn't he? But I think he has a serious bent when it comes to his flock."

"Sheep shearing *is* serious business," Daisy said. "Neither of you will be laughing. Cursing is more like it."

"The winner is the man who shears his sheep the fastest—and properly, I might add," said Charlie.

"That's right," said Mr. King, "a sloppily shorn sheep won't count toward our total."

"Are you sure you're both ready for this?" Daisy eyed them both warily.

Mr. King laughed. "Sheep aren't dangerous creatures, Miss Montgomery. We'll be fine. Aren't you coming with me, the two of you? I've got my eye on a docile ewe for the contest. I want to claim her before Lord Lumley gets to her."

"Of course," said Charlie. "She'd best not be the same one *I* wanted."

"We might have to fight each other for her, eh?" Mr. King grinned.

"I'm game," Charlie said.

"Enough, you two, with your silly threats." Daisy bestowed a polite smile upon Mr. King. "I have to speak to Lord Lumley a moment—about dinner. We'll catch up with you in a trice."

"Very well." He went off whistling.

As soon as he left, she turned to Charlie. "You must let him win."

"Don't be ridiculous."

"I'm certain that if he loses, he'll be unhappy the rest of his visit. What if he cuts it short?"

Charlie blew out a breath. "Then I'm canceling the match. I won't lose to anyone intentionally, Daisy. Don't you know it defeats the whole purpose of the competition and is an insult to the other party?"

"Yes, but—"

"You saw him. This is all in fun. We're joking about it." He rubbed her upper arms. "Please don't worry."

"I know you're right, but—"

"I won't let him win. It will be a fair competition or none at all."

"Even if it means we'll be assured of a happy guest?"

"He wouldn't be happy. No man would be happy to win under false pretenses." She opened her mouth to speak, but he put a finger over her lips. "I promise that if he beats me fair and square, I won't pout. Because I know you'll be happy he won."

"No I won't." Daisy sighed. "The truth is, I'll be rooting for *you*, Charlie. I won't be able to help myself."

He leaned his forehead against hers and groaned. And then he chuckled. "You're killing me, Daisy. You can't have everything."

"I'm sorry." She bit her lip, but he saw a grin lurking there. "It's just that I'm so worried about getting the money. And so confused . . . about you."

He pulled back. "About me?"

She nodded. "I told you I like you—and I do, at least at the moment and against all my better judgment. I'm sure I'll feel differently soon, but—"

"But for now, you can't resist me." He arched a brow. "It's easily understandable."

She slapped his arm. "See? Already I don't like you again."

"Good. The sooner you learn you can't control everything, the more you'll be able to let go and enjoy yourself. Don't you know if you try too hard with anything in life, it usually goes to pieces?"

"Yes, but I don't have trunkfuls of money to fall back on if that happens. *You* do."

Money doesn't protect you from falling for someone and then having your heart broken, he wanted to say. But he couldn't. Mainly because he didn't want to contemplate that he might be falling for *her*.

"Remember, I'm broke at the moment. But even if I gain access to my family's coffers again, having trunkfuls of money won't protect me from everything," he told her instead.

"I'm sure you're right." She sounded a bit blue. "I've seen my share of unhappy rich people. But doesn't money at least lessen the sting when things go wrong?"

"It makes it easier to hide from your problems. And it makes it a damned sight easier not to have to grow up. So is that a *good* thing?"

She narrowed her eyes at him. "You're a clever man, Lord Lumley. I'm dying to be rich, and you're practically begging to be poor."

"I am at the moment, don't forget. Poor as a church mouse." He grabbed her wrist. "You know I want you to call me Charlie when we're alone."

"Charlie," she whispered.

He pulled her close, his lips a mere inch from hers.

He wanted Daisy's high regard. He wanted it badly. It was stupid of him, and he knew that sheer male pride was involved.

But there it was.

He forced himself to release her. "I'd better go. I really don't want our smug American guest to pick out all the sleepiest ewes."

Daisy gasped. "See? I'm afraid this friendly sheep-shearing competition is going to spiral out of control."

"Don't be ridiculous." Charlie tugged on her hand. "Are you coming—or not?"

"No," she said, still looking worried. "Go choose your sheep. I have better things to do."

"Such as?"

She gave a short laugh. "I don't know yet. But I'm sure by the time I get back to the Keep, there will be something."

CHAPTER SIXTEEN

Famous last words.

There was something, all right.

And that something was Perdita.

When Daisy got back to the Keep, Perdita was holding court in the elegant drawing room in the main hall. The room was thick with cheroot smoke, and the smell of whisky was strong. A sideboard groaned under the weight of platters of sandwiches, cheeses, fruit, and Scottish shortbread.

All but four of the gentlemen were playing cards. Those four who weren't were either snoozing or reading.

It was a man's world, and woe to any woman who entered it, except Mona, of course. She didn't give a fig what any man thought.

Daisy stood outside the door with Cassandra, watching Perdita in action.

"She's in her element," Cassandra whispered.

"I know," Daisy said. "Everyone's been sworn to secrecy—are you sure you can keep it a secret, too?"

Cassandra scowled. "Of course. I've kept your secret, haven't I?"

"Yes," said Daisy.

But for how long?

Her beautiful stepsister strolled away.

Meanwhile, Perdita's cheroot hung from her mouth, and she eyed her cards carefully. She had the notice of every person in the room, except Mona, whose gaze was disinterested as she watched the proceedings from her perch near Mr. Woo.

"Ye have a good hand, young laird?" one of the gentlemen asked Perdita.

"Aye," she said in her usual loud voice.

The man from Bavaria, Mr. Gnamm, sighed. "What I would have given to meet your grandfather. Can ye tell us about him, MacFarland?"

MacFarland was the name Daisy had given Perdita.

"*Slainte.*" Perdita raised her glass and clinked it with Mr. Gnamm's, ignoring his question.

"*Slainte,*" he said back.

Perdita took a gulp and went back to her cards.

"Was the old chieftain in any battles?" asked another man.

"Aye," said Perdita.

A footman came up with a tray of sandwiches and held it before her. She moved all her cards to one hand, picked up a sandwich, took a huge bite, put the rest back on the tray, and then held her cards with both hands again, which were large and mannish, like the rest of her.

"What was his preferred weapon?" asked another gentleman.

Chewing slowly, she glared at him.

"Oh, I'm sorry," he said. "Please. Finish your bite. And focus on the game."

She swallowed. Then laid down a card.

There was a collective sigh.

"You won again," said Mr. Woo.

"Aye." Perdita pulled a pile of coins toward her broad chest.

Daisy chose that moment to stroll in. "So, I see you've all met our son of a son of a Highland chief." She got varied responses, all encouraging:

"Fascinating."

"Almost a throwback to the old days."

"What a treat."

Except for Mr. Woo's. "He doesn't say much," he said.

"Of course not." Daisy threw a smile at Perdita. "I told you he's not much of a talker. But he represents a way of life that is fast disappearing. We're thrilled to have him here, aren't we, gentlemen?"

A chorus of affirmations followed.

"You're all brilliant businessmen," she went on. "You've a great deal in common with the old Highland chiefs. They made all their decisions from their gut."

"It's the only way to live," said one man.

"Who knows? Perhaps you each have a Highlander in you," Daisy said, looking around the group.

"Aye!" cried Perdita, her fist crashing down on

the table and her eyes sparkling with approval at Daisy's remark.

One man jumped up. "I feel as if I do have a Highland chief within me. And he wants to go salmon fishing. Will you come with us, young laird?"

"Aye!" Perdita boomed, and pushed her chair back.

Everyone else stood, too, their eagerness to experience the Highland way of life apparent on all their faces. Even Mr. Woo's.

"The footmen will show you the fishing tackle in the shed by the stables," Daisy announced. "And there are two lads already at the burn. They'll lead you to the best fishing spots and give you instructions. When you get back with your catch, we'll have it for dinner tonight. But don't forget: before dinner is the sheep-shearing contest."

"I wouldn't miss it!" one man said.

There were a few shouts echoing his approval, and then they were gone.

Daisy and her stepmother had the room to themselves. Still on the sofa, Mona picked up Mr. Woo's cheroot and inhaled, stared at her stepdaughter, then exhaled. "You excel at this, you know."

"Thank you." Daisy paused. "I suppose." Getting a compliment from Mona was not a good thing.

Mona crossed her legs, as if she were settling in for a coze. "There's something I need to tell you."

"Oh?" Daisy got a bad feeling, but she always did around her stepmother.

Mona took another drag on the cheroot. "It's

time you learned something about that night with Cousin Roman."

Oh, dear God!

Daisy quickly began to pick up empty cups and plates. "No, it's *not* time. Why are you even bringing up such an awkward subject in this place, where we're surrounded by strangers?"

"You'd best sit down."

"No. Please. Not now. I'm not at all prepared. Or interested, quite frankly."

"Sit down," Mona ordered her. "I'm telling you whether you're prepared or not."

Which was typical. Daisy put down the empty dishes and sat, her jaw clenched with distress, her hands balled into fists. It was the last thing she needed, to experience a personal jolt of any kind while the guests were here.

What was wrong with her stepmother? Why was she so . . . unkind?

"Go ahead," Daisy muttered.

Mona gave a little laugh, the kind that gave Daisy gooseflesh. "Cassandra drugged your wine that night," she announced.

Daisy closed her eyes. The words didn't register at first. She had to let them sink in.

Sour, almost bitter, wine.

A drug.

Heavens, she'd never made the connection!

She shook her head and opened her eyes. "What are you saying?"

Mona let out a long sigh, but she seemed to be quite enjoying herself, swinging her crossed leg back and forth. "She drugged you with Roman's cooperation. She wanted you asleep so they could put you in his bed."

"Why? Why would they plot something so wicked?"

"They were hoping you'd appear ruined."

"Obviously, but it boggles my mind that—"

"It's quite simple, really. Roman hoped that perhaps your father would make him marry you. Roman needed the money. And if for some reason Barnabas didn't demand a wedding, Cassandra knew that he'd send you to a school or convent, at the very least."

"She would have enjoyed that."

"Yes. She longed to be rid of you."

"She's awful." Daisy felt outrage, but she also felt a sense of relief that she hadn't been responsible for winding up in Roman's bed. She knew she couldn't have drunk that much wine. And she was sure she wouldn't have gone to bed with Roman, as attractive as he was.

But how could she ever have proven so when the whole night was a blank in her memory?

She never could have. But now . . . now she knew the truth.

Mona inhaled again on her cheroot. "Of course, Cassandra's plan didn't work out quite the way she'd hoped. The fire interfered. No one even noticed you in Roman's bed. So in a way, luck was on your side when you forgot to snuff that candle."

"Luck? *Luck?* There was nothing lucky about any of that night!" Daisy put her head in her hands, then looked up. "Why are you telling me this now? You don't even like me. It makes no sense. It makes even less sense that you're willing to betray your own daughter. I don't trust you."

"I'm telling you because you've made clear your desire to be rid of us, and you're clever enough to find a way. I want you to remember that I told you the truth."

Daisy sighed. "If you knew about this before Cassandra carried out the plan, you're just as responsible."

Mona sat up. "She told me afterward."

"Am I supposed to believe you?"

Mona shrugged. "I have no proof."

"Even if you did find out afterward, you still didn't tell me. Not only that, you've been doing your best the past year to make me feel like a harlot."

"You're bright and useful, and it was the only way I could get you to do my bidding. I was misguided, perhaps."

"Yes," Daisy whispered, and wrapped her arms around her middle. "I should say so. And now— now you're sacrificing Cassandra to save yourself."

"One thing you can't accuse me of is being stupid, can you? I know what side my bread's buttered on."

There was a pause as Daisy tried to adjust to her stepmother's revelations.

Don't trust her, a voice in her head warned her.

Daisy could feel her father's presence as surely as she could see the glow at the end of Mona's cheroot.

I won't, Daisy told herself. *I never will.*

She took a deep breath and faced down her step-mother. "I have to know something. Why would you want to stay? You hate me. You hate Scotland. I think you even hated my father."

Mona didn't deny it. "I'm tired. I don't have it in me anymore to wander the streets, looking for a rich man. And if your Highland venture is successful, perhaps more rich men will come to Glen Dewey."

"Men like Mr. Woo."

"Yes." Mona chuckled. "In London, he might not give me the time of day. But here, in Scotland, in this magnificent setting at the Keep, I look more interesting, don't you think?"

Daisy felt bitter. So bitter. Mona was admitting that she'd married her father for security, not love. Daisy wasn't surprised, but how had her father been so taken in? All she could guess was that it was grief over her mother's death that had made him susceptible to Mona's charms. When the woman wanted to put them on, she had them.

No doubt, she could find another rich, naïve man to entrap.

Despite her wobbly knees, Daisy forced herself to stand and walk about the room, keeping her distance from the woman she despised. "So you're saying that if I show patience with you and see that the gatherings of rich sportsmen continue, that someday you'll marry again and leave for good."

"Yes."

Daisy stopped in front of a large arched window

with a view of Glen Dewey below. "But what of my own marriage? To the viscount? I won't be here to find you a rich husband. I'll be in London. Very soon."

"It's simple." Mona laughed. "You won't be marrying him. All it would take is one word from me or Cassandra to send him running from you, and you know it. So get marriage to him out of your mind."

The woman was diabolical, but Daisy refused to give up. She would best her.

She thought out her next words carefully. "But if you *do* sabotage my engagement and I'm left here to pine away, I won't lift a finger to bring in more rich gentlemen for you. Not only that, I'll find a way to rid myself of you. You'll have to seek your wealthy husband elsewhere. So ruin my life . . . and I'll ruin yours."

"It's a gamble I'll take," said Mona. "You're all talk at this point. You don't have a plan to get rid of me, or you would have by now. And here's a warning: I stick like glue. After a while, you'll realize that the best plan to rid yourself of me is to do exactly what I said you should: bring in more rich gentlemen to a Highland gathering."

Daisy's heart sank. It seemed that Mona had it all figured out.

Mona's smirk sent shivers through her. "I can tell you're seeing sense. And if you get rid of me, at least you'd no longer have to suffer the fate of being my lifelong companion."

"I suppose not." She'd never fall in with that plan.

"Perdita's useless. But she'll have to do."

"And what of Cassandra?" Daisy asked.

"She'll marry the viscount."

"He won't have her."

"All men can be won." Mona shrugged.

"Lumley is too intelligent, too kind, too savvy to fall for Cassandra's machinations!" Daisy felt ill at the thought.

"So was your father," Mona said. "But I got him. Didn't I?"

Daisy was once again rocked to her foundations. "I hate you. You used my father. He was a good man, and he didn't deserve to be so ill treated."

Mona shrugged. "Water under the bridge."

But Daisy refused to give in to despair. "You won't win. I don't know how I'll stop you, but you won't win."

Mona sauntered to the window and gazed out. "I suggest you pull your head out of the sand and listen." She turned around. "You need to understand that Perdita and I aren't the enemy. Cassandra is. I didn't say I longed for her to marry the viscount, did I? She wants to, and what she wants, she gets—especially if you have it first."

Daisy's chest expanded with indignation. "But you're her mother! It's your duty to rear your daughters with principles. And you've done a terrible job, I might add."

Mona inclined her head. "You're not just a little bit jealous that Cassandra is going to get what she wants—and you won't? She's got everything you don't have, you know."

"No, I'm not jealous. The last person on earth I'd envy is Cassandra."

Mona's eyes glittered. "I wasn't going to do this, but you're making me. You Highlanders are a stubborn lot." She reached into her bodice and pulled out a folded piece of paper. "Read this."

It was very old. And somehow familiar.

The seal.

She knew whose seal that was!

Slowly, Daisy unfolded it and immediately recognized the writing as well:

My dear Barnabas,

She's a precious little thing with smoky gray eyes and a tuft of ebony hair. As you desired, Miss Hausenstab is calling her Cassandra and will treat her with the same loving care I've seen her show her own infant daughter Perdita.

I don't know how I can be of service to little Cassandra, but as her godmother, I'll consider it my duty and privilege to keep both you and your sweet baby girl in my thoughts and prayers always.

Your old friend,
Lady Pinckney née Lucy Warren

Daisy's knees began to tremble, and she sank onto the sofa. Mona was Miss Hausenstab. "Where did you get this note?"

Mona sighed. "Didn't you ever wonder how your father and I found each other to marry? It was no mere coincidence."

"Where—did—you—get—it?" Daisy's jaw wobbled.

Mona plopped down on the sofa next to her. "Barnabas kept it in a drawer in his desk, where he kept all his important papers."

"Who—who's Lucy Warren?" Of course, Daisy already knew, but what did Mona know about her?

Mona shrugged. "Some well-born girl Barnabas insisted on having involved in the adoption. I could've done without her interference and was glad to see her nosy self disappear after she saw us settled in London."

Daisy could hardly breathe. "I've got to go."

"It's an awful lot to take in," said Mona blithely. "Cassandra is Barnabas's daughter, your half sister. She's not my daughter in the least. She's actually older than you by three months, but we told both of you she's younger."

"Why?"

"So you'd have the privilege of being the eldest when we married. Barnabas felt he owed you that. It's why you're Miss Montgomery. He didn't want you displaced."

"Does Cassandra know?"

"Yes."

"And she managed to keep it a secret from me? I wonder why?"

"Because I told her if she doesn't, she'll get the same treatment I give you."

"That's a good reason." Daisy restrained a shudder, thinking of the number of times Mona had locked her in her room. "But why didn't you want me to know the truth after Papa died?"

"I was saving it for when I could get the most use out of it."

"Tell me more, please, about how this all started."

Mona lofted a brow. "Are you sure you want to know?"

"Yes."

"Barnabas had an affair with a London actress a few months before he met your mother," Mona said. "Cassandra was the result. Haven't you ever wondered how someone who looks like me could produce such a breathtaking beauty?"

"Not really." Of course Daisy had, but she wouldn't tell Mona that. It would be too cruel.

"At any rate," Mona went on, "after years alone, with occasional money coming in from your father, I contacted him and told him Cassandra was grown. He couldn't resist wanting to see her, and when he did . . . I worked my wiles. It made perfect sense. He was grieving. And he got his daughter back. Somehow, I think he thought she'd fill the hole in his heart left by your mother's death."

Daisy's eyes filled with tears. "Did she?"

Mona shrugged. "I have no idea."

Daisy's heart clenched—she'd thought *she* was her father's North Star, that she'd been the one to pull him out of his grief.

"I—I must go," she said to Mona, and raced from the room.

Her stepmother was right. It was an awful lot to

take in. Cassandra was her *real* sister? Her older sister? Her father's firstborn child?

How shocking.

How terrible.

How *wrong*.

What of Daisy's relationship with her father? Had he loved her less than he'd loved Cassandra? He must have loved Cassandra a great deal to have married someone as unpleasant as Mona.

For the first time, Daisy felt the stirrings of jealousy toward Cassandra.

But she also saw Cassandra in a new light. No wonder her stepsister despised her. In the bosom of her loving family, Daisy had gotten everything Cassandra hadn't over the years.

It all made more sense now.

Daisy needed to say something out loud about the situation, or she would burst from all the mixed emotions she felt. Into the looking glass in her bedchamber, she whispered, "Cassandra is my father's daughter. *My* sister."

Not only did they share the same father, Cassandra wanted to steal away Daisy's viscount!

Daisy's fear and jealousy compounded.

You're being illogical, she told herself. *Cassandra is rude and unhelpful, even cruel. Charlie can't stand her.*

But still. Her own father had been taken in by Mona.

Could Charlie go the same route and be fooled by Cassandra?

The entire revelation was still too big a notion to

take in . . . Daisy would have to spend some time contemplating it.

Meanwhile, she also had to deal with the second verbal grenade Mona had thrown her way. It involved the old letter Daisy still had tucked away in her turret room at Castle Vandemere, the note from Lady Pinckney to Barnabas—the one that had spurred Daisy on to write Lady Pinckney for help with getting the four hundred pounds.

After reading the second letter, now Daisy knew Lady Pinckney was more than someone who'd once been an old friend or paramour of her father's—*she was* Cassandra's *godmother, not hers*.

CHAPTER SEVENTEEN

It was time for the sheep-shearing contest at Castle Vandemere, but Charlie wasn't feeling in a competitive mood. He was worried about Daisy. She'd been acting distracted all afternoon, and he could swear she'd been crying. But she wouldn't tell him anything.

She stayed busy with the guests, which was typical of her.

"You asked for a godmother's help, so let me help," he'd told her.

"No," she'd said flatly. "But thank you."

And moved on.

And then taken a step back. "Sorry," she'd whispered, and thrown him a small smile. "I do appreciate your concern."

Charlie didn't know if he'd ever understand women. He also didn't know if he'd ever understand what being a godmother was about, and he wished with all his heart that he didn't have to worry about such matters.

Except that serving as his grandmother's stand-in had brought him to Daisy, and he couldn't regret that.

Now that the contest was about to begin, he felt compelled to find her in the crowd and reassure himself that she was all right.

A moment later, he saw her in conversation with Miss Cassandra, slightly apart from the crowd, and neither of them looked at all happy.

Mr. King saw them, too. "What are they doing?" He stared at them with his hands on his hips, ignoring the noise of the crowd surrounding them.

"I don't know." Charlie was equally fascinated, but he was trying to be low-key about it.

"They appear to be in an argument of some kind." The American watched the pair avidly. "I wonder who started it?"

"I don't know."

Charlie was glad no one else was paying the young ladies the least bit of attention.

"She's stunning," Mr. King said. "The stepsister. I never noticed her before now because she's always staring daggers at your fiancée. But she has a fine figure. And some spirit, doesn't she?"

"I suppose she does," said Charlie, not willing to dash her character to this stranger. He wouldn't be much of a gentleman if he did that.

Mr. King gave a little laugh. "She's the one who belongs in a peer's bed. Or anyone's bed who's powerful and rich."

"No," Charlie replied strongly. "No, she doesn't.

Miss Montgomery was in her cups when she said that, and I'm sure she regrets it."

They both watched as Miss Cassandra put her nose in the air.

Daisy's throat and cheeks turned pink.

And then the two women walked in different directions.

"They don't like each other," Mr. King said. "That's for certain."

Charlie saw, too, that something ugly was going on between them, but he'd have to stave off his curiosity—and concern—for a little while.

He had this nuisance of a contest to win.

Yes, he liked to be the best at everything, but these were sheep.

Sheep.

If they were dragons, he'd be more interested in looking manly and courageous in front of Daisy and the crowd. As it was, if Mr. King somehow beat him, he'd just be glad his London friends weren't here to see him make a fool of himself—and Daisy probably wouldn't care that he'd lost, either.

"What's the prize if you win?" one of the visiting men called out as he and Mr. King pushed their ewes into position within circles Joe had drawn with chalk on the grass.

"No prize," replied Charlie, "just the glory of winning!"

The man grinned and gave him a thumbs-up.

Charlie was a bit distracted—his first sheep was perhaps more stubborn than he'd realized—and he wondered if his shears were sharp enough. The crowd was also bigger than he'd imagined.

Perdita, dressed in her Highland garb, sat in a large chair ready to cast judgment on the proceedings, although a village elder was the real judge.

Even so, Perdita was obviously in her element.

Suddenly, there was a loud roar of approval—about what, Charlie had no idea.

Mr. King grinned. "Absolutely," he said to the crowd, then looked at Charlie. "What do you say?"

"To what?"

"The loser must buy a round of drinks for everyone at the new pub in Glen Dewey," Mr. King replied.

A handsome man stepped forward. "At the grand opening which I, Gavin MacKee, will hold this very night!"

All the men shouted, clapped, and whistled.

"I'll do one better," Charlie told them. "If I lose, I'll bring down another cask of Joe's whisky to pass round instead."

"Oh no, ye won't, Lord Lumley," Gavin chided him. "I needs must make my living at the pub. Ye'll be buying the round if ye lose, my friend."

"If you don't win today, you need to feel the pain of losing in your pocket, lad!" someone else called out.

"Tha's right," an old man said. "Whichever rich nabob loses must pay!"

The crowd endorsed his remark with a hearty "Hurrah!"

It was a simple, friendly bet.

But it was a dangerous one to Charlie.

He couldn't afford to lose any longer.

If he did, he'd have to borrow money from Daisy. A man didn't shirk a bet. He'd have to buy a round of drinks for the men of the village.

Which would mean he'd lose the bet with his friends in London.

Which meant he'd be thrown onto the Marriage Mart because he was an honorable man, and honorable men confessed when they lost bets.

Why, oh why, couldn't it have been anything but a sheep-shearing contest?

Inhaling a breath, he held his ewe still while the village elder walked to the center of the pen and lifted a scarlet handkerchief high in the air. "Just remember, gentlemen, you're being evaluated on your speed *and* the quality of the shearing. No nicks on those poor ewes, mind you. And the fewer cuts the better. On your mark, get set, go!" The man brought the handkerchief down on the word *go,* and the match was on.

Do it right, Charlie told himself.

Finding the place to start was the hardest part of all. He put his arm under the ewe's neck, just as Joe had shown him. When she tried to leap away with her hind legs, Charlie was able to tilt her back so she sat up like a person. Grabbing a fold of wool and skin on her belly, he made the first vital cut and prayed he wouldn't nick her.

And he didn't. Breathing a discreet sigh of relief, he vowed not to observe what strategies Mr. King employed. Charlie would stay focused. *Extremely* focused.

The crowd called to both of them, and Charlie ignored them as best he could. The ewe struggled more and more as he snipped at her wool with the shears, attempting to get the fluffy stuff off in one, big piece.

He felt the stress build up in his belly and chest, which didn't improve when he lost his grip and the ewe bolted.

He cursed a blue streak in his head. He wasn't laughing at all. Especially when he saw Mr. King's tremendous progress, which he couldn't help observing as he was required to chase after his ewe and bring her back to their shearing place.

A shout went up. Mr. King was done with his first ewe!

Dear God, Charlie thought. *I'm in for it.*

Visions of London debutantes clamoring to marry him besieged him, but he was determined to cast them aside.

A moment later, he'd finished his first sheep. He patted her rear and she ran bawling away, naked as she could be, with just a few little clumps of wool left on her. He thought he'd done a good job, but had he done it fast enough and well enough?

"Only two to go!" he heard Joe call to him.

Bloody hell, this was going to take ages.

And it did. Charlie had never worked so hard in his life. It was meticulous work, all to be done while a sheep struggled beneath his nose. Sweat poured from his brow. His whole body was soaked with it, which made holding on to the next two ewes that much more difficult.

People came and went. Refreshed themselves from a bucket of water, drank from flasks, made comments on their progress.

Meanwhile, Mr. King was slaving away, too. Charlie had no idea how well he was doing, but he suspected they were close. The crowd's teasing remarks ceased. Their noise got louder, more frantic.

Charlie felt panic build in his middle, but he pushed it down once again.

He couldn't lose!

"Charlie!" he heard Daisy's voice call above the others.

He took a half second to look up. She was over by the byre, standing on a low-lying stump so she could see him. Her eyes were lit with concern, and she was biting her lip when she caught his eye and waved at him.

Cassandra stood next to Daisy. She wore a close-lipped smile when she waved at him, too, but her face was tight with something unpleasant.

Daisy glanced down at her stepsister and made a small grimace that Charlie recognized as annoyance and perhaps a bit of confusion.

Why was Cassandra standing so close? Why couldn't she watch the contest somewhere else?

Charlie was indignant on Daisy's behalf. She was only trying to cheer for him, but Cassandra was proving a bit of a bother.

Daisy appeared to give up wondering why her

stepsister was there because she cupped her hands together and called to him, "Win, Charlie, win!"

That spindly utterance, delivered over the roar of the crowd, gave him a tremendous boost, and he went back to work with renewed vigor.

Daisy had no idea what the true stakes of this match really were. If she knew, would she care?

The third ewe bucked and bawled worse than the others. He'd saved her for last because he'd seen her around the pastures. She was bossy, given to bursts of pique.

"Go, Viscount, go!" he heard a little boy scream from his right.

"Mr. King's ahead!" someone else called.

"Aye, and it's close," an old man to the left of Charlie said.

The ewe wriggled so hard, Charlie had to hold the shears up and away. He stumbled backward, the ewe twisted . . .

"Go!"

"He missed a spot!"

"That damned ewe reminds me of my wife!"

"Hurry!"

Charlie had no idea if the crowd was talking about his ewe or Mr. King's, and he certainly didn't know which of them had to *go* or *hurry*.

He reestablished his stance: knees bent, toes in . . .

Sheep locked into position between his legs.

This was it.

Without blinking or breathing, he finished shearing the sheep.

He dropped his shears and looked up and—

Mr. King was shearing the last bit of wool off the right side of his ewe and . . .

It was over.

Over.

Charlie wiped the sweat out of his eyes. His lungs were near bursting, but he forced himself to take slow, measured breaths. Already the village elder and his cohorts were examining the last two sheep for nicks and holding up the fleeces to see how neatly they'd been shorn.

Charlie was sore, but he moved toward Mr. King as if he'd not just been working harder than he ever had before. Mr. King came toward him, as well. His rival looked as worn out as Charlie felt.

They met in the middle and clasped hands.

"It was a fine match," Charlie said.

"It was indeed." Mr. King's handshake was firm but quick.

A little too quick, Charlie thought, to be considered entirely sporting.

He looked over his shoulder—Daisy was still in front of the byre, her hands clasped beneath her chin. Cassandra stood beside her, both her hands resting on one hip, a casual pose that belied her taut expression. Daisy jumped up and down on her little stump and waved again.

He raised a hand to her and grinned, glad he was worth more than a meager hop. He merited full-fledged bouncing, didn't he?

Take that, Mr. King, he thought, remembering that first meeting in the hall at the Keep when Daisy had been so enthusiastic about the man.

But then a drumbeat called his attention in another direction. It was time to find out who'd done the best job shearing.

Perdita stood, her fists on her hips.

The village elder cleared his throat. "The laird has made his choice."

Please let me be the winner, Charlie prayed. He really didn't want to have to buy that round at the village pub.

He thought of Daisy, at how fresh and real and feisty she was, and felt a keen ache to win the bet he'd made with the other Impossible Bachelors. There was no way he wanted to enter the London Marriage Mart and wed a simpering miss.

Ever.

He bowed his head and awaited his fate.

"The winner is . . . *Lord Lumley*!" cried the elder.

"Aye!" Perdita gave a mighty growl and punched the air with her fist.

When Charlie raised his head, he found himself grinning from ear to ear.

He'd won. Thank God.

He immediately turned around to see Daisy. There she was, smiling at him! She looked a bit strained because Cassandra lingered at her elbow, but that smile lit every corner of his heart.

The fact that she was happy delighted him no end.

He winked at her. She blushed, which made him wish he could go over there right now and receive a celebratory kiss.

Later, her expression said.

Later, he confirmed with his eyes.

Which was exactly when Miss Cassandra gave her a lovely little push, causing Daisy to stumble off her stump and teeter backward into a slippery patch, where she landed flat on her rear end into a pool of mud.

CHAPTER EIGHTEEN

Daisy was happy for Charlie. She really was. She said, "I'm happy for Charlie," through gritted teeth under her breath all night.

She'd be happy for Charlie if it was the last thing she did. She'd *forget* what happened to her with Cassandra. She'd *forget* that Cassandra had been so wicked that she'd pushed Daisy off her stump.

And she'd forget that when she'd fallen in the mud, tears had come to her eyes and Cassandra had stalked off, laughing.

Charlie, of course, had been carried off with the crowd of men to the pub. Daisy ran into Castle Vandemere for a quick change of clothes and a long hug from Hester, and wondered why she'd never known there was such a thing as grown people pushing each other.

Joe had said when both parties did it, it was called wrestling.

"But when one does it, it's called spitefulness," Hester told her.

Back at the Keep, Daisy decided the only way to get through the evening would be to avoid Cassandra at all costs. She'd think rude thoughts about her. She'd also pity herself and wonder how life would ever get better. And she'd stay busy in the kitchen scrubbing pots so she wouldn't cry.

When Charlie returned with the other men to the Keep after an evening's celebration at the new pub, Daisy was still busy scrubbing pots in the kitchen, but she'd gotten over pitying herself. Hard work tended to do that to a person.

And it might have helped that when Cassandra had walked by the kitchen an hour ago and seen her scrubbing away, she'd actually put her head in the door and said, "I'm sorry I ruined your ratty gown. Now maybe you'll be forced to get a decent one."

And Daisy had said, "If that's you trying to be nice, you're doing a very poor job. Why do you bother with me, Cassandra?"

Cassandra shrugged.

Daisy's heart pounded with fury. "Should I tell you what I'm thinking?"

"Go ahead," her new sister said, tossing her head.

"Very well." Daisy crossed her arms. "I wish you'd eaten that mud I fell in and gotten sick the same way you and Cousin Roman made me ill by giving me that drugged wine."

Cassandra had bitten her lip at that and stalked on.

Meanwhile, the cooks had made a hearty lamb stew and bread, which they'd kept warm for the men's—and Perdita's—return.

A few rounds of card playing followed, and as usual, Daisy didn't go to bed until the last guest had retired.

"I've arranged a surprise for you," Charlie said to her at his bedchamber door. "You deserve it after all your hard work today. And your mishap."

"What mishap?"

"You know."

She bit her lip. "Did you see it happen?"

He nodded.

"Why didn't you—"

"I knew you wouldn't have wanted me to," he said.

She looked down at the ground, remembering that feeling of being covered in mud.

"You're right," she replied with a sigh. If anyone had gotten near her at that point, she would have screamed.

"I wanted to be with you," he said. "Honestly. But then I got pulled away, down to the pub. Will you tell me why it happened?"

"Eventually," she said.

He pulled a curl off her forehead.

"When will I get my surprise?" she whispered.

"I'm not telling," Charlie said back, and slipped into his bedchamber. He'd told her he'd linger for twenty minutes and make a bit of noise for Mr. Woo next door before he sneaked upstairs to her bedchamber through the hidden staircase.

When Daisy entered her room, she saw a lovely copper tub standing before the fire. Curls of steam wafted upward from the water's surface. A fluffy towel and bar of soap were laid on a chair.

Charlie, apparently, couldn't wait. He appeared a few seconds later. "Your bath, my lady."

For a moment, neither one of them spoke. A bit of peat on the fire flared, and a log shifted.

"How wonderful," Daisy said, feeling out of breath.

Charlie smiled softly. "You need it after the day you've had. But our restrictions still stand."

"What restrictions?"

"If you recall our conversation this morning, you said that we wouldn't touch each other tonight, and I agreed."

Daisy thought back. Or tried to. It was difficult to concentrate when he was so near. "Oh," she said. "You're clever, aren't you?"

"More desperate than clever, actually."

"Desperate for what?" she whispered.

"For you. It's why I'm bringing out the screen. If we can't touch each other, we certainly shouldn't see each other, either. Much too tempting, don't you think? And after your bath, we'll extinguish the candle and take to our own sides of the bed."

She gulped. "Yes. You're right, of course."

He pulled out an exotic painted-silk screen from a corner and placed it in front of the tub. "I promise I won't peek."

"Thank you, Charlie," she said softly, feeling shy of a sudden.

"You're welcome," he said, and left her to her ablutions.

Behind the screen, she could see nothing of him. But she heard him walking about the room. And then she heard him pull up a chair and place a candle on a small table that she knew was not two yards away from her tub.

"You'll wait?" she asked him from behind the screen. She was glad he couldn't see her blush.

"Yes," he said. "I've a good book to occupy my time."

"Very well." Slowly, she untied her ribbons. The fire hissed and crackled. The clock on the mantel ticked slowly. She also heard the flick of pages turning as Charlie read his book.

Her gown fell to the floor. She shivered, even though she didn't feel cold.

"Daisy," Charlie whispered.

"Y-yes?"

"You *are* beautiful, you know."

Her breath seemed to stop. "Thank you," she whispered back.

And then she realized he must be able to see her figure outlined on the screen by the fire behind her. She tried to look through the screen to see him, but she couldn't. She could *feel* him, though. His presence filled the room.

Carefully, she ascended a little stool and slipped into the tub.

"Oh, this feels good," she said.

"I'm glad," he answered back.

She closed her eyes, and for a few minutes, there was nothing but a comfortable quiet. Charlie turning his pages. The fire, lapping at the peat and logs.

This bath really was what she'd needed. She'd

worked hard today. And fought hard, as well. Her limbs ached.

When she reached for the soap, the sound of water droplets seemed to echo loudly through the room. She ran the soap down her arm. And then the other. And submerged her arms again, reveling in the sensation of warmth and the lavender-scented bar.

But she no longer heard pages turning.

She sat for a moment longer.

"Charlie?" she called softly.

"Yes?" he replied.

She laughed. "I—I thought you might have fallen asleep."

"No," he said.

But his voice sounded almost too serious. Actually, *tortured* was a better word.

She blinked in the sudden knowledge that he—

Well, he was sitting on the other side of the screen, wasn't he? And he knew she was on this side, stark naked . . .

"Charlie," she said.

"Yes?"

"Can't you—can't you come round the screen?"

There was another long silence.

"No," he finally replied.

"But I want you," she whispered. "I want what we had last night. And on the Stone Steps." She waved her hands through the steaming water, making small ripples.

There was another silence.

"We still can," he said. "In a way."

She stopped moving her hands through the water. "How?"

"Simply remember us together. And your body will do the rest."

She was intrigued, and without thinking, ran the soap over her breasts. A dart of pleasure flickered between her legs, and she wanted him to come to her.

So badly.

"Charlie," she whispered, hearing the plaintive need in her own voice.

"I want you, too," he said. "Very much. But you yourself said we can't have each other that way tonight."

"It's not fair," she said.

"Fair has nothing to do with it. But you can lean back, Daisy, and shut your eyes. Let your body take over."

She sighed with frustration—but also with pleasure at the thought of their being together. "What will *you* do?"

"The same. But you have to promise me one thing."

"What?"

"No matter what, you won't stop imagining until you're—" He hesitated.

"Until I'm what?" she asked breathily.

"Until you're satisfied," he said.

Satisfied.

She touched her stomach and let her hands reach to the curls between her legs. Charlie had kissed her there three times now. She ached for him to do it again.

"I—I promise." She licked her lower lip and felt her legs fall apart.

"Think of me," he said again. "And I'll be wishing I were with you—the way we were last night."

She heard his boots come off. And then he tossed his breeches over the top of the screen. And finally, his shirt wound up there, as well.

"You're naked," she whispered.

"I know." His voice was rough. "And I'm staying right here. With you. Watching you. Pretend *I'm* touching you, Daisy."

She'd never felt so wanton. Never felt so heavy with desire, immersed as she was in the water, which touched every part of her like a kiss.

Silence reigned once again, and then she sighed out loud, her breathing coming faster as her hands roamed her body and she thought of Charlie.

"Are you still watching?" she said.

"I can't . . . I can't keep my eyes off the screen."

"I want you," she whispered.

"I want you, too."

"I—I'm going to—" And then her body arched like a rainbow over the water. *"Charlie,"* she moaned as she crested in a wave of sensual pleasure—and sank back down, her mind drifting, even as her body did, cocooned by the warmth of the water and the knowledge that she was discovering new depths—and a tender passion—with her viscount.

CHAPTER NINETEEN

A week later, Charlie opened one eye and saw Daisy curled next to him, sleeping peacefully. No wonder she hadn't woken yet. Yesterday had been another long day with the visitors, a large part of it spent indoors because of rain. And it was followed by another heady night of passion between them which demanded to be sated several times over.

As if she knew she were being watched by him, Daisy opened her eyes and smiled. "It's a *braw, bricht* day, I can tell already," she said. "It has to be. Tonight's the *ceilidh*."

When she looked at him then, with all that happiness and hope shining in her eyes, he realized something very important: he loved her. He loved everything about her.

The knowledge shook him to the core.

But he couldn't think about it now. The feeling was too precious. He must savor it alone today. Explore what it meant.

"As it's our last day at the Keep," he said, "I think I'll go fishing. Alone."

"Alone?"

He nodded. "I have some thinking to do."

"About what?"

He kissed her. "Life, I suppose. And how magical it can be when you're sleeping with the same beautiful woman every night."

Daisy sighed. "I don't know how I could have survived the past week without our nights together."

"You've had some shocking news to digest. Who ever would have thought your worst enemy would turn out to be your very own sister?"

She grinned. "I know. The Fates have a diabolical sense of humor, don't they? Along those lines, I can't help thinking it would be perfect if Mr. King proposed to Cassandra tonight. He'd take her away to America. And I'd never have to worry about seeing her again. I suppose I should be sad, as she's my sister, but I'm not. We're still not talking. Except for this odd comment she made to me days ago about my needing to buy myself a nicer gown. It wasn't exactly spiteful sounding. It was almost as if . . . she *wanted* me to have a pretty frock." She bit her lip. "I'm sure I misunderstood her. But there's a chance I didn't, of course, and the truth is—I want *her* to have a pretty frock, too. For tonight. Every woman should look beautiful."

"Including yourself," said Charlie. "Do you have a new gown?"

"No."

Charlie sighed. "You should get one."

"Too late," she said nonchalantly, then sat up on her elbows. Much to Charlie's delight, she forgot to pull up the covers, exposing her beautiful, pert breasts to the morning light.

"Oh, dear," she whispered.

"Oh, dear, is right," Charlie answered her. He leaned down and kissed her neck. "Somehow I can't think about your new sister at the moment. Or your lack of new gown, as much as that dismays me. I want to talk about us. You've made me the most creative lover in the world."

"Have I?"

"Indeed you have." He ran a hand over her silken breast. "We've been sleeping together—"

"We've done *more* than sleep together—"

"Yes, for over a week now. I believe we win a prize for showing incredible ingenuity and forbearance. You're as virgin as you ever were."

"What's the prize?"

He whispered in her ear.

"Oh, I adore that notion!" She grinned again. "Remember the night we weren't allowed to touch each other?"

"How could I forget? It was all your fault, by the way."

"What you're suggesting now is even more torturous!"

"And you love it."

She pulled him closer until they were nose to nose. "I do."

It was hard to believe the days had flown by so fast, and their guests appeared to be more enthralled

with the Highlands than ever. The village had out-
done itself in welcoming their visitors by heaping
lavish attention upon them at the Keep, on the hunt,
and at the games which followed.

And through it all, Mr. King had spent every
moment he could with Cassandra.

At the hunt, Mr. King brought home the largest
buck, but Cassandra hadn't appeared to be impressed. He'd also participated in all of the games
afterward . . . the caber tossing, stone lifting, and
speed races, and won his share of glory. But Cassandra merely watched all the proceedings with a
smug smile and showed no apparent favor to him
whatsoever, which only served to pique his interest
in her more.

"Do you think Cassandra favors him?" Daisy
asked Charlie now.

"I think she might. I got my first inkling of that
yesterday."

Daisy sucked in a breath. "Do you really
think so?"

Charlie shrugged. "She allowed him to walk her
home from the village. You know what happened
to *us* on that walk home."

Daisy blushed. "The Stone Steps. But surely
Cassandra wouldn't—"

"Wouldn't be so . . . wanton?" He kissed her nose.

"Yes," she said, and pushed him playfully away.

"Well, whatever happened on the way home, she
spoke to him all through dinner."

Daisy bit her lip. "I really think she likes him."

"Did she say much else?"

"No. Although she blurted out that she thinks he's very, very rich. What do you think that means?"

Charlie grinned. "Knowing Cassandra, she means she's interested in becoming his wife."

"I do believe you're right. So there's room for hope there. I wonder why she gave up on pursuing you? Ever since our mud escapade, she's avoided you like the plague."

Charlie brushed some hair off Daisy's forehead. "I've no idea. Perhaps she's being a good sister."

"Hah," said Daisy. "I'm sure she has a nefarious motive. Although a tiny part of me is rather curious about this new Cassandra. She's as rude as ever and takes great pleasure in laughing at other people's shortcomings, but she hasn't engaged me in direct insults in days. I almost miss them."

"I want you to know," Charlie said in all seriousness, "that even before this conversation, I'd planned to ask Mr. King exactly what his intentions are—tonight before the ball in the privacy of the library. Cassandra is not my sister, but now we know she's yours. And as you're my grandmother's goddaughter"—*and the woman I love*, he thought—"I feel a certain responsibility toward her."

Daisy blushed so red, her ears turned pink.

"What is it?" he asked her.

"Nothing," she choked out.

"Are you sure?"

She wore a pensive expression. "About being your grandmother's goddaughter—"

"Yes?"

She stared at him a moment, then shrugged. "I'm glad I am, that's all."

"I'm glad, too," he said. "I never would have met you, otherwise."

She kissed his cheek. "I appreciate your concern about Cassandra, but please don't corner Mr. King. He's a sophisticated man. He'll show his colors tonight without needing any push. Just you wait and see."

Charlie hesitated. He couldn't forget what the Virginian had said about Daisy on the first day they'd met. Yet Mr. King's remark—when Charlie thought about it—was typical of a man of the world speaking to another man of the world. Should he really have held it against his visitor all this while?

Yes, said a voice in his head. *Don't make excuses for him. It was in poor taste. And it says something about who he is and the rules by which he plays.*

"I think waiting for him to make the first move with your stepsister is a mistake," Charlie said.

"Why?"

"He's toying with her. He can go home and say he had an amusing time in the Highlands with a local English girl. I know his kind. Rich, powerful . . . bored."

"Oh, Charlie." Daisy sighed, the bedsheet wrapped around her lovely form. "You mean well, but you're wrong. He's *devoted* to her."

"I know it seems that way. But you don't know how men in his position can be."

"Every sign he's shown has been so clear—he's in love!"

"Love?"

Daisy nodded. "Of course."

Charlie sighed. "It could be mere infatuation. What do you know of love?"

She stared at him, at a loss for words.

"That's too hard a question to ask me," she said eventually. "I'm too busy to think about love—I have to think about securing a castle." A small squiggle of annoyance furrowed her brow. "What do *you* know about love?"

He didn't know what it was—yet—but he knew he loved her. He loved her so much, he couldn't live without her.

So what should he say?

"Nothing, I suppose," he said, feeling as if that were the truth. For now.

"We must take a gamble, then," said Daisy. "I've already begun a secret project to make Cassandra look extra beautiful tonight."

"Oh?"

"The women of the village have been making her a special gown in secret. And Mr. Glass has donated a gorgeous pair of slippers for her—they're exquisite!" She clapped her hands in delight. "Of course, I won't tell her I thought of it. Let her think someone else did. It would be most awkward if she knew—"

"I'm afraid you're setting her up for failure."

Daisy sucked in a breath. "That's a terrible accusation to make."

"I know you mean well." He took her by the shoulders. "But trust me on this. I *am* the type of man I'm warning you about. When I'm not here and not in my parents' bad books, I'm a rich man about town with not a care in the world. And I'd do exactly what I think Mr. King will—leave her without remorse."

Daisy's eyes widened at that. But he'd had to tell her the truth.

He also had to remind himself of the truth.

I am *that man.*

Would Daisy be that woman, the one he'd leave behind so he could keep his freedom?

Shaken by questions he wasn't sure how to answer, he rolled out of bed and got dressed. Daisy was silent, watching him with large eyes.

"I think I'd best go now," he said. He tried to smile at her. But it was difficult somehow.

She nodded. "All right," she said in a sad whisper.

Charlie hesitated. "There's something you should know," he said. "I haven't told you because it's a moot point, really. But it may help you understand." He sat on the edge of the bed. "My friends in London put me up to a bet. They dared me to spend nothing until I return to London. It shouldn't be difficult, as I was cut off from my family accounts, right?"

She nodded, her gaze wary.

"But I'm a wealthy man on my own, and I had enough money stashed that I could have gotten here in comfort. Perhaps I could have even scraped together your four hundred pounds."

A small pucker formed on Daisy's brow.

"But I took their challenge. I got to Scotland on the back of wagons—"

"One of them must have carried turnips," she murmured, a small grin curving her lips despite the bleak tone of their conversation.

"Right." He gave a short laugh, remembering. "My point is, I took the bet. And if I lose, I go on the Marriage Mart, which to me . . . is anathema."

The remnants of the grin on Daisy's mouth disappeared.

"The bet was meant to prove to myself that I'm more than the balance in my accounts," Charlie struggled on, hating how with every word he spoke, the atmosphere in the room became more depressing. "But to the world, the wager must appear shallow. Especially because of the stakes."

"If you win this bet, you can dine out on it for months," Daisy said slowly. "Telling stories of your little adventure. And all your wealthy friends will tell you how much they admire you for enduring the hardships. And you'll say, 'Wouldn't you have? Considering what I would have lost—my freedom.' And then you'll pull out your purse of gold coins and buy everyone a round of drinks."

"Yes," he said. "It will likely go something like that."

They stared at each other a few moments.

"I'm glad you told me." Her brow was smooth, and her eyes revealed nothing.

For the first time, he couldn't tell what she was thinking.

But it couldn't be good.

When she rolled over and faced the wall without kissing him farewell, he left the room without another word.

Looking out her window at the Keep, Daisy could see people streaming up from Glen Dewey, everyone in their finery. She wore one of Perdita's muslin gowns, cut down, along with the thistle pin Hester had given her. She felt a twinge of remorse that she hadn't spent more time on her appearance, but she hadn't had time.

Besides, she'd felt rather numb all day. Her talk with Charlie had left her feeling terribly blue and unsettled.

She didn't like what she'd heard, that Charlie was capable of attaching himself to people and then leaving. And the bet he was embroiled in was proof that he was a man who lived for adventure—and who didn't want to marry.

He'd never pretended to be anything else, even in their most intimate moments, when their eyes would lock and something magical would thrum in the air between them.

So why had she felt on the verge of tears since the morning?

When Perdita came unexpectedly to her bedchamber dressed as the Highlander, her gait was slower than usual, and she twisted her tartan sash in worried fashion.

"Is everything all right?" Daisy asked her, glad to get away from her own glum thoughts.

"No." Perdita sank onto the bed, a picture of

misery. "I need to tell you something. It's very important."

Daisy sat next to her. "What is it?" She had no idea—it could be anything.

Perdita heaved a huge sigh. "I can't be the . . . *me* I want to be."

Daisy was silent a moment, taken aback by the raw emotion in her stepsister's voice. "What do you mean?"

Perdita shook her head. "It's complicated. I've always said you're the plain one, but we both know I am. You just don't try very hard. If you did, you'd be beautiful." She looked at Daisy with genuine frustration and concern. "You should try. It's not right to hide. I know Mother is the one making you so afraid to be the young lady you were meant to be."

Daisy was touched at the sisterly advice. "You're very kind to care. I—I didn't realize I was hiding, but you're probably right. Perhaps I should try harder. And you're *not* plain."

"Oh, yes I am. I'm more than plain. I'm ugly."

"Perdita—"

Her stepsister held up her hand. "It's true. But that's all right. Because I've found a way to like who I am."

"Tell me."

Perdita chuckled. "I love playing the son of a son of a Highland chief. No one makes fun of my loud voice and my big shoulders." Her face lit up. "You should have seen me on the hunt. I was good, one of the best hunters there. Men were coming up to me and complimenting me on my skill."

"That's wonderful!" Daisy marveled at how attractive Perdita was when she was enthused. She didn't at all resemble the dour girl Daisy had always known.

"But I can't be a Highlander forever." Perdita's expression drooped. "For one, I need to be able to say more than *aye, nay,* and *slainte.*"

"True."

"And"—Perdita paused, as if it were hard for her to say—"as the Highlander, I can't win the man I want."

"Oh, dear," Daisy said. "Do you still admire Mr. King?"

Perdita shook her head. "I thought I did, but he laughs like a donkey. And he has a *tendre* for Cassandra."

"Right." Daisy tried not to chuckle at the description of Mr. King.

"So on the hunting trip," Perdita went on, "I did my best to meet the other men. And I found one I like even more than Mr. King."

"Who?"

"The Spanish marquis. He asked me to call him Pablo, but of course, I never did. I said nothing beyond *aye, nay,* and *slainte.*"

"How difficult that must have been."

"It was. He talked long into the night about life while I listened. We looked at the stars, and he taught me the different constellations. He also told

me stories about his boyhood at his castle in Spain.
I fell in love with him more each night."

"You did?" Daisy felt a glimmer of hope for her
sister. She had a heart. That was good to know.

Perdita nodded. "But it's hopeless. He admires
me because I'm a fierce Highlander. He asked if I
would care to go shooting with him on his estate in
Spain. He told me I would enjoy his cigars and
brandy, and that the women in Spain were beautiful." She gulped. "He can't like me . . . that way, as
a woman. We speak only man to man."

Daisy laid a hand on her arm. "Oh, but he does
like you as a woman! I saw him looking down your
gown the very first night. And he was most attentive to your needs. He pulled out your chair—"

"He *did* pass me the salt and pepper without my
having to ask."

"Yes, and don't you remember he said, 'How do
you do?' when you first sat down?"

"I forgot about that."

"He saw you as a woman, I promise you. And he
liked what he saw."

Perdita perked up. "Are you sure?"

Daisy nodded. "Most definitely. He even asked
after you several times when you were purportedly
ill, which leaves me no doubt he was interested in
pursuing your acquaintance." She sighed. "I wish
you could tell him who you really are. I'm so . . .
sorry. If he finds out we were fooling him—"

"He'll be angry," said Perdita. "All the visitors
will be. They'll feel we were making fun of them,

and then they won't pay us any money. Which means we'll be back where we started."

"Perdita—" Daisy felt a terrible jolt of guilt. "I want you to be happy. And there must be a way out of this dilemma with the marquis." She bit her lip and thought for a moment, then gave a little chuckle. "Perhaps the son of a son of a Highland chief can't come tonight. It's his turn to be ill. Surely no visitor will penalize us for not having him at the *ceilidh*. You've been so good all week long. It's time for Perdita to reemerge from the sick room, don't you think?"

Perdita smiled. "I like that." She took off her cap, and her frizzy brown hair fell about her shoulders. "But won't they recognize me?"

"I very much doubt they will," Daisy said. "First of all, they have no reason to suspect that you'd ever have call to pose as a man. But more importantly, you look like a woman in love."

"I do?"

"Yes. You're softer. In every way. Even your voice."

Perdita blinked rapidly. "I like being soft," she whispered, which was still a bit loud. But she was doing better than she'd ever done before.

"I think you should stay seated in an inconspicuous spot," Daisy said, "away from blazing candles, somewhat in the shadows. That way we'll have no fear of your being unveiled as our Highlander. And you'll also appear quite mysterious."

"I've heard that men love mystery," Perdita said. "They told me themselves, on the hunt. I heard some shocking things about how they feel about women."

"I'm sure you did." Daisy patted her hand. "Speak only to the marquis, whom I shall send your way, I promise. When he asks you to dance—and he will—tell him you will dance only outside, under the moonlight."

"But it's summer in the Highlands. It will be day all night long."

"Oh, that's right." Daisy bit her thumb. "Never mind about the moonlight. But dance close to him."

"I see."

"And then when you're dancing . . . kiss him." Daisy thought about how much she loved kissing Charlie.

"*Kiss* him?"

"Yes. Lean forward and kiss him. Be bold as brass. Sometimes being bold as brass can be a good thing. Especially when time is running out."

Perdita laughed. "You're right. The men on the hunt said they like modesty, but they also like women who aren't afraid to enjoy the realm of physical pleasures. They want both, they said."

"Yes. It's confusing, isn't it? A woman must be all things to them. But what do you have to lose? The marquis leaves tomorrow. After you kiss him, perhaps something else will happen. Perhaps a true attachment will form. And that's what you want. Sometimes to get what you want, what you know is right for you, you have to risk everything."

Tears formed in Perdita's eyes. "This is my only chance."

"Perdita?"

"Yes?"

Daisy smiled at her. "I hope all your dreams come true."

"Really, Daisy? You don't hate me?"

Daisy shook her head. "Absolutely not. I used to, I must admit. Until quite recently. But I happen to think your mother was a very bad influence on us all. I haven't tried as hard with you as I should have." She hugged her.

Perdita hugged her back so hard, it hurt, but Daisy managed to refrain from gasping.

"Mother *is* a bitch, isn't she?" Perdita said.

It was most definitely a rhetorical question.

They both laughed together.

"Somehow I don't think she'll ever change," Daisy said. For the first time ever in their whole lives, a beat of cozy sister silence passed. "Now where is Cassandra? We need her help getting you ready. And then we must see that *she's* ready."

"She found a lovely new gown and slippers on her bed," said Perdita.

"Interesting," said Daisy, and left the room with a secret smile.

It seemed that all the women who were now gathered in the ballroom for the *ceilidh*—except for Mona, who was already drunk and sitting in a corner pouting—practically glowed with good cheer, their beautiful gowns giving them the confidence to act like young girls again. The men jostled each other, eyed their newly beautified mates, and looked more lighthearted than Daisy had seen them since her father had died.

As soon as the musicians finished setting up their corner, she knew the *ceilidh* would be a roaring success. The visitors would leave with many fine memories of their Highland experience, and the villagers would be more united than ever.

Anticipation made the room hum with excitement. Peering around heads and shoulders, Daisy looked for Cassandra and Mr. King in the crowd. Although Charlie had warned her that rich, powerful men typically entertained themselves with many women, flirting shamelessly with them and pretending devotion to their every need and want, Daisy didn't want to believe it of Mr. King. She hoped he'd come to care for Cassandra.

The pipes began their droning. The fiddlers practiced a few notes.

The crowd grew louder than ever.

In a moment, Charlie would call the room to order and open the *ceilidh* with her.

But first, where *was* Cassandra? Daisy saw Hester in the corner, speaking with Perdita, who sat docilely in her chair, far away from the action. Next, Daisy swung around and saw the Spanish marquis, at the other end of the ballroom. There was Mr. Woo and every single other visiting gentleman except Mr. King. Joe was ensconced in a group of men obviously talking shinty, as one of them swung an invisible shinty stick.

All the village women were there, including a new mother who looked dazzling in her crisp new gown from Mrs. Gordon's shop.

The footmen and maids were scattered about the room, already serving punch and various savories and sweets. Charlie was speaking to the head musician.

Daisy stood on a chair. She was starting to get a tad worried.

Cassandra was missing. And where was Mr. King?

They weren't in the ballroom. She hastened out into the hall. But there was no butler. The man she'd assigned that position had joined the festivities, and why not? He wasn't a *real* butler, after all.

She went back through the ballroom and through a door leading to the back gardens. No one was there, either, save a young lad and lass from the village. Daisy caught them kissing, and they both drew apart.

The girl gasped. "I'm sorry, Miss Montgomery."

"It's quite all right," she said. "I mean . . . you should probably come inside, both of you." She was beginning to panic. "You haven't seen Miss Cassandra, have you?"

The girl shook her head. "No, I haven't."

"I saw her with Mr. King," said the boy. "Just a few minutes ago."

"Where?" Daisy could hardly breathe. She had no idea why she was panicking. Mr. King was foolish and prideful, but he was also clever and accomplished. She wasn't bad to have hoped for a match between him and Cassandra.

Yet at this moment, she felt as if she'd made a huge mistake—and possibly thrown her half sister to a lion.

"He was walking her to the stables," the boy said. "I caught a glimpse of them as I was coming round the east wing of the castle."

Daisy pushed right past them and ran to the stables.

But when she got there, it was too late.

CHAPTER TWENTY

Something terrible had happened—and was still happening—at the stables. Cassandra lay sprawled on the ground, either dead, injured, or in a faint. A freshly ridden horse stood calmly below a tree, its reins tethered around a branch, while two men fought fiercely near her prone figure.

Daisy's heart stopped. All she could see was Cassandra.

My sister, she thought, *and Papa's daughter.*

"Stop it!" she shrieked at the men, not even aware of who they were. "Don't you see she needs help?"

She rushed forward to Cassandra's side. Luckily, her lips were pink, although her cheeks were pale, and she was breathing. Quickly, Daisy scanned her face, her neck, and her shoulders, relieved to see no visible injuries—yet.

She leaned down and kissed her cheek. "Cassandra," she breathed.

Cassandra's eyes fluttered open. "Daisy," she whispered.

"Are you all right? Do you hurt anywhere?"

Cassandra closed her eyes. "I—I fainted, is all. I'll be all right."

Daisy squeezed her hand, and Cassandra squeezed back.

Tears pricked Daisy's eyes. She wouldn't cry. She needed to be strong, and there were still two ridiculous men involved in a vicious fight that continued unabated not many feet away.

"Back off," Daisy ordered them. Of course, the dunderheads ignored her. "I said, back off! You're too near the lady!"

Still, they continued hitting and pushing each other. As she stared blindly at them, their faces came into sudden focus.

Mr. King was one of the men. He was an expert pugilist, it appeared. He hit the other man in the jaw and sent him sprawling. While the man on the ground groaned, Mr. King stood still for a moment, gasping for air.

"Stop it, please, you two," Daisy said.

"Y-yes, please stop." Cassandra's voice was a mere whisper.

Mr. King said nothing.

The man on the ground rose to his feet, swaying. He pointed down the mountain. "Get out," he said to Mr. King in guttural tones. "And never come back. If you stay, I'll kill you."

Daisy gasped. And not just at his strong words and vehement manner.

It was Mr. Beebs.

Oh, God, Mr. Beebs—the white-haired overseer of the Keep, back a day early!

Mr. King wiped his brow with the back of his arm. "Who are you to speak to me so? You vile rat. The lady and I were merely—"

"Don't you dare mention the lady and yourself in one breath," Mr. Beebs said in a low, threatening tone. "Get out, I say. Get out before I call the constable. You're trespassing on private property. And you've assaulted a lady."

"I didn't assault the lady. A kiss between two consenting adults is not an assault."

"Not an assault?" Mr. Beebs's voice was menacing. "I know what I saw. The lady wasn't at all interested in your so-called kiss!" His chest heaved. "Now do I have to take a whip to you to get you to depart?" He stumbled to the stable door, opened it, and retrieved a whip.

Mr. King spat on the ground. "What insanity is this?" He looked at Daisy.

She merely stared back, shocked at how twisted his features were.

"You said she was fit for a peer's bed," Mr. King sputtered. "Or the bed of someone rich and powerful. I took you at your word."

Daisy felt her face flame red. "I—I was wicked to say that. I wish I never had. I didn't know you'd—"

Cassandra moaned.

"Don't engage him, Miss Montgomery," Mr. Beebs snarled. "He's got no excuse for his behavior.

He's a cur." He snapped the whip in the air. It made a wicked, impressive sound.

Perhaps there was more to Mr. Beebs than Daisy had supposed.

Mr. King backed up a step.

Perdita rushed in and stopped short then, panting for breath. "What's wrong with my sister?" she yelled in her fiercest Highlander voice, which made even Daisy tremble.

"She'll be fine," Daisy assured her. "Please get me a fresh bucket of water and a rag. And bring out several men who can carry her to a soft bed."

"I can carry her myself. And I will clean her wounds myself." Perdita picked her sister up with ease. "Aye, you'll be all right," she said softly.

"Thank you, sister," Cassandra whispered.

As Perdita lumbered toward the Keep with Cassandra dangling from her arms, Mr. King stared after them. "Wait a minute. I recognize her—him. That was the son of a son of a Highland chief. And he was wearing a *gown*." He turned to stare at Daisy.

She took a deep breath. "Her name is Perdita, and she's more a warrior than you'll ever be."

Mr. King narrowed his eyes at her but said nothing.

And no wonder. Mr. Beebs hovered nearby, whip at the ready. "Pack up your things and go," he commanded the American. "You can travel by the midnight sun."

Mr. King felt his bloodied lip, looking first at Mr. Beebs, then at Daisy.

"Huh," is all he said. There was disgust in his tone, as well as some hubris gone terribly wrong.

Daisy knew what that *huh* meant. She knew very well, indeed.

Mr. King walked away, slowly. And when he was out of reach of the whip, he turned. "Don't expect a farthing from any of the bird-watchers," he said. "And none from the anglers, either. I'll be sure to let them all know they've been duped. Highlander, indeed." He gave a bitter laugh. "This whole week has been a joke, hasn't it? What else did you invent to lure rich visitors up here, Miss Montgomery? The avid hunters, the cheery cooks, the bright, happy village . . . was all that a put-on, as well?"

"No," she insisted. "The residents of Glen Dewey may have fallen on hard times, but—"

"There *is* no Highland magic," Mr. King said flatly, and disappeared into the garden leading up to the back of the castle.

Daisy could hear the distant rumble of footsteps and voices, people descending the steps of the Keep and talking in hushed tones.

Her heart sank. The villagers were leaving. The *ceilidh* was no more.

CHAPTER
TWENTY-ONE

As soon as Charlie got the word in the ballroom of a fight out at the stables and a possible injury to a young lady, he rushed to the scene. Only Daisy was there.

"Are you all right?" he asked her.

His whole body tensed for her answer.

She nodded quickly, and he felt a great rush of relief. When he took her hands—what had become to him her very precious hands—he noticed her fingers trembling.

"Are you sure?" he whispered.

She nodded, but there was something still wrong. She didn't quite meet his eyes.

His heart sank. Their talk of this morning . . . it had changed things. He wasn't sure what to do about that. It was why all day he'd been miserable, even as he knew that he'd done his job—their moneymaking scheme was destined to become a great success.

Or so he'd thought.

Mr. Beebs held a whip dangling from his hand. "Miss Montgomery," he said in husky tones. "I'm so sorry I ever brought him here as a guest."

She had no trouble meeting his eyes. "Don't be. You couldn't know what he was like." She hesitated and inhaled a great breath. "Thank you for saving Cassandra. I can't thank you enough."

"You saved her?" Charlie asked Mr. Beebs. "From whom?"

"Mr. King," Daisy interjected.

"Where is he?" Charlie spun to search the grounds for signs of the man's imposing figure.

Daisy laid a hand on his arm. "Mr. Beebs took care of him already."

"So I did," said the man with no swagger. He tossed the whip toward the stables. "Thank God I got here in time."

"The guests—" Charlie began.

"I think they'll leave without paying." Daisy's voice was small.

"I think you're right, Miss Montgomery." Mr. Beebs sighed.

Charlie raked a hand through his hair. "Why didn't I demand half the money up front? What was I thinking?"

Daisy shook her head. "Who'd have imagined this sort of outcome? Don't berate yourself."

But her words were no comfort. He'd let her down. And his grandmother, as well. All because—

The truth was he hadn't taken this whole enterprise very seriously. He'd been more interested in flirting with Miss Montgomery.

Daisy blinked rapidly at Mr. Beebs. "We won't have the *feu* duty by the first of July."

Mr. Beebs winced, his expression most sympathetic. "I'm sorry, Miss Montgomery. I did my best to help you get it."

She sank to the ground and let out one, small sob. "I'll do anything, Mr. Beebs. Anything." She lifted her head. "You know that bird you've been seeking so avidly? Well, I think I found one. I've been keeping an eye out all week. I know exactly where its nest is."

"Do you?"

She nodded. "I'll show you—if you can let us stay another year. We'll hold another Highland venture soon, and we'll get you your money—"

He shook his head. "I can't do that."

Daisy wiped her eyes with a shaky hand. "What if I—what if I put in a good word for you with Cassandra?"

Mr. Beebs froze. "I—I—"

Daisy smiled through her tears. "You're a good man, Mr. Beebs! I wouldn't be lying. She saw you rescue her."

"You can't make someone love another person." Mr. Beebs drew himself up as if he were shocked she'd even suggest such a thing. "No matter how many good words you put in for them."

Daisy shrugged. "I suppose you're right." Her buzzing-bees-and-honey voice cracked. "Oh, Charlie. If only you had your money."

Charlie's chest tightened. This was the real Daisy. Desperate. Willing to do anything—she'd said so herself—to get her home back.

What did he think of her now?

He sympathized with her plight, yes, but he also felt the old wariness creep back in, the suspicion that she was like all the other women who'd dared to get close to him—after money. Property.

Things.

He crouched next to her. "You'll be all right," he said quietly, and looked up at Mr. Beebs. "You won't kick them out of Castle Vandemere, will you?"

Mr. Beebs's expression was grim. "I've no choice. The laird doesn't appear to take the slightest interest in the properties. His men of business handle all legal and financial matters pertaining to the estate. They're sticklers for doing everything by the rule book."

"Can't you contact him?" Charlie asked.

"His people are hefty gatekeepers," said Mr. Beebs. "And in fact, I had no idea who he was until I met my contact in Edinburgh this past week. According to him, he's extremely wealthy and has better things to do, I suppose, than worry about a couple of castles rich in heritage here in the most magnificent part of the country." His tone was wry. "To tell you the truth, by allowing you here, I've been taking shameless advantage of his negligence."

"Who is he?" Charlie asked.

Daisy looked up. "Yes, who?"

Mr. Beebs swallowed hard and cocked his head to the side. "It's you, Lord Lumley."

CHAPTER
TWENTY-TWO

"You don't mean that," Daisy said to Mr. Beebs. She looked back at Charlie.

His face was white as a sheet.

Mr. Beebs nodded his head somberly. "After I found out the news in Edinburgh, I came back as soon as I could to apologize for allowing the hunt party here without your express permission—as property holder—to host such an event."

Charlie lifted up from his haunches and stood staring at the fortress that was the Keep. And then at the stables. And finally, at the turrets of Castle Vandemere in the distance. And ran both his hands down his face.

"Oh, God," he said in a ragged whisper.

Daisy simply couldn't speak. She was so shocked, she felt nothing.

Charlie, in legal possession of both the Keep and Castle Vandemere!

She couldn't believe it.

It was the irony of all ironies. An irony big enough

to shake her out of that dream world she'd been living in with him the past ten days.

She turned to him, her heart in her throat. "You didn't even know these properties fall under your protection?"

His eyes were dark, hooded.

"Well?"

He shook his head.

She found she was clenching her hands stiffly at her sides. "That's outrageous. Simply . . . *awful.*"

His facial expression became glacial. "It never occurred to me that this could be my Scottish property. Why should it have? I'll admit it's shocking to find out this way, but truth be told, I'm not surprised. I accrue many estates."

"How could you neglect a property such as this?" Daisy cried. "What have you been doing the last five years?"

"Living my life the way I want to." Charlie forced himself to sound calm, although he felt anything but. "I've also stayed busy making a great deal of money, so I won't apologize to anyone for the fact that I've neglected to visit."

Daisy's chest heaved. "You sound so . . . spoiled."

He felt wounded to the core by her assessment, considering how much hardship he'd faced getting to Scotland in one piece—and after all the efforts he'd made to help her.

"Perhaps I am," he said. "But I've never brokered an inappropriate business deal. You'd already made a bad move encouraging a match between Cassandra and Mr. King, but how swiftly you volunteered to put in a good word with her for Mr. Beebs so you could remain at Vandemere. It goes against all principle. And it shrieks of opportunistic behavior."

He'd thought he'd loved her. But maybe that had been infatuation. Because now when he looked at her, all he felt was betrayal.

When would he ever learn?

"You talk of principle and opportunism?" Daisy's lips were white. "You may follow the proper rules of business, but you've neglected much higher principles. Castle Vandemere—and the Keep—have been wallowing in stagnation ever since you've taken possession! To collect properties without a care as to what they mean—to the local community, to the history books, to the people who've polished and swept and repaired those places because they love them—is a dastardly crime. And to think that all those times I was cursing the owner of the Keep for neglecting to appreciate it, I should have been cursing you."

Her words flayed him, but she would never know it.

"I rue the day I volunteered to be at your beck and call, Miss Montgomery," he told her. "Now if you'll excuse me, I have an enormous castle to inspect. And a smaller, crumbling one, as well."

He looked at Mr. Beebs. "Meet me in the library with any documents you have verifying my claim to the estate and the accounting books. I want to know exactly how much I pay you and what sort of drain on my income the property has been—it's obviously not generating a farthing."

Daisy stomped her foot. "You find out you're master of this glorious estate, and the first thing you want to do is complain about how little money it produces for you?"

Charlie ignored her. "And Beebs, after our meeting, just"—he waved a hand in the air—"just pack your bags."

Mr. Beebs froze. "Am I fired, my lord? I did allow strangers to stay here, didn't I? I can see how you might have a problem with trusting me to be your overseer."

"Right," said Charlie gruffly. "I'll give you severance and a reference. But it's best that you go."

Mr. Beebs made his way toward the castle, and although his back was straight, he bowed his white head when a bird flew by—which wasn't natural in Mr. Beebs. Most likely the man felt despair.

But Charlie assured himself he'd done the right thing. He couldn't keep on a man who obviously had little respect for him.

Charlie felt like a bloody fool. He'd have to behave more responsibly and then hire someone who didn't know the extent of his negligence.

Daisy turned to him, fire in her eyes. "Look at you," she hissed. "All you care about are things."

He cast her a sideways glance and started walking toward the Keep's front entrance. "Things?"

"Castles. Money." Tears blurred Daisy's vision. "Who cares about the people in them? Or *not* in them, for that matter. All the villagers left here disappointed tonight. Did you even notice? And Mr. Beebs . . . he was trying to be kind, helping me keep Vandemere, so he allowed us to use the Keep."

Charlie kept his eyes straight ahead. "You were the one after property and money, not me."

Daisy felt a stab of pain near her heart. He seemed so removed from her already. He was once again the viscount, the smug, world-weary one who'd appeared on her doorstep in tattered clothing.

"Only because I care about my home—and Joe and Hester," she tried to explain for the umpteenth time. "I wanted to make a life for us that wouldn't rely on the whims of my stepmother. You have no reason to be so angry."

Charlie stopped and looked coldly at her. "Don't you see? Finding out I'm responsible for the well-being of this vast fortress and Castle Vandemere—and that I shirked my duties here—is the most humiliating moment of my life. I've brought dishonor to my family and misery to Glen Dewey."

"Charlie," she whispered. "Neither one of us is bad. Please don't be so hard on yourself. Or me."

His expression was inscrutable. But then he walked on.

"Charlie! Is that all?"

He stopped one more time, no warmth on his countenance. "Stay in the castle for as long as you wish without paying the *feu* duty."

"That's not what I was going to ask." The castle was the last thing on her mind. Daisy prayed for courage. "What about . . . us?"

"What *about* us?" He lifted his chin. "I told you—I'm a rich, bored bachelor. Not to be trusted."

"But I"—her voice was a bit wobbly—"I think I might be in love with you."

There was a long stretch of silence.

Daisy had no idea those words would come out of her mouth, but they had. And she knew they were true.

She *did* know what love was. It was standing by Charlie now, when he was at his lowest ebb. It was giving him the benefit of the doubt, even when he didn't believe in himself. It was wanting to be with him completely and forever.

When she looked at him, she realized love was so many other things. The wave of his hair. His strong jaw and warm, brown eyes. His grin. His smile. His mouth, his laugh, his funny jokes—

And his trying so hard to be a good, honorable man!

"I know you didn't win that sheep-shearing contest simply to avoid losing the bet with your Impossible Bachelor friends," she told him.

"That's exactly why I tried to win it."

She shook her head. "You did it for me, too. You wanted to please me. And you did it for *you*. Because you want to be the man who strives, Charlie. You don't want to be that indolent bachelor with no purpose other than counting your gold coins."

He lowered his brow. "I appreciate your concern. As I said earlier, you may stay in the castle."

How those words hurt!

"You think that's why I said 'I love you,' don't

you?" She gulped back more tears. "You think I want to marry you so I can get Vandemere back for good."

He said nothing at first.

"Well?" she demanded to know.

"You love your home," he said eventually. "And you want what's best for Hester and Joe."

Meaning, she'd do anything—even pretend to profess her love to a wealthy viscount—to possess her childhood home.

Charlie turned on his heel.

Daisy's heart was hammering so hard, she could barely breathe. "You'll never change, will you, Lord Lumley?" she yelled after him. "I don't want your castle. And I have officially absolved you of any responsibilities toward me."

"Don't be ridiculous." He kept walking.

She scampered after him. "It's not ridiculous. It's the most intelligent thing I've ever done. I'll make my way through the world without being beholden to you, your grandmother, *or* your property overseer."

"You're acting impulsively," he replied, deigning to glance her way.

"No I'm not." She brushed by a magnificent rhododendron bush. Her cheeks, she was sure, flamed as brightly as its flowers.

"I'm acting like myself," she insisted, "a Highland lass who loves her family; and a woman who chooses to believe in the goodness of people rather than surrender to cynicism, which is more than I can say for you."

Without waiting for his reaction, she picked up her skirts and ran. She ran all the way back to Castle Vandemere, her eyes streaming with tears.

And when she got there, her beloved lemon tree at the back door of the kitchens was ripped up by the roots and broken in half, the sole lemon to have ever grown upon it stomped into a pulpy mess on the ground.

CHAPTER
TWENTY-THREE

A week later

Charlie stood in front of the Keep and looked out over the glen. Far off, a little dot in the distance, with smoke curling from its chimney, was the modest cottage Daisy was subleasing from a tenant farmer. Mrs. Montgomery, Perdita, Cassandra, Joe, Hester, and all their pigs, sheep, and goats lived there with her.

Charlie liked coming out here each day to check on her. As long as smoke was coming from the chimney, he assumed everything was all right.

Well, as all right as it could be.

He hadn't been over to Vandemere yet to check the condition of the grounds and the actual living quarters. Going there brought back too many painful memories.

He'd hate to see it without Daisy in it. Empty. Hollow. Without the sound of her laughter.

He wondered, not for the first time, how she was

managing to pay her current lease. Most likely, the eleven pounds she'd saved toward the *feu* duty was coming in handy at the moment.

Miserable and out of sorts, the state he'd been in since Daisy had left, he shoved his hands in his pockets and began his daily walk down to the village. Every day since the debacle at the Keep, he'd endured the unspoken question he'd read in the villagers' eyes: why hadn't he gone back to London?

He endured . . . and he ignored.

They were cold to him. He was an absentee property owner who didn't give a fig about their well-being. They felt he was responsible for the Keep's stagnation and, in an indirect way, the derelict condition of Castle Vandemere, even though the residents were supposed to maintain the castle and the grounds. That didn't matter.

He was the laird, and their beloved landmark was in sad shape.

As such, he was going to have to endure their disapproval.

They were also upset about the ruined *ceilidh*. He couldn't blame them for that. They'd been looking forward to some merriment, and a wicked visitor—a guest he should have kept his eye on, as host—had ruined everything.

But Charlie thought they were primarily angry with him about Daisy's moving the family out of Castle Vandemere. No one had liked to see that happen. It had been reassuring to the village to look up the mountain and know the family was there, including Joe with his small flock of sheep on the hillside.

Now the last local tie to the Keep and the castle had been cut.

And it was all Charlie's fault.

Silence greeted him when he entered the new pub.

Gavin MacKee, the owner, barely nodded his head. "We hear you're looking for a new title holder to take your place."

"Yes, I am," Charlie answered him. "With the properties as they are. If I can find someone."

The room was so quiet, no one moved. Not a single man picked up a drink and set it down. Outside, the wind howled and gray clouds scudded across the sky.

It was a miserable day, in more ways than one.

Charlie sighed and looked down at his boots rather than at Mr. MacKee and his customers. *Their approval of you doesn't matter,* he told himself. *You'll be out of here soon and back to your life in London, a bit worse for wear but wiser.*

But then a penny on the floor caught his eye.

It was as good a distraction from the tension bowing his shoulders as any.

Of course he'd pick it up. He was damned rich, but a penny was still a penny. He twirled it on the counter and remembered his lucky penny, the one that had been snatched from him on the way to Glen Dewey.

Without that lucky penny, a fortress and a castle had landed in his lap.

But he'd lost Daisy.

His Scottish grandfather's words came back to him: "Here's your lucky penny. What you see is what you get. Dinnae forget that, laddie."

What you see is what you get.

Charlie looked closer at the penny. It was dull. It had seen many hands. He spun it again, and in the light of the candle, for a brief moment, it became gold.

What you see *is what you* get.

Somewhere in his hurting heart, a flame of understanding lit. It wasn't the luck Granddad had wanted him to hold on to. Charlie now had a sneaking suspicion the old man hadn't believed in luck.

And it wasn't even the penny.

It was the philosophy: how you perceive the world is how the world will be.

If you feel lucky, you'll be lucky.

But if you don't, you won't.

What you see is what you get.

You see betrayal all around you, you'll get betrayal. You see distrust, you'll get distrust.

And if you see love . . .

A picture of Daisy's face swam before his eyes. Daisy, concerned for him. Daisy, being brave and saying she loved him, even when he'd been nowhere near the man she deserved.

He jumped up from his chair and flipped the penny to Mr. MacKee. "Here's your lucky penny. What you see is what you get. Dinnae forget that, laddie."

Mr. MacKee caught the penny handily. "Where

are ye going so fast? You look on a mission of some sort."

I am, thought Charlie, *to get love.* But now was not the time to announce that fact to the world. The getting would take him some planning. Some time.

And a great deal of effort on his part.

"Don't worry," Charlie told the room. "I'll be back to finish that pint. I'm just going down the road to visit the mayor. And Mr. MacKee, the next round's on me." He dug a sovereign out of his pocket and laid it on the bar.

He'd gotten it from the small safe at the Keep, the one Mr. Beebs had used to store money to pay laborers. That pint would be the first thing Charlie had purchased since leaving London.

"Why the sudden change of heart, my lord?" the barkeep asked. "Ye've been so dark and grim."

Charlie nodded. "I have, haven't I? But I've got a lot of work to do. There's no time to be blue."

"What kind of work?" asked one man.

"Fixing up the Keep and Castle Vandemere." Saying the words out loud brought home to Charlie how right his plan was. "I want them sparkling, in tip-top shape, before the Londoners arrive."

"Londoners?"

Yes, why not?

Charlie scratched his head. "I think it's a good idea they get up here before the snow comes, don't you?"

"I suppose, but why are they coming?"

Charlie grinned. "To see the properties, of course."

"I thought you were getting rid of the castles, 'as is,'" said Mr. MacKee.

"I thought so, too," said Charlie. "But not any-more. By the way, I'll be holding a ball after the Londoners get here. A small hunt, too, if the deer are running. You're all invited."

He left the pub then, but not before he heard Mr. MacKee say, "He's a bit crazy, that one."

"But I like him," one of the customers said.

He heard them all laugh in a good-natured way.

Which was why walking down the high street, Charlie began to whistle.

Daisy scrubbed and scrubbed, but the ink stains on her favorite gown—the strawberry-striped one she'd made from the settee—wouldn't come off.

She knew very well Perdita had ruined the dress, just as she'd done a week before with Daisy's lemon tree. Her stepsister had been a holy terror since the night of the *ceilidh,* when the international guests had learned that Perdita's Highlander was a woman dressed as a man.

According to Hester, the Spanish marquis had laughed until he cried. But the other men were highly incensed at being taken for fools.

No longer was Perdita fawning and obsequious to Cassandra and Mona. No, she began to treat them poorly, the way she'd always treated Daisy, at least until that special chat they'd shared at the Keep.

Back at Castle Vandemere the evening of the visitors' rapid departure, she'd vented her spleen on Daisy. "I take back all the nice things I said to you today. Now that the Spanish marquis has laughed at me, I hate you more than ever for raising my hopes about him."

"I'm sorry," said Daisy, and she had been. But it had been difficult to care after the day she'd already had.

Meanwhile, the very next morning, with no money to be had, Daisy convinced her household to depart Castle Vandemere before they were thrown out by Lord Lumley. Gathering up every coin they possessed—and three pairs of candlesticks—they paid six months' rent to a tenant farmer in the glen and moved into Rose Cottage.

Space was limited, so Daisy and Cassandra shared a straw tick in the loft while Hester had her own small palette right next to theirs. Joe slept on a blanket by the fire. Mona had the only private room, which contained a comfortable bed she shared with Perdita.

It was as if Lord Lumley had never appeared in their lives. They were back to the old days but even worse: the worse being not their cramped new living arrangements, which were bad enough, and the precarious state of their future, which was quite slippery, but what was happening with Cassandra.

For the first time since Daisy had known her, Cassandra appeared genuinely sad.

She was done making fun of Hester and Joe. Completely finished with insulting Daisy. Every day, she made a feeble attempt to be rude, but she couldn't quite manage it.

"I'm perfectly fine," she kept saying when Daisy asked.

But it was so clear from her troubled, forlorn gaze that she wasn't.

Daisy didn't know what to do.

The worst was when Cassandra came to her one evening, with tears trickling down her cheeks, to apologize about the trick she'd played on her with Cousin Roman.

"We never talk about it, but we both know we're sisters," Cassandra said. "And when Mr. King frightened me so much, it made me think how afraid you must have been that night when you woke up in Roman's bed."

Daisy acknowledged this was so, but she felt compelled to apologize to Cassandra about her role in the debacle with Mr. King, as well.

"You already said you were sorry," Cassandra said, wiping her eyes. "You told me that day. But the truth was, I *was* willing to marry and bed him because he was rich and powerful. I simply had no idea he was also a very bad man, and that—"

"And that what?" Daisy had asked her.

"Nothing." Cassandra refused to confide in her further. "And it's best we not talk much. Mother will be angry if we're . . . getting along."

"I agree," said Daisy. "Are you all right, though, Cassandra? I mean, I know you know the facts of your birth."

Cassandra rolled her eyes. "I'm *thrilled* that she's not my mother. It's been the only thing that's kept me sane all these years."

And so they went out of their way to ignore each other.

Mona, meanwhile, lounged about the cottage as if she were still ensconced at Castle Vandemere. She was waiting, she said quite frequently, for a turn of events.

"A turn of events," she proclaimed, "that will land us in clover. Daisy"—she never neglected to look at her with narrowed eyes—"don't forget your purpose: you're my companion for life unless you produce more rich gentlemen for me to meet."

Her attempt to lure Mr. Woo to the marriage altar had failed miserably.

Daisy immersed herself in work around Rose Cottage and spent all her free time with Joe and the sheep. Occasionally, she'd steal glimpses up the mountain to the Keep and Castle Vandemere when she pretended she wasn't really looking. But she couldn't resist—something was happening up there. All kinds of work was going on at both places. She even tried to figure out if any of the tiny people she saw moving about up there was Charlie.

"I see you looking up there, Miss Daisy," Joe said one afternoon while fixing his pipe.

She couldn't deny it. When she went to the village, she heard the gossip. Charlie hadn't left for London, as everyone had expected he would. Old Mrs. MacLeod said that try as the villagers might to ignore him, they'd given up because he was employing every man in the village and glen who wanted work.

The biggest gossip in Glen Dewey, Mrs. MacAdoo,

said he was cheerful, as if "nothing in the world were botherin' him."

And Mrs. Gordon confessed to Daisy one day that every woman in the village found him entirely charming.

All observations that both infuriated Daisy and broke her heart into even tinier pieces.

"He's fixing up the Keep and the castle," Mrs. Gordon told her with some satisfaction. "And then he's bringing some Londoners up to see it."

"Possible buyers?"

Mrs. Gordon shrugged. "That's what they're saying."

"And then he'll be gone forever," Daisy said with feeling.

Mrs. Gordon cast a glance at her. "Aye. He just might."

She saved sharing the news with Hester until Mona had gone out with Cassandra and Perdita to the village to sell eggs, a chore which Mona had at first been reluctant to perform but which she'd eventually agreed to—because it meant she could visit with old Mrs. Dingle, a former London lady's maid who was nearly as judgmental as she was.

Hester's face was lined with concern. "And how will you feel about the viscount's leaving, lass?"

"Hmm," Daisy said. "Let me think on this." She tried to roll out some dough for pasties, but she quit and burst into tears. "I'll be miserable. That's what."

Hester put aside her own work, which was making the delicious filling to go with the dough. "Och, it's difficult to be in a houseful of brokenhearted women."

She hugged Daisy close and let her cry for a minute.

"I know Perdita's pining after the Spanish marquis," Daisy said. "But he's long gone. I feel terrible for getting her hopes up about him."

Hester patted her shoulder. "Ye were only trying to help. No, lass, I'm not talking only about Miss Perdita. I'm speaking of Miss Cassandra."

A heavy weight fell on Daisy's heart at the thought of Cassandra unhappy. "I've been concerned about her, too," she said. "I think she's having trouble getting past that night with Mr. King at the *ceilidh*. It must have been traumatic for her."

"Oh, she's weathered that crisis just fine." Hester sprinkled some flour into a bowl. "She's broken up about Mr. Beebs. She gave her heart to him long ago."

Daisy gave a little laugh. Poor Hester!

"Cassandra doesn't fancy *him*," she told her dear friend kindly.

Hester shot her a sideways glance. "Don't get all superior. She does. Every time he rode by and waved at her, she pretended she scorned him. But she didn't. I could tell by the way she'd come into the kitchen, all breezy and free and pleasant. It was the only time she'd ever be that way, and although it lasted only a few minutes, I knew Mr. Beebs had caused it."

Highlanders were awfully forthright. And damned perceptive.

Daisy sighed. "I—I did see her paying attention to him after he saved her from Mr. King, but I thought it was because she was grateful."

Hester nodded knowingly. "It was more than that, and it's cruel to pretend it's not happening. Ye've got to say something to her. Let her air her grief."

"Oh, dear." Daisy bit her lip. "I feel terrible that all this while, Cassandra's been suffering in silence."

Daisy knew how it felt to love someone and then realize it was over. It was a living hell, was what it was.

"Mr. Beebs may be older, but he's not a bad man," Hester reminded her. "You have to let Cassandra fall in love her way, not yours. Or anyone else's. *If* you care about her happiness."

"Of course I do, but it doesn't matter anymore. He's gone."

Hester made a scoffing noise. "He's not gone. He's away, not thirty miles from here. He's managing a property in Glen Muldoon."

Daisy stared at her. "How would you know?"

Hester shrugged. "I'm an old woman with my ear to the ground."

Daisy paused at the small window near the fireplace and looked up at the Keep. She could swear she saw Charlie on the sweeping grassy lawn, looking out over the glen, and he was looking at her little cottage.

"What are you going to do about him?" Hester asked her.

"I don't know," she said with a shake of her head. "I really don't."

"You'll think of something." Hester squeezed her shoulder. "And while you do, I'll ask a man in the village to set off first thing tomorrow morning for Mr. Beebs."

"Will you?" Daisy felt so grateful.

"We've got to get Miss Cassandra happy."

Daisy glanced once more at that little stick figure on the hill in front of the Keep.

If it were Charlie, was he thinking of her?

Or had she already become a distant memory?

She didn't have time to think any more on the matter, however, because Cassandra came running to the door of the cottage, a bright smile on her face and a piece of paper fluttering in her hand.

"Come outside," she said. "Look what Mrs. Skene's son brought by."

"A message from Mr. Beebs," said Joe, hobbling as fast as his legs would carry him. His broad face beamed.

"He arrived back in Glen Dewey today." Cassandra's voice trembled a wee bit.

"He did?" Daisy exchanged glances with Hester.

"Yes," said Cassandra. "He's working up at the Keep again, and he's to come see me in the morning. He says Lord Lumley is perfectly amenable to the idea—in fact, he insists upon it."

"That's marvelous news!" Daisy hugged her.

Hester chuckled. "Oh, I like when a man doesn't need any coaxing to come see his lady love."

Cassandra hugged her, too.

"It's a *braw, bricht* day," said Joe, doing a little jig, which he somehow managed even with his lame foot. *"It's a* braw, bricht *day!"*

"Yes, it is, dear brother," Hester murmured, her cheek still resting on Cassandra's.

Daisy gazed with them, off into the distance, to the moor and the sky and the craggy mountains rising high above the loch.

It *was* a beautiful day, a day which would make even the most despairing woman in love dare to hope for a happy ending, especially when she knows the man she adores has righted a wrong—and has made sure she knows about it!

CHAPTER
TWENTY-FOUR

A month later

Charlie paced about his bedchamber at the Keep; he'd installed himself in the one where he'd shared so many passionate moments with Daisy. The invitations to the *ceilidh* had gone out that very morning. The event would be held three days hence, following two days' hunting with his male guests and some of his good friends in the village.

But would Daisy come?

He had no idea.

She must. She simply must! He wanted her at the center of his life. It was why he'd been working so hard all these weeks, day in and day out. Along with every other able-bodied man in the area, he'd been revitalizing the Keep but spending even more time restoring Castle Vandemere—fixing its sagging drawbridge, cleaning out the smoking chimneys, and rebuilding the crumbling hearths.

He'd done it for Daisy. He'd done it to show her

that he wasn't afraid to lavish his money on things she loved. He would spend money freely because he knew she would love him even if he never fixed Castle Vandemere.

He trusted her, and he loved her.

But how to explain all this to Daisy? How to make her see that he'd changed? He was still the same man—ridiculously wealthy—but he was a *new* man. He'd always known his wealth didn't define him, but he'd also never been sure what *did*.

Now he knew. And he trusted that his actions would show other people what kind of man he was, too.

He could let go of that wall he'd put up between himself and the rest of the world. He could let go and let people in.

Somehow he would prove all this to Daisy at the *ceilidh*.

He wondered if he'd taken too big a risk staying away from her so long. It had tortured him, this separation. What if it hadn't bothered her? Perhaps she'd already forgotten about him.

Not that he'd had much time to dwell on that concern. His guests from London had arrived. His grandmother, God bless her, had made the long trek up to the Highlands. She was Daisy's godmother, she'd said in her return letter to him, and she wanted to see her for herself after all these years.

Several family members had accompanied Grandmother—two of Charlie's sisters and their husbands, as well as their children. And then there were his best friends—Harry, Nicholas, and Stephen. They'd come up with their wives and children, as well. Even Stephen's new baby had made the trip.

The Keep was loud and noisy at the moment. He loved being with people who loved him, people who wanted him happy. And it made sense that when you were taking a massive gamble, you'd surround yourself with people who love you even if you were to fall flat on your face.

"So you're back to spending money like water," Nicholas told him with a chuckle.

They were in the library—just Charlie and his very best friends.

"It needed to be done," Charlie replied. "My parents have restored my access to the family money, now that I've explained that I've . . . matured. I'm drawing funds from a bank in Edinburgh."

"You lucky dog," said Nicholas. "This is a magnificent place. How you could have overlooked it in your portfolio of properties—"

"It's easy when you're as rich as Charlie," Harry said. "You have an entire staff handling everything from business matters to the color of your coats."

Charlie shifted uneasily. "Yes, well, I won't be allowing that to happen anymore. I'm going to be much more hands-on from here on out. It's my life, and I won't have anyone else shape it for me."

"My," said Harry.

Charlie watched as his friends all exchanged surprised glances.

"Why the change of heart?" Stephen asked.

Charlie chuckled. "Because of this journey north. I've had opportunity to, shall I say, reflect."

Harry laughed. "The trip's obviously been full of lots of surprises."

"Yes," Charlie replied.

"So have you solved Miss Montgomery's problem, whatever it is?" Stephen asked.

Charlie took a swig of Joe's fine whisky. "No. Not yet."

"When will you?" Harry asked.

"I hope to soon," Charlie said vaguely.

"What's her problem, exactly?" Nicholas leaned back in his comfortable club chair and waited.

Charlie was dreading this part. "She wanted to raise the *feu* duty for Castle Vandemere so she wouldn't lose her home. That's it in a nutshell."

And then he explained what he knew about the history of the property and how he'd unknowingly acquired it five years before.

Harry shook his head. "So you're the one she owes the money to?"

Charlie nodded, feeling a bit sick to his stomach. "Yes. Neither of us knew that, of course. I was to help her earn the funds."

And then he told them all about the international visitors and the attempt to create a Highland experience for them. "It started off well but turned into a huge disaster."

He told them the details, including the portion

about how Miss Montgomery and her family vacated Castle Vandemere. There was an uncomfortable silence in the room.

Charlie winced. "I told her she could stay, but she refused. And now they're all living in a little cottage in the glen, and I hear they could put down only six months' rent. I have no idea what will happen to her after the lease is up."

The silence went on for a bit longer.

"Well?" Charlie looked around at his friends. Every one of them was brooding, staring at the floor or at his boots or the fire.

Finally, Harry cleared his throat. "It seems to me she's much worse off than she was when you came up here to help her."

Nicholas shook his head. "God, man, this is a disaster."

"A veritable catastrophe," echoed Stephen.

Charlie stood up. "That's not the worst of it." He went to the fire and turned around to face them. "I love her. I love her desperately. And she hates me. I'm almost sure of it."

"Why?" asked Nicholas.

Charlie sighed. "She told me she loved me, and I—I rejected her. I told her I couldn't trust her, that I would never know if she loved me or simply wanted Castle Vandemere back."

"You ass," said Stephen.

Charlie rubbed a palm over his face. "I deserve that," he muttered.

"Yes, you do," Stephen said, "but every man in

this room has been an ass to the woman he loves. So cheer up. We'll help you get through this."

"Right," said Harry.

"With flying colors," added Nicholas. "You'll win her back."

"I already have a plan," Charlie said.

"That's what this is all about, isn't it?" asked Harry. "Rebuilding and inviting us up here. Entertaining us in style and throwing a lavish ball."

"Yes," said Charlie. "It's all to win the girl. But it's funny. If I can get her back, I'm confident it will be on my own merits. Not because of the money."

"That's the spirit," Stephen said. "And that's the kind of girl we want for you, someone who loves Charlie-the-charmer and merely puts up with Charlie-the-moneybags."

"Yeah." Harry rolled his eyes. "The moneybags is a bit sickening, but we'll endure him."

"Right," said Charlie, throwing an unlit cheroot at Harry and hitting him in the forehead.

Harry leaped from his chair and put Charlie in a headlock, which Charlie promptly broke and then pinned Harry to the floor. But then Harry swiped him with a strong leg thrust and rolled away, in the process knocking over an end table with a vase on it—a vase Stephen caught handily.

While Charlie and Harry lay breathless on the floor, Nicholas put his foot on Harry's stomach. Stephen did the same to Charlie.

Nicholas raised his glass, and Stephen followed suit, replacing the vase with his snifter.

"Come on, now," said Harry. "We need to join you."

So Nicholas and Stephen let their two friends stand and take their own glasses to the air.

"To Charlie," Nicholas said. "He lost his bet to us in a very big way."

"Slainte," Charlie said.

And as his friends repeated the toast, he felt a spark of hope.

CHAPTER
TWENTY-FIVE

When the invitation to the *ceilidh* at Castle Vande-mere came, Daisy pulled out a sheet of paper, a quill, and ink to write a reply on behalf of all the residents of Rose Cottage. She noted without surprise that Mona wanted to go, of course. She was still hoping to meet that rich man who'd carry her off.

"I'll never get a better chance," Mona said, "at least while I'm stuck in this godforsaken land. Besides, I'd like to see the improvements the viscount has made."

Daisy turned to Perdita. "Do you want to go to the dance?"

Perdita merely glowered at Daisy and broke a larch twig in half. That was her new job, providing kindling for the fire. Hester had been the brilliant one to come upon that solution to Perdita's tirades. But as big as Perdita's supply of twigs had become—she'd filled five large fish baskets—the practice hadn't seemed to alleviate her general pique one bit.

"Very well," Daisy told her. "You may stay home if you wish. But I think you're foolish to do so. The Spanish marquis isn't the only man in the world."

"He is for me," Perdita said, snapping a particularly sturdy twig.

"Well, nothing's stopping you from writing him then and confessing your true feelings," Daisy replied smoothly.

Perdita sniffed. "I already did. I've received no reply." She broke another twig.

"Where did you send it?"

"To the Spanish Marquis. Castle de Salazar. Spain."

"That's all you wrote as the address?"

"Yes."

"Perhaps it will find him. But it's not been more than five weeks. He's still traveling."

Which was why Daisy had written him herself. The day after he'd left, she'd sent a missive with Benjamin MacAdoo, one of Mrs. MacAdoo's sons, to carry with him on his trip south via horseback. He'd surely overtake the more lumbering carriages of the international visitors. Benjamin had reported back that he had, indeed, met up with the Spanish marquis and delivered the letter himself.

But nothing had come of it, sadly.

Daisy would never let Perdita know.

Cassandra was happily dusting. Mr. Beebs had come round to see her enough times that any day now, Daisy expected a marriage proposal.

"And you, Cassandra?" she asked her. "Do you want to go to the *ceilidh*?"

Her sister turned to her, her eyes bright. "If Mr. Beebs will be there."

"I'm sure he will."

"Will you go?" Cassandra asked her.

Daisy tapped her quill on the edge of the ink pot. "I'm staying behind."

Cassandra's eyes widened. "But why?"

Daisy shrugged and pretended to be indifferent. "I'm not fond of Scottish dancing. All that hopping and leaping and, well . . . sometimes it's simply too much for me."

"Ye know darned well you can hop and leap with the best of us," Hester said.

"I'm sure I could if I wanted to," said Daisy, "but I don't. I'm preoccupied with . . . sewing. So everyone, please leave me alone about the *ceilidh*."

"How's the whisky making going, Joe?" Daisy asked to change the subject, but she was also truly interested.

"Verra well," he replied. Perdita's larch twigs were spilling out of the latest fish basket, and he was stacking them back neatly. But not nearly fast enough to keep up with Perdita. Talk of the *ceilidh* seemed to have riled her more than usual. "Now we just have to wait ten years."

"Ten years?" Daisy couldn't believe it.

"Tha's how long it takes me to make a good batch," said Joe.

She tried not to sigh with impatience. "But we need money sooner."

Joe shrugged. "Whisky's currency around here. We can always fetch the casks in the secret cellar in Castle Vandemere, if no one's found the stash yet."

A thrill went through Daisy. "You never told us there was a secret cellar!"

"A course not," Joe replied. "It were a *secret*."

"Oh. Right." She'd never be able to keep a secret about a hidden cellar!

Hester nodded. "You'll have to steal it during the *ceilidh*, Joe. We meant to take it with us, but Miss Perdita was caterwauling so loud, I couldnae think straight. Och, how I miss her Highlander days. She was a braw, brave lad for one golden week."

Perdita snapped another twig and narrowed her eyes at Hester.

"I like your idea about retrieving the whisky, Joe." Daisy finished writing her reply to the invitation by signing it with a grand flourish. "There."

She leaned back to admire her work and hoped that Charlie would be able to tell by the extravagant loops beneath her signature that she wasn't missing him in the least.

She made one more loop to remind him that he'd crave her company terribly at the *ceilidh*, and then asked Perdita to deliver the note to Mrs. MacLeod, who no doubt would be collecting a whole stack of them for a group of boys to carry up to the Keep later that afternoon.

The very next morning, the residents of Rose Cottage received an unexpected visitor. They knew Mr. Beebs was coming with his usual bunch of flowers. But this time he brought a lovely older woman with him. She was tall and graceful and dressed so fashionably, the humble cottage looked more humble than it had ever done.

"I'll leave you to get to know one another," Mr. Beebs said after he'd made the introductions.

Lady Pinckney tilted her head in a friendly manner and smiled at them all. She had the same eyes as Charlie: a rich, warm brown. "It's a delight to meet you," she murmured.

Daisy curtsied, but she forgot to breathe. She gave a nervous smile but couldn't speak, and her hands grew cold with nerves.

"Your eyes haven't changed," Lady Pinckney said to her. "So expressive they were, even when you were a baby."

"R-really?" Daisy was amazed. "But—"

She wasn't her goddaughter. Cassandra was. She stole a look about the room. Where *was* Cassandra?

And then she caught some movement outside the window and saw Cassandra hand in hand with Mr. Beebs. They appeared lost to the world as they moved through the small garden.

"No buts, Miss Montgomery," Lady Pinckney said. "Now come with me. We have some talking to do. And when we're done, I have something to give you."

"Now just wait a minute," Mona broke in rudely. "This girl doesn't have my permission to leave yet." She looked over Lady Pinckney with a disdainful eye.

Lady Pinckney trained her own intimidating gaze on Mona. "She *will* come with me. Oh, yes, one thing more. You, Mrs. Montgomery, are not invited to tonight's *ceilidh*."

Mona would have gasped, but she was apparently so shocked that she merely gulped.

No one else said a word. Perdita broke a stick in a malevolent fashion but froze in place when Lady Pinckney cleared her throat with authority.

"Come, Daisy." She moved toward the door. "I won't bite, you know." She threw a warning glance at Mona. "Unless highly provoked," she added, then turned her back and glided regally outside.

Daisy followed as if she'd had a spell cast upon her.

At the door, she looked back to see that the room seemed to be under a spell, too. No one said a word. They were still, their eyes wide with either respect, fear, admiration, or hatred, depending upon who they were.

And then she had the sad thought that Charlie must have gotten a great deal of his strong will from his grandmother. She'd bet Lady Pinckney had the same sense of adventure, too, that Charlie did.

Indeed, it seemed that Lady Pinckney was a real force of nature, and Daisy felt rather proud of her connection to her—even though she'd been highly mistaken as to that connection, which was really no longer a connection at all.

The knowledge that all her ties to Charlie's family were broken made Daisy miss him more than ever.

In the fresh outdoors, Lady Pinckney insisted

on taking off her bonnet and walking in the sun. "I like how Highland lasses wear braids and forsake bonnets," she said. "It's perfectly charming."

"I'm glad you think so," Daisy replied.

With a hefty sigh, the lady linked her arm with hers. "What am I to do with you, Daisy?"

"I—I don't know what you mean."

Lady Pinckney laughed. "Of course you do. I want you to come to my grandson's ball. Yet you wrote a note declining."

Daisy bit her lip. "I didn't know you'd be there. Had I known, I would have . . ." She hesitated.

"Accepted?"

They were strolling along a slow-moving burn, the sun casting dots of gold on the water.

"No, my lady." Daisy looked bashfully at her. "I would have declined—but gone in disguise so I could peek at you."

"Pooh," said Lady Pinckney. "You've no reason to hide from Charlie. And please call me Lucy."

"I daren't. You're a lady, my lady."

"I insist. *All* my goddaughters do. Before I was a lady, I was a girl. Just like you. And I still am, beneath all the folderol that goes along with being a member of high society."

"All right." Daisy chuckled. She *adored* the woman already. "But, Lucy, I'm not hiding from Charlie. I love him, actually." She stood still, and felt tears prick her eyelids. "But he thinks he'll never be able to trust me because I wanted Castle Vandemere so badly. It would always stand between us. Did I marry him for a pile of stones I happen to adore—or not? He'd always ask that question."

Lucy pursed her lips. "All his wealth has made him quite defensive. So many women have come after him just for his money, you know."

"I've no doubt," said Daisy. "That's what I wanted from him, too." She picked a leaf off a nearby chestnut tree and folded it, over and over. When she was done, she looked up at Lucy. "But I want him more. *So* much more. I tried to tell him that, but he didn't believe me."

Lucy waved a hand. "If it's love, nothing will keep you apart. It takes the power out of fear. And pride. And all those important objections to being together that turn out to be not so important, after all."

Daisy pondered that a moment. She wasn't sure what to say.

"Look," said Lucy. "I've got you a lovely surprise in a box under the shady tree behind the cottage. I want to be there when you open it."

Daisy was excited, yet scared.

"Be at ease, child," said Lucy. "This is a lovely surprise, and you've been too responsible for far too long. It's time to have fun."

She sat down beneath the tree and patted the ground beside her. Daisy sat, too, and Lucy handed her the box, which she opened with trembling fingers.

Inside was an exquisite ivory gown made of the most luxurious satin with beautiful little embroidered sleeves and gold beads sprinkled over the hem and bodice. It looked as if it had been sewn for a princess. Daisy had never seen a garment so beautiful in her entire life. She pulled it out and held it up.

It appeared to be just the right size.

"You're going to wear this to the ball," Lucy said, "and someone is going to do your hair—I insist—and adorn it with flowers. And then you're going to wear a beautiful pair of slippers Mr. Glass, the cobbler, is making for you right now."

"Oh, my." Daisy could hardly speak. She took a moment to compose herself, then said, "Thank you so much, Lucy. It's the most wonderful surprise I've ever received."

She folded the gown with care and put it reverently back in the box.

"But I can't accept." She bowed her head. "*I'm* not your goddaughter. Cassandra is."

Lucy laughed. "You're both my goddaughters, silly! Didn't Charlie tell you? He thinks I have only seven. But I have fourteen."

"Fourteen?" Daisy barely restrained a gasp.

"Yes, indeed." Lady Pinckney chuckled. "I'm thrilled my little surprise appeals to you. I had it altered a bit, the waist moved up, and a few panels of the skirt removed. It was slightly out of fashion."

"It was?"

"Oh, yes. This dress belonged to your mother."

"It *did*?"

Lucy nodded. "We were very good friends."

Somehow that idea made no sense to Daisy.

"Let me explain," said Lucy. "Your father and I

were infatuated with each other at one time. But we were far too young and interested in life to want to marry, so you know how it goes . . . we went our separate ways. Years went by, and I married, but Barney still hadn't. He had that affair with the actress—you know how that turned out. And then a few months later, he met Catherine, who bowled him over right away. He told me it was a good thing we hadn't married because what he felt for Catherine was bigger than anything he'd ever felt before. He couldn't even express how big. I really didn't mind a bit his saying that because I was desperately in love with Charlie's Scottish grandfather, and I knew just what Barney meant."

Daisy inhaled a little breath and blinked, over and over.

Lucy became a big blur.

"Dear? Are you all right?" Lucy hugged her close.

It was several minutes before Daisy could speak. "This is too much," she eventually whispered against Lucy's shoulder. "I'm simply happy."

She closed her eyes and tried to take it all in.

Lucy squeezed her close, and the affectionate touch helped calm Daisy's jangled nerves.

A moment later, Lucy sighed. "There's something very serious I must talk to you about. I'm shocked at how bamboozled we all were by Mona all those years ago when she adopted Cassandra. Charlie's told me she's been terribly wicked to you. I think after Barney married her and realized her true colors, he was too embarrassed to tell me he'd been so taken in. She needs to leave this place. Immediately."

Daisy sat up. "I wish she would. But, Lucy, I can't let Perdita and Cassandra go with her. Perdita might seem awful, but she's not rotten to the core the way Mona is. I can't give up on her. Not yet. And Cassandra's my half sister. She's come leaps and bounds from what she used to be. I think she'll be marrying Mr. Beebs, so she'll be happily settled."

"You do whatever makes you happy, dear."

Daisy bit her lip. "I've never had anyone say that to me before."

"Well, get used to it," Lucy said briskly. "No more living in Mona's dark shadow. Now will you pull me up? I'm rather stuck beneath this tree!"

Daisy laughed and did just that.

She felt the opposite of stuck—she felt free.

CHAPTER TWENTY-SIX

It was time for the *ceilidh*. Charlie had spent the last two days on a wildly extravagant hunt with his best friends and his sisters' husbands, as well as some excellent friends he'd made in the glen. In his tramps through chilly burns and over rocky terrain, he'd released all his nervousness about his plans to win Daisy back and surrendered to the elements.

A dose of the Highlands was what he'd needed . . . it felt right in his very bones that he was still here in Scotland and working to improve the state of his property and the climate of his adopted village of Glen Dewey.

His heart filled with pride in his new home when he sang along with his hunting companions the well-known verse by Robert Burns:

My heart's in the Highlands, my heart is not here;
My heart's in the Highlands, a-chasing the deer;
Chasing the wild deer, and following the roe,
My heart's in the Highlands, wherever I go.

Every hunter knew he mustn't force, but lure, his target to him. Tonight, at the *ceilidh,* Charlie told himself, he would open his heart, and he hoped Daisy would accept it.

And then he would make her his.

Now his friends and family were gathering for the great event in the hall at Castle Vandemere, which wasn't half as vast as the one at the Keep. But Charlie found it much more inviting, perhaps because he'd asked his sisters and his friends' wives—Poppy, Molly, and Jilly—to decorate the space for him. They'd hung wreaths and stuffed vases with beautiful flowers and made stunning collections of candles that warmed every corner of the room.

But when the party arrived from Rose Cottage, Daisy wasn't among them.

"Where is she?" he asked Joe and Hester.

His female guests hovered behind him. All of them couldn't wait to meet Daisy, who they knew was meant to be his bride—if he could convince her of that fact.

"She's at Mrs. MacLeod's, getting her hair done," said Hester, "and och, she looks so beautiful. Wait until ye see her. Her slippers look like they were made for an angel."

Grandmother smiled. "Mr. Glass says he never sells them to a woman herself. They must be bought *for* her by someone who loves her very much. He asks the buyer to describe this special woman, and he listens with his heart. From there, he makes her a unique design."

"I've got on a pair of Mr. Glass's slippers myself,"

said Cassandra, and pointed her toes. "I've never found out who chose them for me. They appeared on my bed the night of the last *ceilidh*."

All the women from London rushed forward to see them.

"They're magnificent," said Poppy. "And so perfect for you." She flashed a brilliant smile at Cassandra. "I'll tell Nicholas about them right away."

"I must have a pair of Glass slippers, too," exclaimed Molly. "I'll tell Harry. I wonder what they'll look like?"

Charlie immediately told his sisters he'd let their husbands know that they must pay a visit to Mr. Glass's cobbler shop, as well.

Then he leaned over to Cassandra. "Daisy chose them for you," he told her.

Cassandra drew in her chin. "But we hated each other at that time."

"I know," said Charlie. "But she said her papa would approve, and that when she described you to Mr. Glass, she looked at you through your father's eyes as best she could. So in a way, they're from him."

Every woman there got tears in their eyes, Cassandra most of all.

Jilly bit her lip. "They'd be all the rage in London. I'm going to get a pair for my dear friend Otis."

Cassandra tilted her head. "A man?"

Jilly nodded. "But he's not just any man. He'll be able to carry them off. You'll see. You'll have to come visit us."

"Thank you very much for the invitation." Cassandra smiled. "But I'm a Highland lass now. My heart is here, and here I'll stay." Charlie saw her look over at Mr. Beebs, who'd turned out to be not only a very responsible overseer but her hero as well.

When Cassandra disappeared into the crowd, Molly spoke first. "I wonder where Miss Montgomery is?"

"I don't know," Charlie said, and tried not to be nervous.

But it was difficult when he had her ring in his pocket—the one she'd given to Mrs. Gordon to pay for all the villagers' gowns. He'd bought it back. He wanted to propose to her tonight—

If the moment were right.

He had a long way to go before he'd know.

Another half hour went by. The *ceilidh* was well under way, and everyone was having a marvelous time.

Or so it seemed. His friends and family seemed on edge, especially Grandmother.

"She's awfully late," Grandmother fretted, which was rare for her.

"I know." Charlie patted her hand. "I can't help but worry."

One by one almost everyone from Rose Cottage came up to him and said they wondered what was taking Daisy so long.

"Mrs. MacLeod must have had to start her hair over again," said Hester.

"Or perhaps her hem fell," said Cassandra, "and she's repairing it."

But then Mayor MacLeod and his wife arrived—without Daisy.

"Where is she?" Charlie asked them.

Mrs. MacLeod gave a little gasp. "Why, I thought she'd have been here by now. She left a good while ago with her mother and Miss Perdita. They happened to come by the hoose while I was fixing her hair. Said they were going late to the *ceilidh*."

"Mrs. Montgomery wasn't even invited to the *ceilidh*," said Charlie.

Mrs. MacLeod expelled a worried breath. "That's what Miss Montgomery told us, but then Mrs. Montgomery took off for Castle Vandemere with Miss Perdita by her side. And Miss Montgomery said she couldn't let them go alone to wreak havoc among your guests, so she asked me to hurry and pin up the last curl, which I did with all haste. And she went running after them." She took another breath. "Then old Mrs. Buncombe came over and the mayor had to help her retrieve her stubborn cow from the High Street. By the time we'd finished, they'd disappeared among the rocks and scrubby pines up on the mountain."

"What?" Charlie felt his voice grow cold. "They left the road?"

Mrs. MacLeod put her hand to her mouth. "I suppose they did. All the locals know the shortcuts. It never occurred to me to worry."

"They're on the mountain." Fear ran its cold finger down Charlie's spine. Something wasn't right.

"Get all the men outside," he told the women surrounding him. "Tell them we need to find Daisy. I'm leaving now."

And he raced outside. He'd have to do this fast.

If Mona attempted any sort of escape from Glen Dewey after wreaking havoc, there was no one in the village to stop her on her way out—except old Mrs. Buncombe, who was feeble and half blind.

But knowing Mrs. Montgomery, Charlie thought she was so off kilter she might just want revenge— and to hell with escape.

He would check his and Daisy's special spot first. The Stone Steps. They were on the way up the mountain, and if Daisy were in any sort of trouble, he hoped she'd try to make her way there.

And then he thought of the bog.

No. She was too wary to go near it. Thank God for the Highland summer nights and their light. She'd know that copse of trees, and she'd steer clear.

He hoped.

Once she'd caught up with her stepmother and step-sister, Daisy quickly gave up trying to convince them not to go to the *ceilidh*. Neither one was listening to her anyway.

"Ouch," Mona said after a few minutes of bickering with Perdita, and began to hobble.

"We should stick to the road," Daisy said. "You're less likely to get injured."

They'd come to the Stone Steps.

"I'll sit here for a moment," said Mona. "And then we'll be on our way again." She winced. "I think I twisted my ankle."

Daisy crouched before her. "Let me see."

And was suddenly lifted up like a sack of flour

and thrown over Perdita's shoulder so hard, she felt one of her slippers fly off her foot.

"What are you *doing*?" Daisy cried, upside down. The blood immediately began to pound in her head.

"Ssshhh!" Perdita said. "No yelling."

"Of course, I'm going to—"

But Mona wrapped a gag around her mouth so fast, Daisy nearly choked. And when the shrew tied it in a tight knot at the back of Daisy's head, she felt the first stirrings of genuine fear overwhelm her fury.

Mona wanted to hurt her. This wasn't a prank.

Daisy knew this without question.

Perdita strode forward, her grip tight on Daisy's legs, and try as Daisy might to beat her with her fists, she could get no traction as she bounced along. Her flailings didn't make a dent in Perdita's determination to hold her fast.

And then Mona deftly slid a noosed rope over her hands and pulled it tight, effectively tying her hands behind her back.

Daisy did her best to scream with the gag, but the sound was muffled and came out weak. No one at any distance would hear her.

She bucked and writhed, but Perdita merely held her tighter and kept walking.

Daisy was getting dizzy. Spots of red and black appeared before her eyes.

"Hurry," Mona hissed at Perdita. "We've only a few minutes before the sun goes down."

"I'm hurrying," Perdita said. "Why can't we just kidnap her and sell her as a slave?"

A slave?

"I know what I'm doing," said Mona. "A slow death by bog will give me great pleasure. And there will be no evidence."

All Daisy could see was down. And below her, the ground turned from grassy and rocky to bracken covered. And then there were tree trunks.

This was the copse not far from the Stone Steps. The one with the dangerous bog.

Binney's Bog.

Daisy kicked and screamed to no avail.

Mona laughed. "You're angry. Well, now you know how I feel. For twenty years I've endured you, and I've had enough. Hurry, Perdy. If we're going to make a run for it, you've got to do this fast. I'll wait for you in the village."

"No!" cried Perdita. "Aren't you coming with me?"

"I said I'll wait for you," Mona said through gritted teeth, and left without even saying good-bye.

Perdita hurried, which meant Daisy was scratched by twigs and branches. It got darker and darker in the woods. Finally, Perdita put her down. Daisy's chest heaved as she tried to inhale through her nose.

Don't panic, she told herself.

Perdita was breathing hard, too.

Daisy blinked over and over. "Please," she tried her best to say. "Please." And then she looked down at the gag on her mouth.

"You want to talk?"

Daisy widened her eyes and jumped up and down.

"I'll let you say one thing," Perdita muttered, "but that's only because a prisoner usually gets one last chance to say something. I read that once."

She looked away from Daisy and gave what sounded like a snort. And then suddenly a series of sobs erupted from her homely face. "Daisy, I don't want to do this. But I'm scared she'll kill me if I don't. I'm *scared* of her." Tears streamed down her cheeks. "If I let you talk, do you promise not to yell for help?"

Daisy nodded her acquiescence.

Perdita stuck her finger between the gag and Daisy's cheek and pulled the cloth away from her skin for a brief second.

"The Highlander would never do something so cowardly," Daisy said quickly.

Instantly, Perdita scowled. "I'm no Highlander. Just ask the Spanish marquis. He hates me for pretending to be one. And it's all your fault."

She tightened the gag, and now Daisy was the one to cry.

Perdita took a moment to wipe her nose on her skirt, then suddenly her shoulders sagged, her anger forgotten. She turned to Daisy. "There's one last thing I have to tell you. I'm sorry I burned down your mother's bungalow."

Daisy felt a jolt run through her, causing her knees to buckle. Perdita had caused the fire—and not she?

"Even Mother and Cassandra don't know I'm responsible," Perdita said in a whisper that was loud enough to bounce off the trees. "You left it darkened, and then went inside to play cards with Roman and Cassandra. And I decided to go out there to cut up the dresses you'd made. I had to light a candle to do it. But one dress caught on fire, and then everything went up in flames. It was an accident, and I'm sorry. Not because you lost your dresses and the bungalow, but because I know I"—she let loose with a sob—"I'm the one responsible for your father's death. He was a good man. And I'm bad."

Daisy inhaled a breath as best she could through the gag, but the shock of Perdita's news made her limbs tremble violently.

She hadn't caused the fire.

She'd been carrying a burden of guilt so heavy that it had crushed a part of her heart, making her afraid to love again, and it had all been so unnecessary.

Dear God, how could this be?

Tears sprang anew to her eyes, but they were tears of relief. She already knew she'd not been responsible for winding up in Roman's bed. That had been Cassandra's doing.

It was an astonishing revelation that Cassandra and Perdita, each in their own way, had unwittingly set the tragedy of her father's death in motion. And neither one had known what the other was scheming—not until it was too late.

But Perdita was sobbing once more, and Daisy had to get through to her.

She nodded her head. "It's all right," she tried to say. But her words were completely garbled in the gag.

"Perdy!" From somewhere below them, Mona's demanding voice called, "Are you done up there?"

Perdita hesitated only a second. She picked Daisy up and then—

Daisy kicked. Her other shoe flew off somewhere in the bracken.

And then Perdita gave a mighty heave-ho, and Daisy was flying . . .

Flying into the bog, where she landed with a mighty squishing noise faceup, thank God. There was a burbling of peat and water around her and the sensation of sinking into cold, mushy nothingness. She heard Perdita crashing through the woods, and she looked up and saw the pale white summer night above the branches overhead.

She was alone, and she was sinking, being sucked beneath the peat.

But before she could register that horrible fact, Perdita came crashing back again, this time toward her, and she was bellowing, "Hold on, Daisy! I'm coming to save you!" in a hopeful, noble voice—

As if she'd never been the one to dump her in the bog in the first place.

Perdita shoved the end of a branch at her, which Daisy couldn't grab because her arms were tied behind her back. So Perdita angled the scrawny limb and then she was caught, just like a trout, her sleeve snagged by a knobby part of the wood that jutted out almost like a hook.

She hung there, moaning and crying, and watching the gray shape that was Perdita apologize for being so cruel to her.

"I *am* the Highlander," Perdita said, holding firmly to the branch. "I hate Mother and her wicked ways. She may kill me, but I can't do this. You don't deserve to die, Daisy."

It was some few minutes that she spoke, genuinely whispering for the first time in her life words of comfort and sorrow and shame that she'd been so stupid and wicked. And then her words melded into more gray forms that were shouting and crashing through the woods. And just when Daisy heard Charlie's voice cry, "Daisy! Is that you?" she let her eyes close and the sound of his voice carry her into a sweet, black nothingness.

CHAPTER
TWENTY-SEVEN

The hot bath had restored a healthy glow to Daisy's cheeks. Now she lay in her old bed in the left turret at Castle Vandemere, safe and warm, bundled up and sipping a steaming mug of whisky punch Hester had concocted for her.

Charlie couldn't believe how close she'd come to being taken away from him.

"You'll stay here," he said, doing his best to sound stern. "No going off to Rose Cottage."

She gave him a tentative smile. "All right. I'll stay in my room one night, and then go back."

Not if he could help it.

The *ceilidh* had disbanded—again. His family had returned to the Keep. He was here alone with her, except for Hester, knitting in her old kitchen, and Joe, who was busy putting back all the whisky from the secret cellar he'd removed not an hour before. Charlie told him he wanted everyone to return to Castle Vandemere and so there was no need for Joe to confiscate it in the first place.

Charlie pulled Daisy's new slipper out of his coat. "Here," he said, feeling awkward. "I found this at the Stone Steps."

Daisy sucked in a breath. "Mr. Glass's slipper. I kicked the other one off by accident, before Perdita got me to the bog."

He chuckled. "We'll find it in the morning, you can be sure of that."

"Thank you."

Her expression was drawn, and she was so quiet. So meek. It worried him.

He cleared his throat. "I'm glad you changed your mind and were planning to come to the *ceilidh*."

Her smile was tentative. "Your grandmother—my godmother—came to visit me. She brought me a beautiful gown"—her eyes filled with tears, and he took her hand and squeezed it—"that my . . . my mother once wore."

Charlie held on to her hand. "Grandmother told me the story. And she showed me the gown. I'm so sorry it was ruined."

Daisy wiped a tear away from her eye with her free hand. "I'm sad about the gown, but it saved me, in a way. My sleeve got caught on the branch Perdita was using to prop me up. It was like a hook, and I was the fish. A very grateful fish."

"You always were the fish I wanted," Charlie told her.

"Yes, Mona tried to tempt you with more elegant fish that day we ate the trout we caught together, but you were stubborn."

He grinned, and she grinned back.

A little.

Actually, not very much.

He suppressed the feeling of panic that swelled in his chest and contented himself with the knowledge that she hadn't released his hand.

He mustn't be selfish. She'd just been through a horrible trauma. He shouldn't expect to see her happy grin so soon after.

But the truth was, her happy grin was what he lived for.

He wanted her to be his lover and his wife, his companion and his very best friend. And he wanted her to know all this . . . but was it the right time?

Or a very wrong time?

She sat quietly watching him.

"So you liked the slippers?" he asked her.

She nodded. "They were exquisite. And such a gift. It's uncanny how well Lucy knows me—even though she hasn't seen me since I was a baby."

Charlie took a deep breath. "*I* commissioned those slippers."

Daisy's eyes widened, and she pulled her hand out of his. "You?"

"Yes," he said. "I bought them for you. With money."

"That's the usual way you buy something," she said pertly. "Oh, unless you're in the Highlands. And then you can buy things with whisky. That's what Joe says."

This time her grin was definitely a grin.

"I was too green to know that," Charlie replied, his heart warming. "And even if I had, I wouldn't have done it. I wanted to use money. I wanted to lose the bet I made with my friends in London."

"The bet," Daisy murmured. "You aren't supposed to use money, especially to help Lucy's goddaughter."

"Yes, I know. Because if I do, I'll be thrust onto the Marriage Mart."

"Poor you," Daisy said, some of her old sparkle reemerging.

He pulled a tendril of hair off her face and tucked it behind her ear. "You see, there's this girl I love. And I was very *afraid* to love her, even though she's the most perfect girl in the world."

"She is?"

"Oh, yes. Perfect for me. But I was hiding behind a silly mask—the mask of the misunderstood man of wealth—and I was using it to avoid facing the truth."

"What *is* the truth?" Her face was so close to his, her breath warmed his cheek.

"The truth is," he said, rubbing her shoulders, "that I was afraid I was worth nothing beyond my riches. But it was easier to blame the opportunists who longed to pilfer my wallet than to blame myself for allowing my life to mean nothing."

She nodded.

"Remember you asked me what kind of man I was?"

"Yes, I do."

"At the time, I really didn't know." She reached

up and stroked his cheek with her palm. He grabbed her hand and held it over his heart. "But I know now. It's why I'm rebuilding Castle Vandemere and the Keep. I'm building a life for my perfect lady and me, right here in the Highlands. I'm no longer afraid she won't love me without my riches. I know she loves who I am, the man who is poor without her."

"Charlie."

They kissed—a sacred, wondrous kiss. Her lips were soft and warm, a haven for his hungry soul.

Just as he'd wrapped her in his arms, a droning began beneath the turret window. It was like a swarm of sleepy bees buzzing out of tune.

Daisy pulled back, a question in her eyes.

"I told three pipers to stay," he whispered. "You haven't forgotten *The Legend of the Two Lovers at the* Ceilidh *on the Last Night of the Hunt,* have you?"

She shook her head, her eyes bright.

He got down on one knee next to the bed and pulled her father's ring from his coat pocket. "Darling Daisy, I love you with all my heart and soul. I long for you to do me the great honor of being my wife, to have and to hold for the rest of my life, with many of those years spent right here at Castle Vandemere with the children and grandchildren I hope to share with you. Will you marry me, my Golden Girl?"

"Oh, yes, my Golden Prince," she said softly, tears in her eyes.

His heart nearly burst with happiness at her answer, and he slid the ring on her finger.

She stared at it, her mouth agape. "Papa would be so happy!" she finally said. And then she laughed and wriggled up through the bedclothes to her knees and flung her arms about Charlie's neck. "I love you to pieces," she said with the grand abandon he'd come to cherish.

And when their lips met again, the poignant, wild notes of "Will Ye Go, Lassie" floated up to them on the brisk mountain air, a Highland song celebrating a *braw, bricht* love—the kind that lasts forever.

EPILOGUE

Christmas 1828

"*Now?*" Charlie whispered in his wife's ear.

It was half past twelve a week before Christmas.

"Tell me when we're going to get another chance," Daisy whispered back. "The weather's been so fine, tonight I'm sure all the guests will arrive." She beamed round the long plank table situated in the cozy kitchen at Castle Vandemere, where they took their noon meal. "Davy, you, Padric, and Duncan will chop down the mistletoe."

"Yes, Mummy," said Davy.

Daisy absolutely refused to let her children call her Mother. She'd made the decision to be the *informal* mistress of a charming Scottish castle.

Davy scooted back his chair and tipped his chin to his brothers. "If either of you dares throw a snowball at my back, I'll rub your faces in it. Promise not to?"

Padric and Duncan exchanged a wicked glance. "We promise," Padric said.

"Me, too," echoed Duncan.

"No making promises unless you mean to keep them," Charlie interjected.

Padric's brow furrowed. "All right, then, Davy. I take it back."

"Me, too," Duncan said once more.

Daisy and Charlie exchanged dry glances.

Davy narrowed his eyes at his brothers. "I won't let you shake the mistletoe down if you're going to be that way."

"Is that right?" said Padric. "Just try to catch me. I'm going to beat you out there."

"Me, too," said Duncan.

It was all he ever said. Every day, Daisy hoped he'd say more.

All three boys bolted from the table.

"Boys!" called Charlie, and the three of them stopped as one, hurried back to the table, and the two older ones said in unison, "Delicious dinner, Mummy. May I please be excused?"

"Excused?" added Duncan, after the fact.

Daisy and Charlie exchanged a secret, happy glance, then Daisy returned to Mummy mode. She knew that if she mentioned Duncan's triumph to him that he would be mortified. So she simply nodded graciously, and they took off like a shot again.

"Now be nice to each other!" she called after them. "And don't go out without your scarves and mittens!"

Two hasty *Yes, Mummy*'s followed.

Duncan was silent, as usual.

But . . . he was improving. Daisy was so glad for that.

She turned to the girls. "Meg and Laurel, you're in charge of Kathleen and Elizabeth. Take them to the attics, please, and allow them to help you bring down the Christmas boxes. They're big enough girls now."

Kathleen gasped with pleasure. Elizabeth laughed and clapped her hands.

"Don't you dare break anything," said bossy Laurel to her two younger sisters.

Meg patted Laurel's hand. "The way you did last year?"

Laurel blushed. "I—I forgot about that."

Charlie arched one brow at Daisy.

She gave a little chuckle.

Their children provided them with endless entertainment. But they were also a handful, as children tended to be.

Daisy and Charlie had a pact, that no matter how many children they had—and seven in seven years seemed quite a lot—they would never, *ever* stop whispering sweet nothings in each other's ear and keeping their marital bed warm.

It was a challenge, but having a love nest helped.

"Shall we?" Charlie held out his arm to his wife.

Daisy took it. "Yes, my dear."

"Where are you going, Mummy?" asked Elizabeth. She had very sharp ears as blindness had made her sensitive to every sound.

Daisy refused to feel guilty about leaving her

youngest daughter in the care of her big sisters. "Your father and I have some catching up to do. Won't you enjoy being the big girl while we're gone?"

Elizabeth nodded, grinned, and sucked her thumb. Kathleen yanked Elizabeth's thumb out of her mouth.

And Elizabeth popped it right in again.

As they ascended the stairs, Charlie snorted. "The ones that act like you suck their thumbs to win us over."

"And the ones that act like *you*," Daisy said, "are quite bossy and don't try to win us over at all."

Charlie chuckled and linked his arm through his wife's. "But I love each one of them deeper than I ever imagined I could. I'd lay down my life for every one of those little mites."

Daisy sighed. "Me, too." She smiled as she recognized Duncan's favorite phrase, and her breath caught. "I—I can't wait for tonight. Can you? I'm a bit nervous. I always get this way."

Charlie nodded and patted her hand. "I know. But every time it works out. Love makes that happen."

Daisy's heart warmed. "The same way you and I came together."

"Exactly. Who ever thought we would?" He opened the door to their bedchamber, Daisy's old turret room. A distinct gleam lit his eye. "Enter, my wanton mistress, and I shall lead you to our love nest."

Daisy grinned at him. "I look forward to it, my lord. And may I say yet again that I think you were a genius in your renovations of Castle Vandemere?"

"Yes, say it as often as you like. I never grow tired of hearing of my brilliance." Charlie's kiss was as ardent as ever.

And the joy they shared over the life they were creating together added another level of satisfaction to their lovemaking, leaving no room for familiarity to dampen their enthusiasm for each other.

Daisy's heart immediately quickened when Charlie's capable hand caressed her waist and moved to her breast. Her husband was her respite. The one who gave her strength when she was depleted.

He was her one, true love.

And as for Charlie, he loved Daisy more and more each day. She'd made him fully a man.

Without her, he was nothing.

Slowly, they made their way across the room, kissing all the while. Charlie reached behind his wife and twisted the knob to the closet door.

Locked, of course. No one other than they had ever seen inside.

Sighing with pleasure—Charlie was kissing the pulse point on her neck—Daisy reached out to a nearby shelf without looking, grabbed the key, and placed it in his hand. They nearly stumbled across the threshold, but it was their love nest, after all, and they knew every little thing about it.

Once inside, they broke apart and Charlie locked the door again, Daisy behind him and holding on to his belly all the while and rubbing wide circles over it with her palms. When she moved her hand lower, Charlie laid his head on the door and let out a pleasurable groan before he turned to her.

"Minx," he said, his voice hoarse with need. "Attacking me while I'm securing the door."

"It's why you never let *me* secure the door. I think you quite look forward to my little attack."

"I confess you're right," he said, and immediately began to disrobe her.

She was untying his cravat when their bedchamber door was flung open.

"Mummy! Daddy!" It was Davy's voice. "I see the visitors! They've arrived in Glen Dewey!"

"Where are they?" asked Padric. "I could swear Elizabeth said they went upstairs."

"I think they must have gone outside," said Davy. "Let's check the bungalow first. Mummy's probably showing Daddy her new Christmas gown. And then we'll count all the carriages again."

Three pairs of feet could be heard running down the stone stairs.

Neither Charlie nor Daisy said a word for a moment.

"I always tell them to knock," Charlie said with an exasperated sigh. "I really must get that lock repaired."

"When have we had time since the children have arrived? It's why our love nest is more valuable than ever," Daisy replied with a giggle, and continued her disrobing of Charlie.

"Wait," he said, staying her hand with a kiss to her fingertips. "Should we?"

"Why not? The girls are probably outside, too. No doubt they're all jumping up and down and yelling down to Glen Dewey, as if anyone can hear them. And the horses must rest before coming up the slope."

The two lovers and best friends looked at each other.

"I need this, darling," Daisy whispered, her palms on Charlie's chest. "For the rest of the month, things will be lovely—but crazy. And you never know. If the snow is horrendous, everyone could be here for another month. Or two."

She nearly shuddered. Charlie didn't look thrilled at that prospect, either.

"I adore everyone, of course," Daisy said in sincere tones.

"As do I." Charlie pulled her close and grinned. "But I adore when it's just us even more."

Daisy brightened. "If we're snowed in, at least we'll have plenty of room if everyone gets restless. The guests can always move to the Keep."

"Fine plan." Charlie kissed her temple and nuzzled her ear. "The Beebses will no doubt come to the rescue."

Daisy lifted her neck to luxuriate in his kisses even more. "Of course they will. And they'll be here tonight."

Daisy loved living next door to Cassandra and her husband, whom she'd grown to love as a brother, the same way she loved Cassandra as a true sister.

"Right," said Charlie with spirit. "We have it all worked out. Now, it's time for our own private celebration of . . . things to come." He made a wry face. "In case Harry is anxious to get here, we'll have to make it short."

"But sweet," Daisy added.

"Ah, love, it's always sweet with you." Charlie's enthusiasm always undid her.

He pulled at her laces.

She worked on his breeches.

Eventually, they stood together naked, their bodies pressed together, heat rising between them.

"No time for besotted gazing," Charlie murmured. And lifted his bride in his arms. He walked a few short feet away to the only object in the tiny room—situated beneath the stained-glass window of the Golden Prince and the Golden Girl, which used to adorn the drawing room until Charlie had it moved.

Gently, he lowered Daisy to a cozy feather tick on the floor. The bed was covered with beautiful silken pillows. She laughed as he lowered her, which made him laugh—and then she pulled him right on top of her and rolled beneath him to her belly.

"This way," she said. "It never fails to delight me."

Their earlier days, when they'd been forced to share a room at the Keep and Charlie had kept to his promise not to ruin her completely, had given them a confident enthusiasm for pleasuring each other in all sorts of ways.

When Daisy spread her legs beneath him, her beautiful rear end providing the sweetest cushion for his loins, Charlie felt lust and love for his wife harden the length of him. He kissed her shoulders, her spine, and worked his way down to her feminine core.

Then with great relish, he kissed her.

She lifted her hips as her moans of pleasure increased.

"Your mouth feels delicious, but the other way, darling," she said in a hoarse whisper. "Now. Please."

"I won't object to that," he said, dizzy with wanting her.

When he knelt behind her and allowed the tip of his manhood to tease her, she threw her arms out, the same way she'd done so many years ago on the Stone Steps.

He adored knowing every move she'd make. She was his.

His.

And he would make her his again. Right now.

"More, Charlie. Please." She wriggled her rear to bring him closer.

How he wanted more, as well! Pivoting his hips, he plunged into her, all the while caressing the feminine pearl he knew so well.

Daisy closed her eyes, reveling in the wondrous pleasure Charlie was giving her, and found she couldn't speak anymore. The pleasure built, bathing her in waves of intense gratification, the kind only Charlie could bring her.

She was here. Now. Nowhere else in her mind. She'd learned to let go . . . to be at ease—to believe she deserved all good things—thanks to Charlie's skills as a lover and his devoted attention to her as her husband and best friend.

As their bodies collided in a lush, primal dance, all Daisy's current motherly worries and cares slipped away like magic. All the old fears had long since passed, as well, especially as Mona was in Italy, in a lovely private house that catered to people with disturbed minds.

Charlie had seen to that. Daisy had told him she couldn't bear to think of the harridan in prison. But neither could she let Mona walk the world alone, and either do to others what she'd attempted to do to Daisy, or flounder without a roof over her head and food in her belly.

No. Things were wonderful here in the present. Even more wonderful than Charlie knew.

She grasped the silken pillows and let her dearest companion make her his own. The fingers of his right hand wooed her, driving her mad with longing.

"Come with me, my love," he murmured.

Those words sent her into the realm of utter bliss. She let herself cry out, a lengthy cry of satisfaction matched only by Charlie's own.

Seconds later, without releasing her from their carnal bond, Charlie leaned down and kissed her neck.

"Mmmm." Daisy smiled, her eyes closed. "That was perfect."

"It's your day," Charlie said. "Always." And gave her the tiniest slap on the bottom.

She rolled over instantly, and pulled him down. "It's *your* day, too."

"I've never gotten used to that fact, either," he said, gratitude and love shining in his eyes.

Daisy bit her lip. "I have something very important to tell you, Charlie Thorpe. It's one reason I wanted us to be together . . . before everyone descends upon us."

"Oh?" Concern lit his eyes. "Is everything all right?"

She gave him the sweetest smile in the world. "Yes, it is. Better than all right. We're going . . . we're going to have a baby."

Charlie laughed and kissed her. "I know that, dear. But I don't blame you for announcing it. It's always a miracle, isn't it? Although he's not a brand-new baby. He's a year."

"And he's from Cheapside, like Davy." Daisy wiped away a tear. "I can't wait to meet him."

"Nor I." Charlie chuckled just thinking about it. Every time a new son or daughter entered their family, he was thrilled, so thrilled he teared up upon first gazing at their precious faces.

They were his sons and daughters of the heart.

Of his soul.

As close to him as any child born of his loins could ever be.

Daisy bit her lip. "But Charlie, we're going to have a baby"—she hesitated—"in say, about seven months from now."

She looked up at him, and he drowned in the love, hope, and the bit of anxiety he saw there.

"Oh, my dear," he whispered. "Can that be? After all this time?"

She blinked back tears. "I know. I can't believe it, either."

"You'll be fine, darling. And so will our baby."

She sighed. "I was positive it would never happen. But"—she smiled—"apparently, it was meant to be, after all."

He bestowed a tender kiss upon her lips. "Our family was meant to be. Just the way it is."

"Yes," Daisy whispered, and laid a palm on his cheek.

He pulled her into his arms and stroked her hair. She clung to him, and they lay together a few silent minutes, relishing their bond and the precious children who were now a part of it and those who soon would be.

"I suppose we should get up now," Charlie said, "but I can't regret it. We're about to meet our new son."

Daisy sat up, excited. "I can't wait. And I also can't wait to see the other Impossible Bachelors and their wives and children."

"Don't forget Perdita and her Spanish marquis," Charlie said.

Daisy still couldn't believe the Spanish marquis had returned to Glen Dewey, the very next day after Perdita's assault on Daisy.

Perdita had roared at him to leave, saying she was a no-good, wicked woman who deserved to die for nearly killing her stepsister. But the marquis wouldn't leave. In fact, he'd said he wanted to take her on a hunt—their own private hunt, with Perdita in her borrowed kilt—to discuss the matter. By the time they'd returned with the eight-point buck Perdita had shot, they were engaged to be married.

They visited every two years. Last time, they'd

brought them Duncan, when he'd just turned two. He'd been the son of a former maid at the marquis's castle, a woman who'd run off and simply left him stranded there.

"Thank God Perdita and the marquis were part of that disastrous first Highland experience," Daisy said. "If they hadn't been, we never would have known our son."

It gave her shivers to think how close they'd come to missing out on that chance!

"Dunk's getting closer, isn't he?" Charlie said. "Saying 'Excused' after the noon meal. He's feeling more like one of the boys."

"Oh, the little dear!" Daisy's heart warmed at the thought of him. "Although I will never allow him to forget his native tongue. I'm learning it myself"— she leaned down and stroked the hair back from her beloved's temple—"*querido*."

Charlie accepted her caresses with the ease of a man who believes he deserves happiness and doesn't question it . . . his masculine sense of entitlement still made her laugh.

He opened one eye. "And *querido* means?"

"Dear one. Dear one who longs to take a nap," she amended, "as he always does after he's had a particularly passionate round of loving." She smiled, leaped up, and began to shimmy into her gown. "Just think. I can borrow all the clothes Cassandra wore when she was with child. But I'll also sew myself a few very special gowns of my own."

"Excellent," Charlie said, raising himself up on one elbow. "You deserve those new gowns."

She slanted a pert gaze at him. "I know. And *you* deserve a late night with your friends in the library and billiards room this evening. Please take it, darling. The ladies and I will have a marvelous time of our own catching up. And I must confess, I'm getting rather tired at night. I'll not be up late. Of course, the other women will understand when I explain the reason."

"Who's going to watch all the children?"

"Perdita's nanny."

"Very good." Charlie stood up, too, and put his hands around Daisy's waist. "I'm the happiest man on earth," he said.

She kissed him and allowed him to cherish her by letting him tie her laces.

A loud clamoring came from outside. Yells of delight, the rattle of carriages, and stomping of horses' hooves.

"They're here," Daisy exclaimed, licking a thumb and pushing the hair off her temples while Charlie went even faster with the lacing.

He then hopped into his breeches, tucked in his shirt, and threw on his coat. "Let's go."

"Otherwise, they might guess what we've been up to."

One last kiss, and then moments later, they were on the drawbridge with Joe and Hester. They both waved madly as the retinue of carriages drove up.

Daisy's heart hammered beneath her gown. Their new son was in one of those vehicles.

"Oh, it's a wonderful moment," Hester murmured.

"Aye," said Joe. "Another shinty player for the family team."

Charlie squeezed Daisy's hand. "Gather round, children!" he called to their brood.

They all raced to their parents' sides.

The hired drivers sat stoically in their seats as the travelers stepped out of all the carriages but the first one.

Daisy was fit to be tied.

She loved all these people, but—

Where was that baby?

After what seemed a lifetime, Stephen and Jilly emerged from the first carriage with Jilly carefully carrying a bundle of tartan in her arms. She locked gazes with Daisy, and both of them teared up at the same time.

"Your new son," Stephen called to Charlie, his voice a bit rough around the edges. "He's here to have the Highland experience."

Everyone chuckled nervously.

It was as if time stood still while Stephen and Jilly carried the bundle over to Charlie and Daisy, a trail of visitors following behind quietly, everyone carrying the strain of long-distance travel around their eyes, even the children. Yet every person present wore expectant, happy expressions.

"Your son," said Jilly with a certain reverence. With great care, she handed the tartan-wrapped bundle to Daisy, who got her first glimpse of her son's tiny, perfect face. Charlie put his arm around Daisy's shoulder and took in his son's remarkable visage, too.

Then he and Daisy looked at each other.

Dear God, he was a miracle!

And in that moment, the magic began its work. Love drew the family together around the new baby son, baby brother, baby cousin—

And baby nephew to all his honorary uncles.

"Welcome, Barnabas," Daisy whispered to him.

He looked up at her with solemn eyes.

"B-Barney," piped up Duncan, and tugged at the tartan plaid blanket.

Charlie's face split into a grin. Daisy gave a hiccupping laugh. "Oh, my dear ones," she said to everyone around her. It was all she could think of to say.

But it was enough.

She looked up and saw Cassandra and Ebenezer appear, striding happily around the byre, their oldest child, a girl, tagging alongside them, and their little boy on Cassandra's hip.

Daisy gave Barney to Charlie. He stared at him a moment, then held him carefully aloft. "Look who's here," he called to Cassandra and her family.

Cassandra's face was bright with joy, even more than usual, and Ebenezer beamed. Their little one, Dirk, had his entire hand in his mouth and appeared to have just woken from a nap.

Nicholas and Harry stepped forward, both accompanied by their respective wives, Poppy and Molly, who smiled broadly at Daisy, even as they wiped their eyes with lovely, bright lace handkerchiefs.

Nicholas laid a folded kilt in Daisy's arms. "A

long time ago, we told Charlie that if he won a bet we'd made, we'd reward him."

"He didn't win," Harry said. "He did his damnedest to lose it, all because he fell in love with you."

"But we wanted to give him a present anyway," said Stephen. "We were simply waiting for the right moment."

"It's been an honor to bring you baby Barnabas," Nicholas remarked. "So we commissioned a tartan specialist to design you your very own tartan. The Thorpe tartan."

"Of the House of Lumley," Stephen added. "Charlie, we hope you wear this on the grand days. And on hunting days."

Harry cleared his throat. "And any day you care to remind yourself and the world that you were all brought together for a reason—by love—to create your own very special clan."

"Know that this tartan design symbolizes our esteem and love for you," Molly said softly.

Poppy took Molly's arm. "Indeed, it does."

Charlie couldn't speak for a moment.

"You're part of our clan," he eventually said, his voice full of gratitude as he looked around him. "Every person here today."

He looked down at baby Barnabas and kissed his forehead.

"Thank you," Daisy uttered with feeling as she clung to Charlie's arm. "We love you all."

And then she kissed her viscount, the one that had been given to her. Once again she thanked her lucky stars that the man who'd been the emissary for her godmother had become so much more than a guardian of sorts.

They were true partners.

Soul mates.

She handed off the new kilt to Harry, and with loving care, Charlie handed Barney back to his mother. Together, they laughed softly over their new son's bundled form, then walked over the drawbridge and into Castle Vandemere, the people who were dearest in the world to them following close behind.

Don't miss any of the Impossible Bachelors!

Look for the other books in this delightful series by
KIERAN KRAMER

WHEN HARRY MET MOLLY
ISBN: 978-0-312-61164-4

**DUKES TO THE LEFT OF ME,
PRINCES TO THE RIGHT**
ISBN: 978-0-312-37402-0

CLOUDY WITH A CHANCE OF MARRIAGE
ISBN: 978-0-312-37403-7

Available from St. Martin's Paperbacks